TIPPING POINT

Deborah Aubrey

ISBN-13: 9798527660944
ISBN-10: 1477123456

Cover design by: Art Painter
Library of Congress Control Number: 2018675309
Printed in the United States of America

This book is dedicated to all hardworking secretaries juggling work and family life, and to the lovely secretaries I met along the way, most of whom were, weirdly, called Sue: Sue W, Suzanne W, Susie T, and Susan D x

Tipping Point
Noun: the critical point in a situation, process, or system be-
yond which a significant and often unstoppable effect or change
takes place.

MERRIAM-WEBSTER DICTIONARY

CHAPTER 1

"Mom," came a frustrated voice from upstairs, "Have you seen my bank card?"

"No, I haven't."

"But I left it on my bedside table. You must have moved it."

"Elliot, I can't even get *in* your room, let alone move anything."

"But I definitely left it on the bedside – "

"We're going to be late," Gary hissed, squeezing past me in the narrow hallway (made even narrower by two pushbikes, a set of rollerblades, squash racquets and enough parts from Elliot's car to make a complete new vehicle). "If Alex wants a lift to the train station we *have* to leave *now*."

"Alex!" I screamed up the stairs. "Are you ready? Only your dad's having a hissy fit."

"I am *not* having a hissy fit!" Gary snarled.

"Gaz, you're bouncing up and down like you're on a pogo stick, I'd call that a hissy fit."

"He's *going* to make me *late* for *work*. Can we *please* get a move on?"

"He's your son too, *you* tell him."

"ALEX!" he bawled up the stairs.

"I'm coming!" Alex, 19, tall, angular and massively indignant as only a teenager can be, came pounding down the stairs with all the grace of a baby elephant. "Mom, have you seen my roller blades?"

Still looking at him, I pointed at the floor at the foot of the stairs.

"And my squash racquets?"

I moved my finger an inch to the left.

"And I can't find my black jacket."

I stretched out an arm and plucked it from the coat stand. "Oh look, a coat, on a coat stand, *weird*."

"I never hang it there," Alex said.

"No, you tend to leave it balled up on the stairs like a dead animal waiting to trip someone up."

"Great!" came Elliot's voice from the depths of his room/pit, "You know where all Alex's stuff is but you can't tell me where my bank card is."

"Can we go now?" Gary urged, opening the front door.

"Elliot, we're just dropping Alex off at the train station and then we're going to work. You remember what work is, don't you?"

"Don't nag, I'm having a bad day." Elliot, 18, tall and thin like a piece of string with a face, and wearing an expression of deep angst, appeared at the top of the stairs. "Can you lend me some money till I find my bank card?"

"Oh, for crying out loud!" Gary looked ready to implode when I opened up my bag and started searching for my purse amongst all the detritus. "Can't we just leave the house without all this hassle, like normal people?"

"Here, Elliot," I said, putting a note on the bottom step, "But I want it back when you find your card. Alex, have you got everything?"

Alex stood in the hallway with his huge backpack, equally huge sports bag, squash racket under his arm, roller blades thrown over one shoulder, trainers and several jackets slung over the other, and nodded. He'd been home from university for the weekend.

"Come on!" Gary began pushing us out the door, "Let's get a move on."

The traffic was, as usual, hell into Birmingham city centre. Rush hour, they called it – the irony. We came to a complete standstill on Bristol Street, near Pagoda Island, agonisingly close to New Street Station.

"Traffic!" hissed Gary, "I told you we'd hit traffic! We should have left earlier or gone the other way!"

"But this is the most direct route," I said.

"For *crows*, maybe!"

"I'm going to miss my train," muttered Alex from the back seat.

"And my boss is going to bollock me for being late, *again*," I sighed.

"It's not *my* fault, is it!" Gary cried.

"I never said it was! Did I say it was your fault?"

"*You* were the one who suggested we took this route."

"Oh, so you're blaming me for the density of traffic now, are you?"

"It wouldn't be this bad if we'd have left 10 minutes earlier!"

"Parent-types," said Alex, calmly, "Whilst you two bicker to pass the time, could I just point out that I'm going to miss my train?"

"Do you think I'm *deliberately* sitting in this traffic?" Gary raged, as Alex rolled his eyes and I tried to pretend I wasn't really married to the Man of Fury. "Do you think I *choose* to sit here breathing in exhaust fumes? I'll get out, shall I, and explain to everyone that *Alex* has to catch his *train* and would they mind *terribly* getting out of the *sodding way!*"

Alex sighed heavily. "I'm just saying, if I miss this train I'll have to fork out for another ticket, and I am but a poverty-stricken student."

I quickly twisted in my seat to look back at him, packed like a sardine amongst his weekend baggage. "Do you need some money?" I asked. "Are we not giving you enough to survive?"

"Suzanne," Gary snapped – he only ever called me by my full name when he was Extremely Annoyed, which seemed to be most of the time, "We are *not* giving him any more money, we can't afford it."

"We could – "

"We couldn't. He probably has more spare cash than us. I certainly couldn't afford that stereo system he's got permanently plugged into his head like a life support system."

"It's an *iPod*, dad."

"And how much did it *cost*, Alex?"

"I'm not telling you."

"He's very good with money," I said.

"Good with *our* money, you mean. How do you manage it, Alex? How can you afford all these state-of-the-art gadgets you keep buying?"

"I donate to the local sperm bank."

The silence that filled the car was almost visible.

"You don't!" I finally gasped.

"No, mom, I don't."

"Thank God for that," Gary breathed. "The thought of all these mini Alexes wandering round Manchester is too awful to think about."

"I think it would be quite sweet," I said.

"Don't give him ideas, Suze."

Alex excitedly leaned forward until his head was between the two front seats. "Do you think they pay much for donations, dad?"

"How would I know?"

"No, seriously, do you think – ?"

"Just concentrate on your studies," I told him.

"I could concentrate a lot more if I didn't have to worry about money all the time."

"We are *not* upping your allowance," Gary said firmly.

Alex flopped back into his seat. "Okay then, I'll starve."

"Gary!" I cried, "He'll starve!"

"He won't starve."

"We'll send food parcels, Alex."

"We won't! Let him get a part time job or something."

"I can't *work*," Alex cried in a really high-pitched voice, "I'm too busy studying."

"Studying to be a complete slob."

"Cheers, dad. When I'm earning obscene amounts of money in some global tech company I'll remember you said that."

"Good, maybe you'll pay us back all the money we've squandered on you. Christ!" Gary cried, thumping the steering wheel, "What *is* the hold up? Ber-*luddy* traffic!"

Alex suddenly started gathering his bags together. "Forget this," he said, "The station's not far, I can walk it from here."

He got out of the car in the middle of standstill traffic. I got out with him and say goodbye.

"*Suzanne!*" Gary screamed at my back, "What the *hell* are you doing?"

"Will you be alright, Alex?" I sniffed at my tall, handsome son.

"Suzanne! We're in the middle of a main road, for God's sake!"

"You take care of yourself," I said, giving Alex a big hug. "Eat properly, lots of fruit and vegetables, and stay safe. Carry your mobile at all times, and don't go into any dodgy areas."

"He's 19 for crying out loud!" Gary bawled, "He probably knows more about life than we do. *Now get back in the bloody car!*"

I wiped away a tear as my son, my child, my *baby*, disappeared into the swarm of cars. I'd barely pulled the door shut when Gary crunched gears and turned down a side road, revving the engine and making the tyres scream. Suddenly the road ahead was clear. "I knew we should have come this way," he said, weaving through threads of traffic like a racing driver chased by demons from hell.

I'm sure it was only some remaining semblance of decency that prevented him from actually kicking me out of the speeding car as we approached my office building on Colmore Row. I got out and turned to say goodbye, but he'd already gone, shooting into the city centre like a heat seeking missile.

I sighed and looked up at the third floor, where I would

spend my day typing and dealing with my boss's unreasonable demands. "Day one," I breathed, "Suzanne enters the building and is lost for all time."

* * *

I actually like my job, when I'm allowed to get on with it. I'm a secretary for a commercial property company. It's interesting work, if a little frantic at times, the stress and pressure not helped by my demanding and disorganised boss, Callum Redfern. He's the kind of boss who blames *everything* on the secretary; files mislaid, papers gone awry, photographs lost, it was me. Reports not done on time, my fault. Global warming, I'm entirely to blame.

What Callum lacked in social skills he made up for with copious dollops of biting sarcasm, which he mistakenly believes is 'dry humour'. It's not, it's just biting sarcasm.

"Suzanne," he sneered today, as I walked past his glass office to my desk, "How nice of you to join us. And you're only – " I sensed him glance at his watch but didn't dare look in case he mistook eye contact as my consent to indulge in a prolonged, sarcastic conversation. " – ten-past nine. Well done."

"Yep. Thanks. Nice to see you too."

"I have a *very* important meeting in fifteen minutes," he said. "Perhaps, if you're not too busy, you'd like to get me a coffee beforehand."

I glanced at Sarah, my partner in crime, sitting at the desk next to mine. She tried to pull a face but failed miserably because she's just totally gorgeous and perfect in every way. Even frowning she looks like she should be on the cover of one of those magazines I can't afford to buy. I should hate her but I don't because she's really down to earth and a lot of fun, and you need someone like that when you work for someone like Callum.

I flung my coat on my chair and turned towards the kitchen.

"Resist the urge to spit in his drink," Sarah said with a grin.

I did, but it was a close call with the bottle of bleach the cleaners had left out.

"Right," Callum barked as I walked back into his office, "I have three *very* important meetings today. One at 10 o'clock with James & Barratt, who are *very* important clients of ours. Have you booked a meeting room for them?"

Secretaries before me had fallen like skittles. One had hated him so much she'd deliberately smashed his favourite mug against the counter in the kitchen in frustration, but I was made of sterner stuff – I'd survived teenagers, everything else was a doddle.

"Meeting room 15," I told him, for about the fifth time. "Hot drinks and biscuits provided. Meeting at 12.15pm with Derek Jacobson, buffet lunch, meeting room 23. Taxi booked for 2.30 to take you to the Wragges offices for a meeting with Tom Bruce, Head of Property Finance, about the Lemming development. And it's your wife's birthday today, she specifically asked me to remind you not to be late tonight as she's booked a restaurant for 8 o'clock."

Callum peered at me with his cold, blue eyes. They were always tinged a bit with red, and the white bits looked kind of yellow sometimes. I think he has a drink problem. "What's this?" he said in mock horror, "Efficiency? Surely not."

"You really don't have to check up on me all the – "

"Don't I?" He leaned back in his chair, enjoying himself, "Didn't you once forget to book a meeting room for some *very* important clients, who we consequently lost?"

"That was four years ago, Callum. It was my first day working for you."

"There's really no excuse for gross incompetence," he said, shaking his head, whilst I imagined a large paper knife wedged between his blue/red/yellow eyeballs. "Now, my wife's birthday. Take some money out of petty cash and get some flowers. And perfume. Lacoste, she likes that. And have it gift wrapped. And get a card, a nice one, not sloppy, something *tasteful*, if you know what that is."

"I can't," I dared to say.

"Why not?"

"I have an urgent report to finish by midday, I don't have time." I almost squirmed like a schoolkid in front of the head-master but managed to stop myself.

"Then ask Sarah to do it," he snapped irritably.

Sarah would probably knee him in the balls and rip off both his arms before she'd lower herself to shop for the bulldog. "I think she's busy too."

Callum's eyes narrowed. "I am Head of Department here, a partner," he said, as he said often. "I have three *extremely* important meetings today and I do *not* have time to leave the office."

I drew breath, considered mentioning the entire weekend he'd just had to sort out his wife's birthday gifts, then thought better of it. Gary had a good job and we'd probably survive on his salary alone, but we wouldn't be able to afford the teenagers that sucked at our finances like voracious parasites … but maybe that would be a good thing.

"Maybe Si has time," I suggested.

Si is the graduate who had been with us for three months and who still hadn't figured out how to work the computer sys-tem yet. He wandered around the office like a lost soul, pilfering sweets off the older secretaries and trying to chat up the younger ones, who glared at him like he was carrying the plague. He was sweet, in a stupid puppy kind of way.

We glared at each other over his cluttered desk, my boss and I, before I turned and made a run for it. "Simon!" he yelled, "Get in here!"

"I love Mondays," I sighed, switching on my computer

"Do you want me to do the bomb thing?" Sarah asked.

I grinned. "He might hear."

"He won't, he's too busy giving Simon his orders."

Inside the office a petrified Simon stood in front of Callum's desk, visibly trembling as my boss roared his instructions.

"Okay then," I said.

Sarah pushed her chair away from her desk and pretended

to pull the ring out of an imaginary grenade with her teeth. She lobbed it in the air towards Callum's office, making an excellent whistling noise like a descending bomb, then splayed her hands dramatically as she made an explosive sound. She was very good at it.

Inside the office, Callum turned his head. Sarah ducked down behind her partition, giggling hysterically.

"What's that noise?" Callum shouted, staring straight at me. "I keep hearing it."

"Nothing," I said, "It's just the sound of my computer crashing again."

Behind the partition, Sarah pulled another ring out of a grenade. "Stop it," I hissed, giggling, "He'll see."

Sarah sat up straight and put on her headphones. "Do you think it's sad that the only enjoyment we get at work is throwing imaginary bombs at bosses?"

"Yes."

"One day I'm going to do it for real."

"Don't be silly."

"I have contacts in military establishments, you know."

"Your brother's in the TA, Sarah."

"Exactly."

We both started typing.

"I love my job," Sarah suddenly said.

"Ah, the enthusiasm of the young."

"I'm twenty-three!"

"Ah, twenty-three. You've still got it all to come, grasshopper. Whereas I've seen it all, done it all, can't remember most of it, which is probably for the best."

"Talking of memory," Sarah said, "You do remember that the Big Boss is in the office today, don't you?"

I turned to look at her. "Can't you see the excitement oozing from my every pore? No, really, I may look dead on the outside, but inside I'm screaming like a teenager at a pop concert."

"It's just that ... "

"What, it's just what?"

"Well ... "

"*What?*"

"Well, you know I think you're absolutely marvellous."

"Yes, but?"

"Well," she winced, "It's just that you look a bit ... a bit scruffy, Suze."

"I always look scruffy," I said, "It's my trademark, foisted upon me by my mean git of a husband. And anyway, I'm going for the sympathy vote in the hope the Big Boss will take pity on me and give me a jaw-dropping pay rise."

"I thought you were going to buy a new suit this month."

"So did I, but Gary said we're broke. Still, and forever more."

"What's his problem? Secret drug habit? Gambling debts? Couple of hookers set up in penthouses somewhere?"

I shrugged. "He just says we have big bills and two scrounging teenagers to support." I glanced down at myself. "I don't look that bad, do I?"

"No, no," Sarah said, rather too quickly. "It's just that ... I can't remember the last time I saw a collar like that on a blouse."

"You're too young to remember. I'm into the millennium section of my wardrobe now. Thank God I kept everything or I'd be coming to work naked."

"Suzanne!" Callum bawled from his office, "I can't find the Smith & Smith file."

"I can see it from here," I bawled back.

"Where?"

"On your desk, right in front of you. Move your hand to the left. A bit more. There."

"And where are the plans we drew up for it? Honestly, Suzanne, I wish you wouldn't rifle through my desk."

"I wouldn't touch your filth-laden desk with a bargepole," I breathed. Out loud I said, "Plans are by the photograph of you and your wife in Florida. No, not the fake picture of you shaking hands with Boris Johnson, the other one."

"And where's my bloody mobile?"

Argh! "In your jacket pocket, the right one, where it *always* is!"

"I don't know how you stand him," Sarah said, "I really don't."

"It's easy once the self-esteem has been battered into submission and all shreds of hope have long evaporated."

Callum appeared in his office doorway. He stood there, looked at me, and I knew, knew instantly; it was like a sixth sense. He uttered the words I dreaded more than anything in the world, the words that sometimes kept me awake at night and filled my dreams with terror. He said, "Is my tie straight?"

I sucked in air like a woman about to be tossed into stormy seas. I think my heart actually stopped beating altogether and the blood froze in my veins. From the corner of my stunned eyes, I saw Sarah's blonde head quickly swivel towards me.

"Well, is it?" Callum asked.

"Yes," I breathed.

"Are you sure?"

"Positive."

Callum lifted his chin, stretching out his turkey neck, and plodded towards me like Frankenstein. "It doesn't feel straight to me," he said, fiddling with it, "Just check it, will you?"

I stared at his outstretched neck with revulsion. With enormous restraint I forced myself to stand and approach Callum and nervously stretched out a hand, delicately prodding his tie with a fingertip.

"Is it straight now?" he said, suddenly leaning forward.

The fingertip of my right hand slipped off the knot and touched the clammy, wrinkled flesh above his collar. I gave a whelp of disgust and instinctively leapt back. "Yes!" I cried, "It's straight!"

"Good." And he left the office.

I went back to my desk, traumatised, staring at the hand that had *touched his skin*.

"Don't you ever feel like garrotting him in the neck when he does that?" Sarah asked, passing over the hand sanitiser kept specifically for such occasions.

"Oh yeah, but I have children to feed."

"They're not children," Sarah scoffed, "They're grown men."

"If only they realised that. And anyway, they're not grown men, they're teenagers, an entirely separate species. Not yet fully formed, childhood behind them, they're reaching out, desperately trying to grasp onto manhood but not quite making it."

"Push 'em," Sarah said, "That's all they need, a good, hard shove."

"They're over six foot tall. You don't push people who tower above you."

"Why not?"

I hesitated. "Well, they might push back."

We typed for a while in silence. I finished Callum's dictations and picked another off the software system. "Oh God," I groaned, "I've got one of Pete's."

"Done in real time?"

"Yes. He's just burped. Now he's pausing for thought. A cough. More thought. A sneeze. The rustle of paper, probably trying to find out what he's supposed to be doing. Now he's on the phone, he's saying ... oh God, he's talking to his girlfriend about the sex they had last night!"

Sarah was out of her seat and at my side in an instant. "Let me listen."

"Not for your tender ears, my dear."

"Come on, give me a headphone."

"Too late, he's finished, and so soon!"

Sarah sulked back to her desk. "I thought you didn't listen to the tapes anyway," she said. "You say the words totally bypass your brain and go straight to your fingers."

"It's true, I never listen to the voices in my head, especially not the ones telling me to kill Callum, must kill Callum."

"Don't delete that dictation when you've finished, I want to listen to Peter's phone sex."

"You won't understand the words, little girl."

Sarah leaned across her desk towards me, raising a perfectly shaped eyebrow, and breathed, "Honey, I know *all* the words."

We diligently ploughed through the department dictations. Clackety-clackety-clack. Brain dead. Eyes blank. Typing but barely alive.

Sarah finally tore off her headphones and cried, "God, dilapidations are *boring*."

"I'm doing a schedule of condition," I said, monotone, staring at the computer screen as my fingers flew over the keyboard.

"I give you permission to stop," said Sarah.

"I can't stop. I can never stop. I'm doomed to type until the end of time."

"It's lunchtime, Suze."

"Oh." I pulled off my headphones and inspected them, picking off a tiny speck. "Look," I said, "My brain fell out."

"Nobody will notice." Sarah stood up, pulling on her coat. "What are you doing for lunch, shopping?"

I cried out dramatically, waving my hands in the air. "Ye Gods, no! I can't stand the third-degree interrogation when I get home." I mimicked Gary's deep voice, adding a lisp just for the hell of it. "*What, you bought yourshelf a whole bar of chocolate? How shelfishly extravagant! Don't you realishe how shtrained our finances are?* No," I sighed, "I'll just stay in the office, all on my own, and play FreeCell."

"Come with us."

"Where are you going?"

"To that nice wine bar round the corner."

"That nice wine bar that charges £15 for a sandwich?"

"Yeah."

"I'll pass."

"Oh, come on," Sarah insisted, "I'll buy you a drink."

"Why are you going for a drink on a Monday anyway? Everybody knows that surveyors only get bladdered on Friday afternoons."

Sarah blushed a little and lowered her big blue eyes.

"James McCreath," I grinned. "You only ever go all coy and girlie like that when the handsome Partner and Head of the Management Department is mentioned."

Sarah giggled. "He's treating some of us for helping to get that Faversham deal finished on time."

"But you weren't involved in the Faversham deal, were you?" But I had, I'd done some work on it when the Management Department's secretaries had been sick/busy/too idle. I'd most likely typed up the memo inviting everyone to lunch – I must pay more attention.

"No," Sarah said, "But James said I could come along if I wanted."

"Oh, did he?" I grinned.

Sarah rolled her eyes. "Oh, it's nothing like that. I'm sure it's nothing like that. Do you think it's something like that?"

"I don't know," I said, grabbing my coat, "But let's find out."

* * *

The trendy little wine bar round the corner was, as always, packed to the rafters with suits, all shouting irate orders to the harassed looking bar staff. The table the management department people were sat at was surrounded by a wall of them.

"We've already ordered," James said, helping Sarah into a chair whilst I – ignored and invisible – squirmed awkwardly into another. My elbow knocked a pint glass being held by an enormous suit standing next to the table. His expression as the beer cascaded down his chest could easily have halted a charging rhinoceros at thirty paces.

"Oh, I'm *really* sorry," I gasped, mortified. "Let me get you another drink. I'll pay for your suit to be cleaned, of course, just send me the bill. And you'll need a new tie, too, is it silk? Was it very expensive? Maybe Primark have one similar?"

"Just ask the bar for another pint, Crispin," James cut in, "tell them to put it on my tab. Now, what would you ladies like to order?"

Still glowing with embarrassment, I furtively scoured the menu. The figures didn't seem to match what was being offered.

My eyes searched for something I could afford that wouldn't cause the bank balance to cave in on itself. Maybe a plate of 'hand cut, hand fried potato wedges, delicately sprinkled with sea salt'.

"James is paying," Sarah whispered.

"I'll have the ploughman's lunch," I beamed.

I only vaguely knew the people from the management department as they worked on a different floor. There was James, of course, looking drop-dead gorgeous, as always. He had one of those voices that made you sigh dreamily, just like Sarah was doing now, and it was obvious that James was well and truly hooked on her too. They stared at each other across the crowded table, eyes only for each other.

I glanced around at my 'companions'. There was Cynthia, with the wild mass of hair, who never uttered a word unless it was about her cats. Jody was 18 and had an attitude that would make Attila the Hun flinch. There were three people I'd never seen before in my life and could well have been gate-crashers, and then there was Mark, who apparently had a severe body odour problem, which didn't bother me as I had anosmia, no sense of smell. I tried chatting with him, but it was obvious he wasn't really interested, so I just stared at the people at the bar and tried not to feel awkward as I sipped at the rather large glass of wine that had appeared in front of me.

Sarah was being massively flirtatious, but in a sophisticated, adorable way. The wine she was continually sipping at might have had something to do with it, or maybe she was just drunk on happiness. You could almost see the electricity sparking between her and James, they were practically a fire hazard.

After we'd eaten, James helped Sarah into her coat, his hands lingering for a moment on her shoulders. She giggled coquettishly. Yes, hugely confident Sarah, who was unutterably gorgeous and stood no bollocks from anybody, not only giggled but she did it *coquettishly*. I felt positively voyeuristic, and so did the others, who all coughed awkwardly and made hasty exits.

Not wanting to be left alone with them, I glanced at my watch, feigned surprise, then genuine panic. I was late. Again.

I sprinted back to the office.

* * *

"How nice of you to join us for the afternoon session," Callum began, as I raced past his glass office.

"*Oh, shut up, you old fool*," I hissed under my breath. This in itself should have given me a clue as to my own 'state of intoxication', but, precisely because of my intoxication, I ignored it. I still ignored it when I almost missed flopping into my chair, and continued to ignore it even when Callum came storming out of his office and came stomping towards me.

"Now that you've *finally* returned from your *very* long lunch," he snarled, "Perhaps you wouldn't mind ordering a taxi for the *very important meeting* I have with Tom Bruce at Wragges this afternoon?"

"It's ordered," I said, desperately trying to sober myself by concentrating on my computer screen, which seemed a bit fuzzy round the edges.

"Are you sure?" Callum drawled.

"Yes, I'm sure." My mouth carried on of its own accord after that, I had absolutely no control over it at all. It was like the real me went and stood in a corner, filing its nails, whilst my gob went onto autopilot. "I told you this morning the taxi was ordered. I also told you on Friday morning, Friday afternoon and last thing Friday night. Short of spray painting the words 'TAXI IS ORDERED' across the glass of your office, there's not much more I can do to convince you of this fact."

"Ex*cuse* me?"

I should have noted the dangerous tone of his voice, but I wasn't used to drinking wine, especially at lunchtime, so all the warning signals sank into the bubbling cesspit that remained of my intoxicated brain.

"Look, Callum," the mouth said, "I've worked here for four years and only *once* in those four years have I *ever* forgotten to book a meeting, a taxi, a conference centre or a hotel room. I've never lost a file or a report, all your work is done on time, and I even make coffee for you and serve drinks to clients like some sort of waitress."

I had, at this point, completely disengaged from my own body. The mouth just wouldn't shut up, like it had been waiting for this moment for four long years and finally had its chance. "I'm a bloody good secretary," it snapped, "You've never given me any praise, said please or thank you once, and you pick on me at every opportunity."

The fuzzy brain noticed that several people around us had stood up from their desks and were now openly staring at us over the partitions. And still the mouth wouldn't shut the hell up.

"You're just a bully, Callum Redfern. That's what you are, an arrogant, egotistical, turkey-necked, tie-obsessed *bully*."

There followed an eternity of piercing silence. The entire office was engulfed with it like a throbbing pulse of nothingness. Shock suddenly brought me to my senses. Wide-eyed, I stared up at Callum's surprisingly expressionless face. He didn't seem to be looking at me, he was staring towards the end of the office behind me.

I turned a little in my chair, thinking maybe the office was on fire or something. But it wasn't a fire. It was worse.

It was the Big Boss.

CHAPTER 2

"You did *what*?" Gary cried.

"I … I'd had a drink at lunchtime," I told him. "I wasn't thinking straight."

"You weren't thinking at all from the sound of it!" Gary got up from the sofa and paced up and down in front of the gas fire, running his fingers through his thinning hair. "You bollocked your boss! A *partner*!"

"I … I … "

"What did they do?"

"Well, Callum went to his meeting and the Big Boss just looked at me for a bit, then walked away."

"They didn't say anything to you?"

"I think their expressions said it all really." I winced at the memory, there had been a lot of side-eye looks and pursing of lips. The Head Secretary, Tracey, came running over almost apoplectic with indecision, and eventually fled back to her desk. I just sat there, wide eyed, wondering what the hell had just happened.

"What do you think will happen?" Gary asked now.

"I don't know". I slumped on the sofa and dropped my head in my hands. "I guess he'll just call me into the office when I go in tomorrow."

"And sack you?"

"Not necessarily."

"You bollocked him in front of the whole office and a CEO and he won't sack you? Come on, Suze!"

"There's no need to be so pessimistic."

"No? Do you know how much mortgage I pay on this house?"

"*We* pay?' I corrected.

"I'm out there slogging my guts out every day – "

"You're a warehouse manager, Gary, not a labourer."

" – trying to earn enough for my family – "

"Little wife working full time and still carrying out *all* domestic duties does nothing to help with finances then?"

"You're not *helping* by losing your job!" he snarled.

"I haven't bloody lost my bloody job!"

"You don't know that!"

There was an awkward cough from the living room doorway. "Bad time to ask for money, is it?" Elliot asked.

Gary threw up his arms and collapsed in a huffy heap into an armchair. I instantly went into 'nothing-wrong-here' mode and said, in a voice that sounded artificial even to my own ears, "Not found your bank card yet then, Elliot?"

"No. I think the dog ate it."

"We don't have a dog, do we?" I briefly wondered if the curse of the Chablis was still upon me and that we did, in fact, have a dog but I'd forgotten.

"No, my girlfriend does."

"You have a girlfriend?" I slipped instantly into my Jewish mother act, smiling profusely and oozing hope. "I didn't know you had a girlfriend. What's her name? Where does she live? Why don't you bring her home to meet us?"

Elliot looked at his dad, crumpled miserably in the armchair, then back at me, grinning at him like a demented maniac with tear-streaked mascara running down my face. "You are kidding, aren't you?" he said, and left.

There followed a silence I didn't like, so I broke it by saying, "Just the two of us then, Gaz, eh?"

The look Gary gave me could have frozen a volcano to its

core. I guess the days of excitedly ripping the clothes off each other whenever we were alone and making mad passionate love all day and all night were long gone – in fact, so long gone I couldn't, at that point, remember when we'd last had physical contact at all. Gary, rather scarily, said we were 'too old for all that now'. We were 35 when he said it. I remember thinking, 'Jeez, is that it then?'

"There's a new bottle of single malt whisky in the kitchen cupboard," Gary finally said.

"I know, I put it there, bought with *my* hard-earned money for when your dad pops round."

"Money we're not going to have for much longer," he retorted. "You'd better take the whisky into work with you tomorrow."

"Why? So I can get drunk at my desk and bollock a few more bosses?"

Gary tutted and rolled his eyes like I was an idiot. I hated when he did that. "The whisky is a peace offering for your boss, when you grovel for his forgiveness so that he won't *sack* you."

"I've got a much better idea," I snapped, jumping up and going into the kitchen, returning with the whisky bottle and a single glass. I pounded them both down on the coffee table.

"Great!" Gary hissed. "Get drunk why don't you, see if you can make today any worse than it already is!"

"It couldn't possibly get any worse."

"Couldn't it?" Gary leapt up. "I'm not sitting around here watching you top up your drunkenness, I'm going out."

"Out where?"

He briefly pushed his face into mine as he passed, hissing, "Just out."

* * *

I didn't open the bottle of whisky, alcohol has already caused enough trouble. I drank coffee instead, figuring I needed to be sober when Gary came home so we could sit down and talk.

Except Gary didn't come home until the early hours of the morning, the slamming of the front door woke me up, as it was probably meant to. He didn't come upstairs for a long time. I could hear him moving about in the kitchen, the kettle clicking on, a spoon being dropped into a mug. When he did finally get into bed he slept with his back to me – the familiar marital position of 'not talking, not touching'.

Consequently, I awoke the next morning having had all of five minutes sleep, feeling like a zombie who'd had its brains sucked out, which is pretty much how Gary looked at me too. We sidestepped around each other in the kitchen as we got our coffee and toast, avoiding all eye contact and most definitely not speaking. None of this was my fault, I thought, why should I say anything? Gary was obviously thinking the same thing.

So, without either of us making a sound, we got into the car and drove into the city. The traffic moved like a sluggish river of lava with rivulets of irate lava trying to merge into it. A few car horns were blown and a few expressive fingers were exchanged as we moved from one gridlock to another. And then a car suddenly cut in front of us, making Gary slam on his brakes.

"How rude!" I gasped.

Gary used much stronger language and pounded on his horn, yelling abuse out of the window whilst pointing up at the sky with his middle finger.

"Did you *see* him, the bloody nutter!" he screeched furiously.

It appeared we were on speaking terms once more – our dice with death had brought us back together. We both looked surprised at this unexpected turn of events, like children being made to shake hands and make up by the teacher.

"What time did you come home last night?" I asked, instantly wishing I hadn't in case it started yet another argument – they seemed so easy to start these days.

"About midnight," Gary said.

"My alarm clock said 4.15."

"Then why did you bother asking?"

"I was making conversation." I risked a quick glance at him.

21

He was concentrating on the road ahead, his expression tight. "I was checking to see if my vocal cords still worked."

"Your vocal cords will last longer than you will. You'll still be yakking in your grave."

I wasn't sure how to take this. I wasn't aware that I yakked a lot, neither was I aware that Gary actually visualised me in a grave, yakking away – did he imagine this often, I wondered?

I inhaled, about to ask him if he loved me, then exhaled again. Gary would rather scrub the kitchen floor during a Cup Final than say anything remotely affectionate, especially when he was in such a foul mood.

"So, where did you go last night?" I asked instead.

There was a pause. Gary made a great show of tutting at some driver in front who had committed some unseen sin before replying, "Met some mates in the pub."

"Oh, which mates?" I knew most of the people Gary worked with and wondered which ones might stay in the pub until that late on a Monday night.

"Does it matter?" Gary snapped.

The tension was back. One wrong word here, one wrong move, and we'd be back to staggeringly shitty silence again. I pressed my lips together, determined not to speak. I sensed Gary glance over at me but I didn't dare look back in case it antagonised him in some way.

"Sorry," he suddenly said. "It was Mike and Nick I had a drink with."

I was surprised and instantly suspicious. Gary never apologised for anything, ever.

We pulled up outside my office building. I went to get out, but Gary put his hand on my arm. "Good luck with your boss today," he said softly. "Phone and let me know how it goes."

There appeared to be a heaviness of bowling ball proportions hanging where my stomach used to be. Gary never touch me these days except by accident, and didn't like me calling him at work unless it was a blood-drenched emergency. The heaviness grew heavier when I started getting out the car and he leaned over and said, "You know I love you, don't you, Suze?"

I nodded and walked away, thinking, 'What the hell is going on?'

* * *

I trembled as I stood in the lift and was so nervous I felt physically sick. I gave myself a stiff talking to, trying to persuade myself that I'd done the right thing by standing up to Callum's tyranny at last. By the time I'd reached the third floor I was pretty convinced that someone in the higher echelons would recognise my outburst as proof that I was management material and were already in the process of promoting me.

In my dreams!

"God, Suze," Sarah gasped as I approached our desks, "What the hell did you *do* yesterday?"

"Is he in yet?" I asked, glancing towards Callum's office and seeing it empty.

"No, not yet. What happened, Suze?"

"You've heard then?"

"It's all anyone can talk about! I wouldn't be surprised if it was headlined in the company's newsletter this month."

"Funny," I huffed.

"And you only had one glass of wine too."

"Yeah, but the glasses were big enough to keep a shoal of Koi Carp in."

"Are you normally so aggressive when you've had a drink?"

I shrugged. "My memory doesn't go back that far."

"Oh Suze."

"Don't go all mushy on me, Sarah. Anyway," I said, wanting to change the subject, "What happened to you yesterday to miss all this excitement?" Sarah hadn't come back from lunch at all.

"I ... we ... well ... "

"Come on, spill the beans."

"I had a business meeting with James all afternoon," she said.

"Business meeting? All afternoon? Just you and James, was it?"

Sarah looked away awkwardly. "Yes."

"And?"

"And what? Nothing. He just told me about some changes that are going to be made around here, that's all. And then ... " She paused while her face rearranged itself into a huge, Cheshire cat smile. "And then he took me to a fancy restaurant."

"Sarah!" I gasped. "You've pulled."

"You don't 'pull' a man like James McCreath," she said sombrely. "We were just talking, that's all."

"Did he take you home afterwards?"

"Yes."

"Did he kiss you?"

Sarah suddenly busied herself with a pile of papers on her desk. "It was just a peck on the cheek," she said, blushing. "I've seen him do it to clients loads of times."

"No you haven't!"

The Cheshire cat smile was back. "Oh Suze!" she cried, struggling to keep her voice down, "He's amazing! So intelligent and funny, and *God*!" she gasped, "Totally gorgeous. We just talked and talked and – "

"Ah, love," I sighed, "A wonderful thing, as I recall, vaguely, with the aid of some deep memory regression and possibly dome drug therapy".

"He's just so – oh shit," she cried, 'It's Callum!"

Callum came storming into the office with a face like thunder. I waited for the inevitable sarcasm as he marched passed my desk, but he simply glared at me and sailed straight into his office. Tracey, the Head Secretary, scampered in after him some moments later and I heard him yelling, "I don't want her to work for me any more, get rid of her." I felt sick again.

And then Tracey poked her head out of the glass doors and said, "Suzanne, could you come inside for a moment?"

I stood up like a woman condemned. The whole office watched as I walked slowly towards Callum's office. My legs were like jelly, my insides felt heavy; with a bowling ball of anxiety already in residence I was surprised there was any room left for my internal organs at all.

The glass doors swished closed behind me. Tracey flittered about nervously, but Callum remained motionless and furious behind his desk. He held a letter in his hand. He smiled when he handed it to me.

Five minutes later I came out of the office carrying a written warning for gross insubordination. Callum insisted that Tracey moved me to another department, the *Ratings* department, but I refused because it was basically a filing job with less money and it was in the basement, and suddenly, inexplicably, Tracey was 'sadly' accepting my resignation. Callum looked well pleased with himself.

* * *

"Oh Christ!"

"It's not that bad."

"Oh Christ!"

"Really, Gary, things will be okay."

"Oh Christ!"

"Repeating those two words over and over isn't helping any."

"Helping?" He pulled his face out of his hands and glared at me. I waited for the barrage of accusations to begin, but Gary just put his head back in his hands and gasped, "Oh Christ!"

"Look, I can get another job. Have some faith in me. I'm a good secretary. I can work anywhere."

"Anywhere where they don't mind your references labelling you a troublemaker with a big mouth prone to attacking senior management." With great effort, and what appeared to be a huge amount of willpower, Gary exposed his face again. "Can they just sack you like that? Couldn't you appeal against unfair dismissal."

"Well, they didn't exactly *sack* me." I muttered.

"You just told me you'd lost your job. What *exactly* did they do if they didn't sack you?"

I bit my lip. "They're restructuring," I said.

"And?"

"They're merging my department with the bigger Consultancy department on the fourth floor, who do all the ... big stuff."

Silence. Gary just stared at me, waiting for more. I eventually mustered up the courage to say, "The bigger department already has enough secretaries, so ... " I was almost chewing my lip off at this point. "So they offered me a position elsewhere."

"Where elsewhere?"

"In a different department."

"And?"

"They wanted me to work in the *Ratings* department, Gary. It's a really crap department. It's this really dingy, dark, depressing place in the basement staffed by people who have clearly lost the will to live. It's less money and definitely a demotion."

"So, let me get this straight." Gary grimaced with the effort of understanding. "They're restructuring?" I nodded. "Your position has effectively become redundant?" I nodded again. "So they offer you an alternative position in a department you don't happen to like?"

"*Nobody* likes it, Gary. Even the people who work there don't like it."

"And you said what?"

I had no lip left. I started chewing the inside of my mouth instead. "I said ... I didn't ... want it."

"And they said?"

"They said they had no other positions to offer me and they'd be sad to see me go, but if that was my decision they had to respect it."

"You quit?"

"It was a spur of the moment thing, Gary. I thought if I turned down the Ratings department they'd offer me something else, but ... they didn't."

"Oh Christ!"

"Will you *please* stop saying that."

Gary leapt up from the sofa. "Jesus!"

"Not an improvement, Gaz. We're atheists, remember? Taking deities names in vain does nothing for us."

"Very bloody pithy!"

"How about being on my side, eh?" I retorted. "How about backing me up and saying I did the right thing, that no one should talk to your wife the way Callum does *all the time!*" Gary went all blurry. I was crying. I suddenly felt lost and helpless and a bit vulnerable. "How about you just put your arms around me and hold me tight like you used to and tell me everything's going to be alright?"

Gary slowly came towards me, put his arms around me in a limp, non-committal sort of way, and whispered, "We're fucked."

"No, we're not!" I said, squirming out of his half-hearted embrace. "Nobody's died, nobody's ill, I've just lost my job, that's all."

"You didn't *lose* it, you *gave* it away! How long have they given you? How much notice do you have to work?"

I hesitated, then grabbed the bull by the horns and mumbled, "Taking my holidays into account I've got until ... until the end of the week."

"What?"

"They've given me until the end of the week."

"A week! Oh Christ!"

"It's okay, Gary. I joined an employment agency in my lunch break, there must be *loads* of secretarial jobs out there, just *loads*. I can get a job just like that." I attempted to click my fingers, but they were covered in tears and simply smacked wetly together instead. Gary left the room and shouted furiously up the stairs.

"Elliot?"

"What?"

"Get a job."

"Why?"

"Cos you're a bone-idle slob and it's about time you paid your way around here."

His bedroom door opened quickly and the sound of panic-stricken feet pounded across the landing. "Why do I need to get a job now?" came Elliot's stunned voice.

"Because your mother's managed to lose hers."

"Oh cheers, Gaz!" I snapped, "Your support means a lot!"

"And make yourself useful," Gary hollered up the stairs, "Throw down the spare duvet and a couple of pillows."

"Why?" Elliot yelled back.

"Because your unemployed mother is sleeping on the sofa tonight."

"I am not!"

"You two aren't arguing *again*, are you?" Elliot shouted, "Don't you ever get bored of it? Why can't you just get along?"

"Just do it, Elliot."

"I am not sleeping on the bloody sofa," I snarled at Gary, "I'm not a child that needs punishing because I lost my job!"

"What does mom say about the duvet and the pillows?" came Elliot's voice down the stairs.

"Mom says forget it," I yelled back, "Your father's just being an idiot."

"Nothing new there then," he called back. Feet thudded across the landing and his bedroom door slammed shut.

"I am *not* sleeping on the sofa," I said again.

"Well, you're certainly not sleeping in *my* bed after you've deliberately flung us into poverty."

"It wasn't deliberate, and when did it suddenly become *your* bed?"

"Since you lost your job and lost your right to sleep in it," he bawled.

"You have *got* to be bloody kidding me!"

We stood there, in the middle of the living room, facing each other, both of us fizzing with fury. Then Gary suddenly lunged for the door. I raced after him and we fought our way through it, down the hallway and up the stairs, pushing and shoving each other. As we scrambled onto the upstairs landing, Elliot's bedroom door opened and he came out, holding on to the arm of a young and extremely pretty girl. Gary and I froze in mid-skirmish and stared at them.

"It's okay, Kelly," Elliot said to his wide-eyed girlfriend, "Just keep walking. Don't make any sudden moves, they're very skittish and unpredictable, but they won't hurt you. Straight down the stairs to the front door, and then into the car. You can do this, Kelly."

"Ha ha, very funny," Gary said.

"No," Elliot replied, walking passed us, "It's not funny at all, dad."

We watched them walk down the stairs and out the front door. There was a moment of heavy silence, and then Gary suddenly said, "I've had enough. I'm sick of this."

"Enough of what? Sick of what? You're never here long enough or often enough to form an opinion about anything that goes on around here!"

Without answering and without looking at me, he plodded down the stairs and picked his jacket up from the coat stand. He didn't pause, didn't turn, he just quietly left the house.

* * *

Left alone – unloved, unwanted and unemployed – I did the only thing I could think of, I opened up the bottle of whisky in the kitchen cupboard and sat on the sofa to drown my many, many sorrows. "Never got your hands on my single malt though, did you, Mr Callum-misery-guts-Redfern," I growled as I poured a glass. I took a gulp, then instantly regretted it. It was alcohol that had gotten me into this mess in the first place, more alcohol wasn't going to solve anything. And besides, I didn't actually like the taste of whisky.

I stared at the amber liquid in the glass as tears flooded my eyes. Once they started, I found I couldn't stop. I staggered miserably up the stairs to bed, *our* bed, and cried endlessly into my pillow.

I didn't sleep a wink. First, I couldn't sleep because I felt so desperately alone, then because Gary didn't come home, nor did Elliot, and, overtired and overwrought, I began to worry about them both. The house seemed so empty, so oppressively quiet. I kept hearing noises through my sobs, a crack, a dull thump, a creak. By midnight I was a nervous wreck, convinced we were being broken into by burglars and that I'd eventually be found dead in my bed.

Gary wasn't lying next to me when I woke the next morning. He wasn't downstairs either, he just hadn't come home.

* * *

Thankfully, Callum was out all the next morning doing site visits, so at least I didn't have to face him. Unfortunately, Sarah had booked the day off to have her glorious hair done, so I was on my own. I got stuck into my work.

By lunch time, as the recruitment agency I'd joined the day before hadn't rang with loads of jobs crying out for my skills, I went to join another agency with some idea about lots of fingers in lots of baskets or something. I was wearing my best suit (the one that wasn't too bobbled), my hair was behaving itself for once because I'd thought to drag a brush through it, and I'd touched up my makeup in the office toilet. I was the epitome of the perfect secretary, I told myself.

"I'd like to join," I told the receptionist at the Office Fairies recruitment agency.

The receptionist deigned to look up at me with a loathing only the very young can conjure. I gave what I hoped was my most confident look, just smiling a little so the laughter lines wouldn't emphasis the dark, sleepless circles under my eyes. She looked me up and down. "We only have secretarial vacancies," she said.

"I might be having a rough day," I said, "But do I look like a brick layer to you?"

"Take a seat."

"Will it take long, only I'm on my lunch – ?"

"Take a seat."

I sat. I waited. I flicked through two Cosmopolitans, three Take a Break, a Woman's Weekly, and the promotional brochure for Office Fairies, before a woman with a smile manufactured in some plastics factory came over to me. She sat down and instantly assumed an intimate rapport, as if we'd been friends for years. "Looking for work are you?" she beamed. I was tempted to reply that I'd just come in for a bit of a sit down and a skim through their magazines but resisted. "Yes," I said. "Secretarial. I'm currently working for Richard Sovereign & Co."

"Oh, the commercial property company?"

"Yes. I'm after something similar."

"Why are you leaving Richard Sovereign?" she asked.

"I … He … They're restructuring internally," I told her. "My position has become redundant."

"Oh, what a shame," she said, glancing down at the papers in her hands to hide the fact that she really couldn't give a damn. "If you could just fill this form out, I'll be back in a few minutes." And, with another blatant display of capped teeth, she wriggled off to the other side of the office.

"Excuse me," I said to the receptionist, who didn't look up from the magazine she was idly flicking through. "Excuse me."

The receptionist lifted her eyes and sighed, "Yes?"

"I'm sorry to bother you when you're obviously rushed off your feet, but do you have a pen I could use to fill out this form?"

She placed a pen on the reception desk in front of her and returned to her magazine. I retrieved the pen and filled out the form. Then I sat and waited, and waited.

"Excuse me," I said again, and again the receptionist didn't look up. "I've filled out the form."

"And we're fresh out of medals," she breathed.

"I really need to get back to the office."

"Not really my problem, is it." Stroppy cow!

"If you could just tell that other lady to come back?"

"She's on her way."

"Oh? How do you know that if you haven't - ?"

"She's *on* her *way*."

I had the sudden urge to throw something at her, the magazine rack, or maybe my handbag. Just as I was contemplating the weight and throwing distance of the coffee table, the woman returned and took me into a room kitted out with five computers. "Just a quick typing test for speed and accuracy," she said. "Start when you're ready and give me a shout when you've finished."

I glanced at my watch and settled into a chair. It was too high but I didn't feel I should be dismantling furniture. I put in the headphones, found the squeaky foot pedal, and began. It was all automated. Programmed boxes appeared on the screen giving me detailed instructions on what I should do – listen and type was basically it. I started typing. It was one of those clacky keyboards, which are massively annoying, and the SHIFT key wasn't quite where it was supposed to be, but I got through it. I sat back in my chair and waited. And waited.

20 minutes later, when I was leaning back, staring at the ceiling and humming Queen's *I Want To Break Free*, the woman returned. She printed out my results and glanced at them. "Oh dear," she said, reading them. "You've made quite a few typing errors."

"I'm sorry," I said, grinning confidently, "I've been a secretary for – " I couldn't remember how long. 8 years? 10? "A long time," I eventually said, "I don't make mistakes."

"Well, according to this printout you mistyped over 40% of the words, and you only have a typing speed of 25 words per minute."

"25?" I laughed, "I can type faster than that with my tongue."

"It's all here," she said, waving the papers at me, "There's no cheating the system, I'm afraid."

I gave her my best Forest Whitaker squint. There had obviously been some mistake, I was the fastest typist in the department, if not the whole company, everybody said so. "Those *are* my results you've got there, aren't they?"

She nodded adamantly, pulling apart the two pages she was holding. "Yes, they're definitely – oh, wait, I must have pulled off a previous applicant by mistake."

I nodded, relieved. The woman said, "99% accuracy, typing speed of 95 words per minute, pretty impressive."

I nodded again, allowing myself a tiny smile of satisfaction. "So, what vacancies have you got for me?" I asked.

"What position are you looking for?"

Anything! I wanted to scream. "Obviously a secretarial position, preferably in a property company."

"We've just had a vacancy in for a receptionist at a solicitors' office," she said.

I stared at her for a moment, then shook my head clear and repeated, "Secretary, property company."

"How about a change?" she said brightly. "We have this great vacancy at a prestigious legal firm in Barnt Green."

"Receptionist?"

"Yes," she said excitedly, "Interested?"

"I'm a secretary," I said, as clearly as I could. "I'm a *property* secretary specialising in building consultancy work, which means I work for building surveyors. I have years of experience in property work and I will be an asset to any property company. I am *not* a receptionist, and I don't even know where Barnt Green is."

I left the recruitment agency and joined another one two doors away. There they were so busy talking amongst themselves that no one thought to question my presence in their office for the first 10 minutes, and then kept me waiting to see someone for another 20. By which time, after I'd quickly scribbled my particulars on yet another form and endured yet another typing test (99 words a minute this time, I was in a hurry) I was horribly late getting back to the office.

I tried to sneak discretely to my desk, but just as I was slithering passed Callum's office the mobile phone in my bag went off – Air on a G-string at 297 decibels. Callum looked up from his cluttered desk and caught me in mid-sneak. He gave me an evil-eyed look. 'I'm not bothered' I told myself, trying to stare him out but failing miserably, 'I'm only here for another three days.'

I answered my phone whilst shaking off my coat, noticing all the audio files waiting to be typed up on the dictation system with my name next to them. There were *loads*. "Hello?"

"Suze."

"Gary?"

"I'm just phoning to tell you I'll be home late tonight."

"Oh?"

"Important business meeting," he said.

"First business meeting in 19 years," I drawled. "Coincidence?"

"No, essential."

"How so?"

"I … I can't tell you. It's just important, that's all you need to know, so I'll be late. And I've asked Mike and his missus over for dinner on Friday night."

"You're just a bringer of good tidings, aren't you?"

Callum had strutted out of his office. He glared at me. I glared right back, imaging a large carving knife rammed between his eyeballs. "Are you intending to do any work at all today?" he asked.

"I have to go," I told Gary, "We'll talk later." I hung up. Callum drew breath, about to launch into one of his famous ripostes, when my mobile rang again.

"Well?" Callum drawled dangerously.

"Yes, Mr Redfern, right away." I'd joined three recruitment agencies and I needed a job *so* bad I would have said anything, done anything, to make Callum go away, I *had* to take that call. He gave me a stern look that seemed to go on for an eternity and a half, and then he sauntered *oh so slowly* back to his office. By the time I pressed the green button on my mobile, Air on a G-string no longer reverberated around the office and the caller, whoever it had been, was gone. Ten seconds later it started up again and I heard a loud huff out of Callum's office. I snatched it up quickly.

"Hello?"

"Suzanne?"

"Yes."

"This is TemPers, you signed on at our agency yesterday?"

"Yes."

"We have a permanent position we thought you might be interested in."

"Secretary?"

"Yes, in a large property company in the city."

Excellent. Finally, things were looking up. "Salary?" I asked, like I was in any position to bargain.

She told me. "Where?" I asked, grabbing a pen. The women said a company name I was familiar with, the address and a contact name. "Can I say you'll be there for an interview tomorrow at 10am?" she asked.

10am? Jeez! "Yes," I snapped. "Fine. Thank you. Bye."

Callum peered at me from the other side of the glass partition. I smiled sweetly, put my phone on silent, and started up the first dictation. It was a Pete one, and he sneezed all the way through.

CHAPTER 3

Gary didn't actually come home at all that night, just sent a text saying he was staying at Mike's, and Elliot, sensing the increasing tension in the house, stayed with a friend, and I can't say I blamed him. I was left alone to bite my nails and ponder my future. I was so tired by everything that had happened I went to bed early and slept right through until morning. I caught the bus to work.

Sarah, her hair looking particularly amazing, did nothing but sigh a lot and come over to my desk to hug me since I'd told her I was leaving. "It won't be the same without you," she kept saying.

I tried to make out I didn't really care, but inside I was terrified. It felt like I was on the edge of a cliff about to fall off – or *pushed* off. Two more days and I would be gone, thrust out into the cold, cruel world, alone, friendless and jobless. Alex would have to leave university and work at WHSmith to make ends meet, and Elliot would have to go down the coal mines – did they still have coal mines in the Midlands? I would have to check.

"Have you heard anything about this reshuffle they're having?" I asked Sarah, when we both unplugged ourselves from the corporate headphones for a coffee break. "Has James said anything to you?"

"Shhh," Sarah hissed fiercely, glancing around with wide eyes. "You can't mention him and me in the same sentence, people might hear and jump to all the wrong conclusions."

"Has he?"

"Well ... "

"Come on, Sarah, I *have* to know. I'm losing my job because of it." Well, I was losing my job anyway, but I was suddenly obsessed with the facts. The facts were something I could throw back at Gary whenever he threw my unemployed status at me. I could either tell him, 'Hey, I'd have lost my job anyway, so I'm glad I got out first, good timing, eh?', or else say, 'They deliberately got rid of me for being rude to my boss, so what? I'm a woman of principle, a model figure of feminism and I *will* stand up for my rights'; this said whilst shaking a hard fist in the air.

"I can't," she said, "I promised I wouldn't say anything."

"You can tell me, I won't breathe a word." I mimed zipping up my mouth for emphasis.

"James," Sarah breathed, so quietly I had to watch her lips, "did mention something about the reshuffle when we had that business meeting on Monday."

"And?" I breathed back, "Is anyone else getting moved or is it just the building consultancy departments merging? Is it just me or are there other people involved? Did Callum stitch me up or would I have lost my job anyway?"

Sarah was now so quiet as to be inaudible. She said something which sounded like, 'Edith was going into retail', but my brain managed to decipher, "He didn't go into detail." Then she said, "Eye mooning upta edge munt," which my brain just shrugged at.

"What?"

"Eye mooning upta edge munt."

"I'm sorry, Sarah, you're going to have to breath out when you speak."

"I'm moving up to Management!" she breathed.

"Are you? Oh!"

"Andes Moore." I thought she was saying a name at first and I struggled to think who this Andes Moore was and how they were involved in all this.

"What?"

"Des Moore."

"Andes Moore or Des Moore?" I ask, completely confused now. "Oh, you mean 'and there's more'?"

"I shoo unt really tellu."

"Shouldn't really tell me what?"

"I'm nodshure I shudsay."

"Please, Sarah, speak properly, my brain's about to cave in."

"I'm not supposed to say," she whispered.

"Well, you've started now, you might as well finish."

"I can't."

I snatched a stapler off my desk and shook it menacingly in front of me. Sarah asked, "Are you going to staple me to death?"

I slammed it down. A gruff voice peeled out of Callum's office. "Would you *mind* keeping the noise down out there, *some* of us are trying to *work*."

I tutted. "Come on, Sarah, tell me what you know."

She hesitated for just the briefest moment, before nodding towards Callum's office and saying, "He won't be here for much longer, I can tell you that much."

Joy flooded my body. I couldn't remember the last time I'd felt so happy. I almost heard angels singing Hallelujah in the background somewhere. "They're sacking him?"

"Well, not exactly."

"How not exactly?"

"I don't know all the details, it's just something *James* – " His name didn't even have a sound now, it was just a pronounced movement on her lips. " – mentioned in passing."

"What did he mention? Is Callum being sacked? I *have* to know, Sarah."

Silence. Long. Lingering. Sarah didn't move, didn't blink. I held my breath, waiting, until she eventually said, "He's leaving." I exhaled, relieved, sending up a grateful prayer to the Great God of Justice. Then Sarah added, "He's been offered another position elsewhere."

"Where, McDonalds?" I laughed.

"Senior Partner."

"What?"

"He's taking up a position as Senior Partner at Flogg & Float."

No! It couldn't be! What the hell was the God of Justice *thinking*?

Callum was being promoted? His career had stepped up another notch on the corporate ladder while I was being thrown out like mouldering rubbish? My view of the world changed abruptly. It wasn't fair. It had been *me* who'd corrected all his stupid mistakes in every single report he dictated for the last four years, *me* who'd chased after him about vital appointments and deadlines he'd completely forgotten about, *me* who planned every site visit like a military operation because the man had absolutely no sense of direction. He got promoted, I got kicked out.

"Bollocks!" I snarled.

"What was that?" came Callum's voice from the sanctified domains of his glass office.

I felt a ping in my head. Just like that, *ping*. I don't know what it was, my brain exploding perhaps, or maybe my sanity being stretched too far, like an elastic band that finally snaps. I stood up. Sarah put a hand on my arm but I brushed it away.

"I said bollocks," I repeated out loud. "You're being promoted!"

Callum rushed like a bulldog with diarrhoea to his open glass door. "Who told you that?"

I could feel the vibes emanating off Sarah. "It's common knowledge," I said casually, "Everyone knows about it."

"But ... but ... " he spluttered, "it hasn't been made public knowledge yet!"

"I hope they've got good secretaries at this place you're going to, Callum, because you need a good secretary. I'll tell you this for free though, if you treat her the way you've treated me you won't be a Senior Partner there for long."

"How dare you speak to me like that, *again*," he spluttered, going bright red in the face.

I leaned menacingly across my desk towards him. "I can

speak to you any way I like. What are you going to do about it, have me sacked? Oh, you've done that already. Not a lot left to threaten me with really, is there."

Callum suddenly looked nervous.

"You've got two days of me yet, Callum. Be afraid, be *very* afraid."

His glass door slid shut in front of him like the closing of the final curtain at the theatre and, without taking his eyes off me for a second, he shuffled backwards to his desk and immediately began picking up random papers, his eyes still on me.

"Bloody hell," Sarah gasped, "I've never seen you like this before."

"I've never felt like this before," I said. "I think I've actually lost my mind."

* * *

"Hi, it's me," I breathed into the mouthpiece. "I just wanted to ring you and see how you were. You've eaten, haven't you? Can't have my man going hungry, can I."

"Suze?"

"How's the big meeting going? Are you nearly finished? Will you be home soon?" I was aware that I sounded like a whiney wife, but I really just needed company and a hug, some-one to tell me that that losing my mind wasn't the worst thing in the world.

"Look, I can't talk right now, Suze."

"Ah, heavy negotiations in the boardroom?"

"No, it's just … You're in a funny mood."

"Practically hysterical."

"Yes, you sound it. Look, Suze, I'm busy, okay? I've got to go."

"But – "

Too late, he was gone. I felt numb, slightly panic-stricken, and massively alone. I'd lost my job, now my husband. I sighed heavily. The sound echoed around the empty living room. Elliot was at a friend's house again, Gary was 'working late' again. Maybe I should get myself a dog for company, something to talk to, something that wouldn't answer back or demand money, something that would look up at me with unconditional love in its eyes.

I turned on the TV, flicked through all 137 channels – tumours, births, deaths, shouting, crying, bad acting and canned laughter – and turned it off again. I huffed and inspected the wallpaper, the ceiling, my nails, then got up and wandered aimlessly around the room.

I felt lost. Adrift. I felt so incredibly alone. I wandered into the kitchen and found myself opening a cupboard door, taking down the bottle of whisky. I opened it and tipped it into a glass.

* * *

Way to go, Suze, I thought – or would have thought if my brain had been functioning in any capacity. It was morning. I was lying on the sofa with the bottle of whisky cradled in my arms. I had a hangover the size of Alaska - it was so big there was nothing left inside me except this throbbing, sick feeling. I moved my eyes a fraction of an inch to look at the whisky bottle and pain coursed through my skull. I'd drunk at least two inches, maybe two and a half. For someone who hardly ever drank, that was a lot of alcohol to consume in one go and my body was punishing me for it.

Slowly, like I was made out of glass and might shatter from any sudden moves, I sat up. The house around me was deathly quiet. The horrific clock on the mantlepiece that Gary's mom had given us said it was 6.15 (a.m. I hoped). I noticed nobody had bothered to throw a blanket over me in the night or left a thoughtful glass of water on the floor beside me. My aloneness surged.

I managed to make it to my feet by sheer willpower alone and staggered into the kitchen, where I consumed half a pint of milk, three large glasses of water and almost a whole carton of orange juice, and still felt thirsty. Using the last of the juice I forced myself to swallow two aspirin and a few random vitamin pills in the hope of stimulating my body back to life.

How I made it upstairs I don't know, I just remember hanging off the banister rail a couple of times and used the landing wall as support as I aimed determinedly for the bedroom. There was a hole in the wall along the way and my head rolled into the gap – Elliot's room, just what you needed to see when you were hungover and on the verge of death, a room full of smelly washing, dirt encrusted mugs and mouldering plates.

Gary was in bed, so at least he'd come home. I staggered over and fell across the mattress, crushing his legs beneath me and making him wake with a start.

"What the bloody hell do you think you're doing?" he screamed.

"Dying," I said.

"Christ, Suze, get off my legs! How much did you have to drink last night?"

"I was feeling a bit down," I told him, "You know, with everything that's been going on."

"And you feel better now you've consumed nearly half a bottle of whisky, do you?"

"It wasn't half a bottle, it was two inches. And please don't shout."

"I'm not shouting!"

I dragged a pillow over my head and made some groaning noises.

"Well, you're not lying there all day," Gary said, leaping out of bed, "You have a job to go to, while you still have a job to go to."

"Go on, rub it in why don't you. I don't see how having a day off would – oh *crap*!" I sat up straight, my brain following a few seconds later. "I have a bloody interview this morning."

Gary had already scampered off to the bathroom. The hangover was now just an ignored agony. I had far more important things to worry about.

There was a brief tussle outside the shower cubicle, but Gary managed to get inside first on account of him being already naked and me still wearing yesterday's clothes. I tore them off and stood there, waiting and hissing, "Come on, hurry up, I have to get ready!"

"I need a good, long shower today," Gary teased, slowly soaping his chest. "Yes, a nice long shower to start the day off right."

I opened the shower door, struggling to get in. Gary pushed me out again.

"I need a shower," I whined.

"Tough."

"Get out of the shower, Gary."

"When I'm good and ready."

Furious, I turned on the sink taps. The water in the shower turned into a scalding inferno. As Gary screamed and cursed, I filled the toothpaste mug with cold water and threw it over the top of the shower cubicle. Gary leapt out, howling, and I leapt in.

* * *

"Morning," Sarah smiled cheerfully.

"You're happy."

"I'm always happy."

"That's true, but today you look ... happ*ier*."

"Well, its nearly the weekend."

Nearly the end of my employed life. Oh god.

"I'm glad you're in such a good mood, Sarah, because I need a favour. I need you to cover for me while I nip out for an interview at 10 o'clock this morning."

Sarah's eyes widened. "Cover for you? You mean, pretend you're still here when you're not?"

"Yes."

"What will I tell people if they ask where you are?"

"Tell them I'm in the toilet, or I've taken up smoking and I'm outside having a fag."

"Suzanne!"

"I know, I know, it's a lot to ask, but it should be okay. Poo breath – " and we both glanced at Callum's empty office. " – is in a meeting until 11, I should be back before then."

"Should be? What if you're not?"

"Stall."

"Oh Suzanne! Why didn't you just call in sick?"

"What, and miss out on all the fun that's goes on around here?" I shook my head, feeling my brains physically move inside my skull. "Believe me, Sarah, I've never felt sicker, but I had to come into town for this interview and, with my current run of luck, someone was bound to spot me in town and blab."

Sarah looked nervous and uncertain for a moment, then she said, "Okay, I'll do it, but you get back here as soon as you can."

"Don't worry, I will."

The place where they were holding the interview was only 10 minutes' walk away. At 9.45 exactly I left the office trying to look nonchalant. The Head Secretary walked into my path just as I'd almost made it to the lobby and asked where I was going. To anyone else it might have sounded like a casual query, but to me it came across like a Gestapo interrogation.

"I'm just dropping off some plans that need to be looked at," I told her, rolling my eyes and huffing wearily. I shook my handbag for effect, hoping she wouldn't notice it was so small I'd have been hard pushed to fit an envelope in there, let alone giant site plans. "You know how it is with these last minute reports, all rush, rush, rush, and you have to get them checked incessantly or else the world blows up or something." I gave a nervous laugh.

"So you'll be back in 10 minutes then?" she said. "Only I need to talk to you about a few things, you know, leaving stuff."

"Yeah, yeah, no problem." Bugger!

Outside, the pushchair brigade were out in force, blocking pathways, charging along like cavalrymen and smashing into other pedestrians. I had to step into the road to avoid being mown down, deftly avoiding oncoming traffic. A woman with a clipboard approached me but I waved her away shouting, "Sorry, no time," like the white rabbit in Alice in Wonderland.

I was almost at the office building on Broad Street when a

frail old pensioner reached out a frail arm to attract my attention. I tried sidestepping her but she was pretty nifty for an old person and blocked my path.

"Excuse me, love," she said, her rheumy eyes imploring me. "I'm a little lost."

I didn't have the heart to walk away so I paused for a moment, jumping impatiently from foot to foot whilst the old lady wittered, "I was trying to find the offices where my son works. Only he left his sandwiches on the kitchen table this morning and I thought it would be a nice trip out for me to bring them to him. I don't get out much on account of – "

"Where's he work?" I snapped.

"It's one of those big office blocks, I'm not quite sure which one."

"Name of road?" I could physically feel the precious minutes ticking away.

"Well, I don't really know." She gazed around, confused. As she did, I noticed a commissionaire step out of a building right next to us.

"He'll help you," I said, pointing and making a run for it.

I was going to be late. Fabulous first impression I was going to make, turning up late. Not only that, but because I was now having to run – and it seemed that every single person in the city centre was there only to *get in my way* – I would arrive red-faced and sweating, too.

I arrived, red-faced and sweating, and was directed to a waiting room. There, I tried to calm my rasping breath and pounding heart and compose myself into something resembling an efficient, immaculate secretary. I knew, without the aid of a mirror, that my hair was bouffant and wild after its struggle to keep up with me across the city, and that my mascara was probably, as I sat there, melting down my cheeks, but I didn't dare ask where the toilets were in case I was called into the interview. So I patted my hair down, rubbed fingers under my eyes, and sat, and waited.

And waited.

After twenty minutes of looking at my watch every thirty seconds and feeling like a nodding dog on the back shelf of a car, a top-of-the-range secretary, who looked as if she spent more on shoes than I earned in a month, came to lead me through the reception area and into a meeting room. On the way I noticed what might be my fellow workers – the receptionist, chewing gum and reading a magazine (not even looking up as we walked past, good job I didn't have a tiny bomb in my tiny bag); an open-plan office full of secretaries diligently tapping at keyboards; and several people crammed into possibly the tiniest kitchen the world has ever known.

In a vast meeting room I sat down at a table already occupied by a huge man with no hair, who looked up at me with such seriousness I felt like I was there to ask for a loan. I smiled brightly, trying to ignore the nerves that were eating my insides away, but he didn't smile back. The woman sat down next to him, and the interview began.

I hadn't been on an interview for six years. I hadn't had time to research the company, swot up on interview techniques or give any consideration as to how I was going to present myself. Not only had I *not* updated my CV, but I hadn't even brought the old one with me, and was so vague about my qualifications I'm sure they thought I was making them up as I went along.

I was utterly unprepared and knew within the first five minutes that I was absolutely crap and they wouldn't offer me a position as stamp licker, let alone secretary.

"How would your friends describe you?" the woman asked.

I was completely thrown. Was this an interview or a therapy session? What kind of question was that?

"Your friends," the woman repeated, glancing sideways at the man, who stared at me relentlessly, "How would they describe you?"

"Oh. Well. Erm. Funny, I suppose." As in, totally off my rocker. "Professional." Oh yeah, Callum could vouch for that alright. "Calm in a crisis." Yep, I'd definitely been calm since they'd told me I no longer had a job, mostly alcohol induced calm.

They both looked at me, obviously expecting more. I had no more to give. There was a fine line between 'selling yourself' and being arrogant. I smiled uncomfortably. Neither of them smiled back. I expected them to say thank you at this point, that my dubious services wouldn't be required after all, but they didn't. The interview continued like some merciless form of torture for another 20 minutes.

"What about your previous employment history?" the woman asked. "Can you tell us a bit about that?"

The fact that I hadn't worked at all for the first five years of my sons lives went down a like a concrete weight in a swimming pool. The woman gaped at me like I was some antisocial parasite, probably wondering if her nanny would do the family ironing before teaching both children to walk, talk and play a musical instrument. My part-time work that fitted in with school hours didn't improve matters either, that I'd been employed by some of the top High Street shops barely dragged me above the primeval soup of mankind.

35 minutes.

"If you wouldn't mind doing a little typing test for us?" The implication being that, after all I'd told them, they would be surprised if I could recognise a computer, let alone use one.

"Of course." Shit!

I was led *slowly* into the open-plan office. A few of the women there looked up, but nobody smiled. The atmosphere was strangely oppressive, as if anyone caught talking would be sent to the Head Secretary's office for a good thrashing. I sat down at an empty desk. The chair was too high, the keyboard smaller than I was used to, and the monitor was so far back I could barely see it. The woman gave me the kind of detailed instructions a three year old would understand.

A letter. Formatted to company standards. Full of names I typed phonetically and test words that I, being a property secretary, had no problem with. Whilst I was typing this at the speed of light, the phone on the desk in front of me started ringing and I was thrown into a panic of indecision. Was this a test to see how adaptable I was? Should I answer it or simply ignore it and not let it distract me?

Thankfully, it stopped ringing before I could decide.

Letter accomplished, I was ready to go, I *had* to go. The clock on the office wall told me I had been absent from work for almost an hour. Sarah would be frantic, and Callum was due back from his meeting *at any minute*.

The woman approached my desk (walk *faster*, damn you!). She dragged a chair along with her and sat down next to me (for God's sake, just let me go!). She leisurely began to tell me about the company structure and office procedure, while I sat there, smiling and silently screaming for escape.

One hour. That's how long I'd been stuck in this nightmare, a whole 60 minutes. And then, finally, the woman uttered the words I'd been longing to hear.

"Well, that's all for now, Mrs Philips. We'll be in touch with your agency."

And I was gone. Free. Racing across the city centre back to my office.

Where I was greeted by the desperate face of Sarah and a very apoplectic Callum.

CHAPTER 4

I was home. At last. It had been one hell of a day and I was more exhausted than I'd ever been in my entire life. The house was empty but showed signs of having been occupied at some point during the day. I could tell exactly what Elliot had been doing simply by looking at the mess he'd left in his wake.

There were four half cups of tea in the living room and, strangely, one outside the downstairs toilet. In the kitchen were the remnants of a meal, so at least I didn't have to worry if he was eating properly. A breakfast bowl, a frying pan, two dinner plates and a sandwich plate, along with two more mugs of unfinished tea, were piled up in the sink. The cooker top was smeared with grease and dollops of unidentified gloop, the fridge was almost empty, and the half open freezer door had created a puddle the size of Lake Windermere on the floor. And every single surface was covered with open packets and bread bags, abandoned milk cartons, dirty spoons and knives. A family of flies were happily ensconced in the butter tub, the jam jar and a discarded pizza. Oh, and he'd filled the washing basket.

Nice.

This is what I did most nights when I got home from work, I cleared up after Elliot, who obviously considered it to be part of my motherly duties. He usually stayed out of the way until the debris had been cleared, his presence then so fleeting I barely had time to draw breath, let alone scream at him to be less slob-like, before he was gone again. At which point I'd start dinner, eat dinner, sometimes with Gary, oftentimes not, clear up after dinner, the whole time listening to Gary, if he was there, moaning about his day, then moaning about the lack of milk, before he sighed a bit, tutted a lot and disappeared to the pub/club/a mate's house to watch football/cricket/rugby. I might then get a bit of ironing done whilst watching TV, before falling, knackered, into bed.

Bitter? Moi? No, just very, very tired, today more tired than normal because my life seemed to be collapsing around me like a flimsy deck of cards. I'd slowly, over the last few days, come to realise I didn't actually have a life at all.

I surveyed today's mess and flopped onto a kitchen chair. I really didn't have the strength to slip into the old routine tonight. I'd screwed up an interview, been bawled out again by my boss and, to top it all, as a finale to a Really Shitty Day, my bus home had been late, was packed, and it had rained on the walk to the house. If this was an American TV programme the husband would be pouring me a cool glass of wine right about now whilst the son (who worked as a top chef in a top restaurant) cooked up something delicious for dinner. In reality, I was just knackered and alone, again.

I rested my elbows in two clear spaces on the kitchen table and let my head flop into my upturned hands. "Crap!" I breathed, "Crap, crap, crap!"

When I'd finally got back to the office that morning it was 11.35 and about half an hour later than I might possibly have got away with. Sarah had valiantly done a pretty good job for the first twenty minutes, after which she struggled to fight off the interest of the Head Secretary, a woman from HR who wanted to conduct a leaving interview with me, and several surveyors and other secretaries from other departments who I barely spoke to but had chosen that particular time to acquaint themselves with 'the woman who'd been sacked'. By the time Callum returned from his meeting, cut short because someone's wife had gone into labour, Sarah was on the verge of a nervous breakdown.

When I showed up, breathless, red-faced and sweating, Callum was frothing at the mouth with rage.

"My office! Now!" he barked.

The entire office, which had been a buzzing hive of activity when I'd walked in, fell into an ominous silence. Some people at the far end actually stood up to get a better view of a condemned colleague. I took a deep breath and shuffled into Callum's office. He motioned me to sit in a chair in front of his desk.

"Where have you been?" he began.

"Dentist," I spluttered, bringing a hand up to my mouth so fast I actually slapped myself in the face. "Emergency, the pain was – "

"Why didn't you inform anyone you were leaving?"

"I was just in so much pain."

"You actually passed the Head Secretary on your way out, and yet, strangely, you didn't mention anything about the dentist to her."

"No, I wasn't thinking straight, the pain you see, I just had to get to the – "

"You're lying." He said this with such conviction and absolute menace that I let the hand slip from my face into my lap. "How long have you worked here, Suzanne?" Still that barely restrained fury in his voice.

"Six years."

"I'm surprised you've lasted that long."

"I'm a good secretary," I said.

"Are you? Are you really?" A sinister smirk. "What makes you think you're a good secretary, Suzanne?"

"Why? I'll tell you why. Because if anyone wants any work done urgently they bring it to me, because I'm fast and accurate and I know what I'm doing. Because when someone's computer crashes and the IT department are too busy reading comic books or porn magazines, it's me they come to because I've taught myself to work the stupid system." And, I thought, I'm so professional I've never once, in the whole four years I've worked for you, followed the urge to rip off your sanctimonious face and stomp on it.

"You're only here for one more day," he smirked, "I'm sure I can tolerate you for that long."

Him tolerate *me*. Had the world completely lost its marbles? I felt the now familiar adrenaline coursing through my veins. I could tell, from the nasty grin on Callum's face, that he was just waiting for me to explode again, but I wouldn't give him the satisfaction. Suddenly, instantly, all energy drained from me like someone had pulled out my batteries.

"You know what, Callum," I said, wearily standing up. "You're an odious little rat of a man who doesn't know his arse from his elbow. Belittle me all you want, I don't care. But, if there's any justice in the world at all, you'd better brace yourself, because you're heading for one hell of a fall."

"Says you," he snorted to my departing back, "Some little secretary who, after tomorrow, doesn't even have a job."

I turned back to him, so tired I could have curled up on the floor in his office and snivelled myself into a coma. "I may be a little secretary," I said, "But people like you get where you are because of little people like me shoving your flabby arses up the corporate ladder."

With huge effort, I pulled back the glass door just as Callum stood up behind his desk. "You have an extremely bad attitude, Suzanne Philips. You won't go far, people like you never do."

And here I now sat, at the cluttered kitchen table in my cluttered, empty house, surveying the debris of my youngest son. Gary would tell me to let them clear their own mess up, but it was hard to live somewhere where you had to navigate your way through the prolific encroachment of detritus like an assault course, and besides, I couldn't stand Gary's constant moaning about it (and everything else), it was just easier to clear it up myself.

I stood up from the kitchen chair, headed towards the plate-filled sink, then thought 'Stuff it," and went for a shower instead.

* * *

Gary came home from work just as I was coming down the stairs in my dressing gown.

"Just got up?" he snapped irritably. He stormed into the kitchen, saw the mess, and cried, "What the hell is all this?"

"It's like this almost every night when I get home from work but I, good wife and mother that I am, clear it all up so we can live in relative safety." I said this in the hope of eliciting some sympathy, that Gary would suddenly see what a wonderful wife I was and take me in his arms, swear his undying love and be on my side in my fight against the world. I had more chance of finding an alien artifact in my dressing gown pocket.

"So why haven't you cleared up tonight then?" is what he actually said.

"I've had a bad day."

"*You've* had a bad day? *You've* had a *bad day*?"

Gary glared at me, then pulled his mobile out of his pocket. He punched in numbers, waited, then yelled, "Elliot, get a job! Get one *now!*" He furiously tossed his mobile down. It skidded across the messy kitchen counter and came to rest against the congealed pizza, disturbing the flies settled on it.

"And you!" he said, turning to me, "Have you sorted out a job yet?"

"I went to that interview."

"And?"

"I don't think I'll get it."

Gary snatched up his mobile again, grimacing at the smear of tomato sauce. He punched in numbers, waited with a pinched bum look on his face, then bawled, "Where are you? At your girlfriend's house? How far away is that? 20 minutes? Right, you've got 10 minutes to get home before I start throwing all your belongings out the window. I bloody will! You're wasting time, Elliot, you've now got precisely 9 minutes to get here before I make you homeless, do I make myself clear? Good." He turned to me, anger oozing from him like heat, and snarled, "I'm going out."

"What? No! Elliot will come home, see you're not here, and

bugger off out again, leaving *me* to clear the mess *again*."

"Do I have to do everything around here?"

"Do everything? You don't do *anything*, Gaz, you're hardly ever here. You saunter around your poxy office all day, barking orders, have extended lunches with your mates and no doubt a few of the prettier secretaries, come home when you're hungry, then piss off out for the night. As far as you're concerned, pixies come when you're not here to wash up and clean and cook and take care of the kids and – "

"The house is a mess and my wife is a nag, what reason is there for me to stay?"

"Me," I said. "Stay for me, stay *with* me."

We stared at each other for a long time across the cluttered kitchen. If he left now, I swore I'd divorce him. He must have seen it on my face because he hesitated. Then he huffed loudly and ripped off his jacket. "Just until Elliot's cleared up," he said.

He was *mine*. Adult company. Marital conversation. *Excellent.*

"Wine?" I offered, opening up the fridge.

"Yes, you do. Constantly."

"Humour?" I quipped, "Things are looking up."

I poured Chardonnay into two glasses and handed one to him. "Here's to surviving the teenagers," I toasted, clinking my glass against his. My glass promptly shattered, the Chardonnay adding to Lake Windermere still spreading across the floor.

As I leaned against the counter drinking the last dregs of wine from a mug, Gary sat stiffly at the kitchen table, trying not to touch anything. The clock on the wall ticked interminably. To pass the time I thought I'd indulge in some conversation with my husband, just to see if it was still possible or if you lost the ability after months/years of mutual apathy.

"Gaz."

"What."

"Are you having an affair?"

"What?"

"Are you having an affair? I wouldn't ask, except you've

been acting a bit strange for a while now and you seem distracted all the time."

"Are you mad?"

"Possibly. It's the little things, you know? No sex, no conversation, no real interest in anything at home. You've been drifting away for ages."

"You think I'm having an affair?"

"Yes. Are you?"

"No," Gary said calmly, "I am *not* having an affair."

Silence between us. Then he suddenly leapt up from the table and headed towards the kitchen door.

"Oh don't go," I said, "We haven't talked properly for – "

"You think this is talking properly? Accusing me of having an affair?"

"I thought I'd clear the air a bit while you were here, who knows when you'll be here again. You're around so little I feel I need to compress everything into the short space of time I have before you disappear again."

Gary paused in the doorway. "I'm not having an affair," he said. "The reason I'm not here a lot of the time is I'm out there working to support my family."

"I think we've had this conversation before, Gaz."

"I think we've had *every* conversation before, Suze."

"Yes. Except this one."

The sound of Elliot bursting through the front door with bristling panic shattered the heavy silence that had suddenly fallen between me and my husband, the man I had lived with for 19 years and who, it seemed, had nothing more to say to me.

"My stuff!" Elliot gasped, holding onto the banister rail, breathing like he'd just completed a marathon when, in fact, he'd only run from his car in the driveway. "Did you ... touch my ... stuff?"

Gary, rather eagerly I thought, became engrossed in bawling out his youngest son. "Sort this!" he yelled, pointing at random piles of mess, "Sort that! That! And that!"

I escaped to my bedroom, where I lay on the bed listening to them arguing downstairs.

"You call that clean?" Gary howled, "That's not tidy, no-where near! Do it again!" And Elliot, alternating between impatience, annoyance and general self-pity, crying, "It's clean! It's tidy! What are you, the Gestapo!"

Ah, happy families.

An hour later, while I was watching TV in bed, the cacophony of noise suddenly stopped. I heard the front door slam shut, a car start up, the screeching of tyres tearing off down the road. A brief moment of heavy silence, then the front door slammed shut again, another engine started up and more tyres screeched off down the road.

I was, it seemed, alone. Again.

Naturally.

* * *

"You know, when I was single," I said to Sarah, breezing into the office the next morning, "I was always afraid of going places alone, like bars, pubs, anywhere really. Then I got married and *really* learned how to do everything on my own."

"Bad night?" Sarah ventured.

"You could say that." I slammed my bag down on the table and noticed, with some relief, that Callum wasn't yet in his office. "All my nights are bad lately, and the days aren't much of an improvement. Gary didn't come home until the small hours. I found him lying like a dishevelled tramp on the living room sofa this morning, stinking to high heaven like a rancid brewery."

I had actually sat in an armchair and scrutinised him for some time while he was asleep, searching for any signs of lipstick on his collar, blond hairs on his jacket, tell-tale love bites on his neck. I couldn't sniff him for perfume as I had no sense of smell, but as far as I could see he was clean – well, relatively clean considering he hadn't undressed or showered. Once again, to avoid a dawn scene, I left the house before he woke up and caught the bus to work.

"And as for Elliot!" I was just about to wax lyrical about the joy of teenagers when a trainee surveyor slapped a wad of papers down on my desk in passing and carried on passing.

"Oi!" I called after him, "What's this?"

"It's my revised schedule of dilaps."

"Why is it on my desk?"

"Callum said you'd type it up when I'd finished."

"Did he, and what, exactly, am I supposed to type up?"

The trainee sighed heavily and threw his head back to look at the ceiling. My stress level shot into the red zone. This was my last day (argh!) and I was already drowning in work, I didn't have the energy to deal with attitudes. The trainee came back to my desk, sighed again, and leaned over the sheaf of papers. "Just type up the revisions."

"Type up what?" I said through gritted teeth.

"See these red bits there? Them, type them."

"I can't *read* the red bits. You have to at least make the effort to form letters and words that I can read."

He sighed again. His groin was right next to me, I could so easily have lashed out with a hard fist or a stapler, but didn't.

"This is a schedule of dilaps," he said slowly, as if talking to a child. Don't punch him, I kept telling myself, don't punch him in his man bulge and make him cry, even if he deserves it. "The red bits are my revisions. Just type them up into the document."

"The red bits look like a pen accidentally touched the paper a few times, they're just squiggles. As I don't have a degree in hieroglyphics, you're going to have to make them look more like English."

"This is literally your job!" he said, all high pitched and aggravated. "Just do it."

I snatched up the pages of red squiggles, caught Sarah's 'uh-oh' expression as I stood up and slapped them hard into the trainee's chest, holding them there. "Take these away," I said, in my firmest don't-bloody-mess-with-me voice, "Write it out again using print if you have to, that means capital letters. Bring it back when I can read the bloody thing. Am I making myself perfectly clear?"

The trainee looked at me, shocked. I glared back at him, unflinching. With a final huff, he pulled the papers off his chest and stormed off.

I'd just sat down when my mobile rang. "Suzanne?"

"Speaking."

"It's TemPers agency here. I'm just ringing to let you know about three permanent vacancies you might be interested in, interviews on Monday."

"Great," I said, giving Sarah a big thumbs up. "As long as you understand I don't do reception work."

"Right," the woman breathed, "Just *two* vacancies then."

"Have you heard from that interview I went to yesterday?"

"Ah." Definite hesitation, not a good sign. "Yes, they did get back to us."

"And?"

"And they've gone with someone else."

"Oh." I gave Sarah a thumbs down. I didn't want it anyway.

"First vacancy is at Flogg & Float." The same company Callum was going to! I briefly wondered if it might be worth working there just to annoy the hell out of him, then quickly decided against it - I had my sanity to consider.

"Pass," I said.

"Oh, right. How about … ?"

I was given details of another property company, which I scribbled down on my notepad. Secretary at medium sized company in the city. It was only when the call ended and I hung up that I noticed Callum standing by my desk, diligently reading my notepad.

"Ah, Cromby & Crocket," he sneered. "Bog standard surveyors, treat their staff like slaves."

"You'd fit right in," I said, because it was my last day and I didn't care any more.

And then Callum genuinely shocked me and said, "How about we call a truce?"

"What?" I gasped, and I heard Sarah gasp too.

"Let's stop all this bickering and shouting on your last day."

"You mean, forget the fact that you deliberately conspired to make me lose my job and that we can't stand the sight of each other?"

Callum raised his eyebrows. "Yes"

I had to admit the recent battles, both at work and home, were exhausting. It would be nice to pass my final day at Richard Sovereign & Co in relative peace. So I nodded in agreement, and Callum looked pleased (as far as I could tell). Then he dropped a three-foot pile of filing on my desk, along with the files for 12 full dictations, and sauntered back to his office.

"Make sure you've finished all the filing before you leave," was his final command before his doors swished closed.

"Yes, sir!" I saluted stiffly. "On it right away, sir!"

"Your last day and the bugger has you filing," Sarah sighed.

My last day. Suddenly those three words seemed to sink into my brain and the full meaning slammed into me like a rugby player.

My last day! Oh my God!

After today I was officially unemployed. Jobless. Without work and without regular money. I'd had such a frantic week arguing with Callum and Gary I hadn't really had time to *think* about it. Never again would I walk into the familiar lobby downstairs, stroll like one-who-belonged passed reception, or sit at this desk, *my* desk, with the photos of my family and the miscellaneous paperwork I'd never been sure what to do with.

I tossed the pile of filing underneath my desk and rang Office Fairies. "Any temp work going for Monday?" I blurted.

"Receptionist?" they offered.

"Anything else? I mean, *anything* else?"

"Nothing at the moment, but we'll keep you posted."

By midday I was running on pure adrenaline and scouring the job vacancies on my works computer, which we weren't supposed to do during work time but bugger it, it was my last day. There wasn't much out there except for dead-end typists, wrong-side-of-the-city positions and vacancies offering half of what I was earning now. But beggars can't be choosers, and every time Callum left his office for a toilet break or a meeting I rang after them, one by one.

One receptionist wouldn't even put me through to the HR manager, she said they were busy and couldn't possibly be disturbed. "But they're advertising vacancies, surely they expected some phonecalls?" But no, apparently they hadn't scheduled it into their hectic day. If they were that disorganised I didn't want to work there anyway.

Another was answered by a woman I could only assume was the office cleaner, such was her understanding of the company, the work or the position. She stuttered and stammered a bit, her voice drifting off to a mere whisper at one point as she apologised for knowing absolutely nothing about anything. And, of course, there was no one else around at the moment for her to ask.

A secretarial position for a 'busy' surveyors' office, salary pretty crap but I was in no position to complain about it, a crap salary was better than none at all. A highly excited woman with a screechy voice 'interviewed' me over the phone; typing speed, experience, ability. I casually mentioned that I would be available to start on Monday and her excitability flew off the scale.

"Oh right," she squealed. "Come in on Monday."

"You want me to start straight away?" I asked, daring to smile.

"Well, come in and we'll see what we want to do with you. Try it for one day and see if you like it. In fact, come for a week and we'll slot you in somewhere. Or, better still, we'll put you on contract for a month and take it from there."

"This is for the position in the building consultancy department, right?" I finally managed to ask.

"Well, we might have that position filled but I'm not sure yet, the girl's going to get back to me about it today. But we have lots of vacancies here, management, marketing, residential property, real estate, industrial, they all need good typists."

"Secretarial positions?" I asked.

"No, just typing, basic salary, 8am till 6pm, Monday to Friday and every other Saturday morning for viewings."

I made my excuses and hung up. I was desperate, but not that desperate.

The next one I rang was answered by possibly the stroppiest receptionist in the universe. Information about the position was dragged out of her by sheer willpower and bloody-minded perseverance, and every answer I elicited was followed by a heavy sigh of boredom. I hung up. A receptionist is the face of a company, and I didn't want to work for a company like that. Annoyed, I rang the number again and said, "You have *got* to be the worst receptionist I have *ever* spoken to in my entire life. Just so you know." And hung up again.

Callum's meeting would be drawing to a close soon, so I hastily rang the last vacancy. 'Mature secretary required for valuation dept of small family-run surveyors' the ad said. 'Salary negotiable.'

I managed to make it past the receptionist this time and spoke directly to the Head of Department, who sounded amiable enough. He asked a few questions, I gave a few answers, then I asked about the 'negotiable salary'. "Well," he said (and I could almost imagine him leaning back in his chair and stretching), "It would depend on your age and experience."

"Well, I've given you my age, or a close approximation of it anyway, and told you my experience. What were you thinking of paying a secretary of my age and experience?"

He told me. My first instinct was to laugh, then to question it, hoping he'd maybe missed off a digit somewhere, but no, he repeated it and there was no mistake. "You pay peanuts," I told him, "You get monkeys. I'm not a monkey." And I hung up, depression settling on me like a heavy blanket.

"Anything?" Sarah asked.

"Not a thing."

"You need a drink," she said, suddenly excited.

"I need a new life," I sighed.

"No, a drink, you definitely need a drink."

I looked over at her and the penny dropped like a rock. "Oh no!" I gasped, "What have you done?"

"Nothing," she beamed brightly. "I've just organised a little leaving party at The Old Joint Stock over the road, that's all."

"Oh God." I let my head fall into my hands and resisted the urge to burst into tears. "How many are coming?" Four people, I thought idly, maybe five in the whole company who I was on friendly terms with. Some leaving party that would be.

"Twenty-seven," Sarah said.

I lifted my head out my hands. "*How* many?"

"Twenty-seven people are coming to bid you farewell." She scrutinised my face. "People like you, Suze. Didn't you know that?"

I didn't. I'd probably been too busy to notice, and Callum was always chipping away at what remained of my self-worth, along with Gary. You can't have a good opinion of yourself when all around you people questioned your validity to be alive.

"Is *he* coming?" I nodded my head towards Callum's office.

"He said he'd try and pop in."

"Great."

Sarah's smile waned.

"I'm sorry," I said, "I don't mean to sound ungrateful. I do appreciate it, thank you."

Oh God. My life was falling apart, and now I had to go out and celebrate it.

CHAPTER 5

Lunch that Friday afternoon on my last day at Richard Sovereign & Co started at 12.30, when Sarah and a few other over-excited secretaries dragged me out of my chair and out of the office. Callum didn't have a say in the matter, he simply watched me being manhandled from the building from the relative safety of his office (never interfere with secretaries *en masse* seemed to be his motto – picking on secretaries *individually* was more his forte).

In the reception area there was a veritable gaggle of people waiting for me. I was surprised at the number who had turned up to 'see me off' – but then, alcohol is always a big incentive. As we made our way across the foyer downstairs I could actually hear 'Here come the girls' playing in my head, and for the first time in a long time I felt good, despite being the scruffiest one in the pack. In a giggling, screeching mass we made our way across the road to The Old Joint Stock, halting the traffic on Colmore Row.

I kept trying to get my purse out of my bag (not that it had much in it) to buy a round of drinks, but my attempts were thrust aside as every single secretary *fought* to ply me with alcoholic beverages – and who was I to argue? Senior Associates and even a couple of Partners wandered in to wish me farewell, including James, but I didn't get a chance to talk to him or even thank him for the enormous umbrella cocktail he had sent over –

Sarah whisked him into a corner, where they whispered and giggled interminably. Callum, however, was noticeably absent and I hoped it stayed that way.

I suddenly found I was enjoying myself. Two surveyors, young and obviously unable to hold their drink well, whispered that they thought I was 'really quite attractive' (for a woman of my age, I thought), and that they admired my 'fortitude and tenacity' in working for Callum.

Others said, "You strut into the office every day with your head held high." I didn't tell them it was because I was usually late and looking to see if Callum was in his office yet. "You have your own individual style," someone else said (bag lady, I thought). More people than I could count told me that I was funny, "Always rely on you, Suze, to cheer us up when we're down, and to keep our spirits up when we're fighting deadlines." I was really surprised. I was just doing my job.

"They're idiots to let you go," a secretary from Accounts told me.

"You're the best secretary we've got," said Si, the trainee.

"It is *me* they're all talking about, isn't it?" I whispered to Sarah, when she managed to tear herself away from James. "It's not someone else's leaving do they think they're at, is it?"

"I can't believe you're asking that," she said. "You're a nice person, Suze. People like you because you're easy to like."

"Just my luck to find this out on my last day, eh?"

"You've no self-confidence, that's your trouble."

"Gary took it, along with my ego and most of my sanity."

"You should get those things back, Suze. You deserve to be treated better than he treats you, I've always said so."

I admired her 23 year old wisdom and gave her a big hug.

At 1.45pm I spotted Callum out of the corner of my eye slinking through the entrance doors. He surveyed the now drunken throng, marched with some determination to the bar, then approached my table.

"All the best in your new job," he yelled above the crescendo, "Wherever that may be." He plonked a half pint of lager down on the table, where it stood out like a sore thumb amongst the cocktails, the brandies, the whiskies and the fancy coloured alcohol in tall glasses – not all of them mine. Twenty-seven pairs of eyes stared at the lager. A hush fell over our corner of the bar. One of the more 'vocal' secretaries bawled, "Bloody hell, six years and all you get is a bleeding half of lager."

"Cheers, Callum," I said magnanimously, raising the glass of a particularly large cocktail, complete with an umbrella and a swizzle stick exploding with coloured foil, "It's been .... " I left the sentence hanging in the air as I searched the ceiling for the right word. All the girls burst into screeches of laughter. Callum promptly turned and left.

By 2 o'clock, when I tried to leave and get back to the office on time, I was physically restrained in my seat by several of the 'serious revellers'. Half the crowd returned to work, but half stayed, and the drinks just kept on coming. By 3.30pm I'd reached the stage where I was hugging everybody – secretaries, bar staff, random customers – and telling them all how much I loved them, *really* loved them.

The mobile of a secretary called Julie, who worked in the Development department, rang. She answered it, listened for a few moments, then stared, horrified, at me.

"My boys!" I gasped, instantly sobering up. "Is it one of my boys?"

Julie shook her head. "It was Callum," she said, putting the phone back in her bag. "He got my number off my boss because he didn't know yours."

"What's he want?"

"He wants you back at the office immediately to type up some urgent letters."

Everybody laughed. "He wants me to *work* on my *last day*?"

"Of courshe you're going to rush back" said a particularly inebriated secretary from the Industrial Agency department, "But firsht – "

"Another drink!" they all yelled, and another round was ordered. Followed by another.

And another.

I eventually staggered, with some considerable assistance from Sarah and two other secretaries, back to the office at 4.30, more than a little tipsy (Sarah kept laughing and saying I was such a lightweight in the drinking department). Callum, spotting me weaving unsteadily towards my desk, hiccoughing madly and still declaring my love for everyone, came out of his office wearing his 'bloody-secretary' expression. 'Here it comes', I thought, 'the final bollocking'.

I flopped loosely into my chair, and suddenly there were people all around my desk, smiling and chatting excitedly. "Callum?" came the voice of a tall Partner at the far end of the office, "Would you do the honours?"

Honours?

Callum coughed – nervously or furiously, it was hard to tell. Then a massive bouquet of flowers appeared out of nowhere, followed by several wrapped parcels and an envelope the size of a garage door.

"Suzanne," Callum began, reading off a piece of paper. "We've all clubbed together – "

"Even you, Callum?" I giggled, sliding sideways on my chair. Sarah hitched me back up again. "You've put in *hic* money, for me?"

"Yes, Suzanne, I bought the flowers."

"Oh," I sighed, tears stinging my eyes as I buried my face in the colourful petals, "You bought me flowers*h*!"

"As a token of our appreciation for the work you've done here."

"You appreciate me, Callum?" I was crying now. "Why didn't you ever tell me? It could have all been *sho* different. I just thought you were a miserable old *sh*od who – "

"We wish you all the very best in whatever you decide to do next," Callum cut in.

"I'm going to practi*ch*e poverty," I burped, "I think I'm going to be very good at it."

"And – " Callum glanced at a piece of paper in his hand before continuing with grim determination, " – we hope you'll keep in touch."

"Keep in touch?" I was being handed tissues, paper towels and toilet rolls by secretaries who were also beginning to cry. "We could do lunch shometime, Callum. I'd like that. Would you like that? Me and you, doing lunch, after all these yearsh."

I was, at this point, face down on my desk, crushing the bouquet of flowers, pressing various paper products against my eyes and up my nose, and really crying.

"Aren't you going to open your presents?" a surveyor asked, desperate to distract me.

I lifted my heavy head, spinning with regret and alcohol, and began to tear at the wrapping paper. A bottle of whisky from Management. A bottle of vodka from Property. A bottle of brandy from Corporate Real Estate and, finally, a bottle of Jack Daniels from the Ratings department.

"Are you lot trying to tell me shomething?" I slurred.

"Yeah," Sarah snapped, eyes narrowed as she surveyed the crowd, "They're trying to tell you they're all mean buggers by giving you the freebies left over from Christmas."

"No!" I gasped.

"No," cried the crowd as one.

"Open the card," someone said.

Three people helped me sit upright and thrust the giant card into my hands. The same people helped me to pull the card out of the envelope and open it out. Inside were a multitude of illegible scribbles that wavered before my bleary eyes. "Oh," I said, "That'sh sho lovely, thank you."

"Speech! Speech!"

Callum suddenly looked terrified. I shook my head, fighting back the urge to throw up. "No shpeech," I said. "Thank you for the card and the booze and the flowers, they're all lovely. You can all go away now."

And they did. Except for Sarah, who was frantically dabbing at her eyes with some of my paper products, and Callum, who suddenly looked sheepish and awkward. "Well," he said, shrugging. "It's five o'clock, I guess you can go home now."

With a huge wail of emotion, I leapt out of my seat. Callum jumped back like he'd been scalded. I caught him, wrapped my arms around him and gave him a big hug. "Bye, Callum," I said. "Bye, boss."

Behind me I heard Sarah say, "Take no notice, she's drunk."

I was helped into a waiting taxi by Sarah, my best drinking buddies from Management, a large bloke from Valuation who I'd never seen before, and the building commissionaire. I remember crying a great deal, telling everyone I loved them a great deal, and telling Sarah what a fabulous/special/wonderful human being she was a great deal. She came with me to make sure I got home safely without passing out or throwing up. I don't remember the journey home at all.

Elliot's car wasn't in the driveway as I staggered up it laden with bags of alcohol, a massive bouquet of flowers and a giant card, so I guessed, in my hazy stupor, that he was out. Gary's car was there, and so was another one. I used the unknown car to assist my navigation to the front door, setting off the car alarm, which tore through my throbbing head like a hot skewer. I struggled to turn and wave at Sarah as the taxi pulled away, and to get my key out of my bag and fit it into the keyhole that kept moving. I think it was only sheer luck that I eventually fell through the door into the hallway.

No welcoming committee, no flowers, no hugs, nothing. I clinked my way across the hallway to the living room door to announce my arrival, and found Gary sitting rigid in the armchair, glass of wine in hand and a hugely pinched expression on his face. On the sofa were an indeterminate number of people.

"Ah, Suzanne," said Gary, his voice syrupy sweet but his burning eyes telling a completely different story. "You're home. At last!" He gave a simpering laugh while I tried to figure out what was going on. "We were all waiting for you."

I tried to focus on the people sitting on the sofa – like the keyhole, they kept wavering. When the smudges of their faces came into focus I realised it was Gary's mate, Mike, from work, and his wife, Rhona.

"Oh hi," I said, moving unsteadily - and probably unwisely - away from the doorframe. The room started spinning and I stepped back, desperately grasping for the doorframe again. The bottles in the carrier bags clanked loudly against the wall. Petals fell off the bouquet.

"Mike and Rhona have come for dinner," Gary said with a rictus smile, "You know, like I told you the other day, only, guess what, there's no dinner."

"No." I was confused.

"You were supposed to cook dinner, weren't you, Suzanne?"

"Was I?"

"Yes, I told you Mike and Rhona were coming, didn't I." That simpering, embarrassed laugh again.

"Oh. Yes." I had a vague memory but nothing definitive. "You said somebody was coming." I nodded at them and burped. "But you didn't say I was *cooking* dinner."

Gary leapt out of his seat, grinned and said, "Just be a sec" to Mike and Rhona, and literally pushed me down the hallway into the kitchen, bottles clinking madly and petals flying all over the place.

"What they hell do you think you're doing?" he snarled in my face. "I *told* you they were coming and you haven't prepared anything! Then you stagger in as pissed as a newt. I'm *so* embarrassed."

"Gary, when, exactly, was I supposed to prepare anything?"

"Last night? This morning? I don't know!" He was waving his arms around now, full of fury but fighting to keep his voice down. "You should have done *something*. Why didn't you leave work early?"

I put my bags of leaving presents and enormous card and flowers down on the kitchen counter. Gary didn't appear to notice any of it. I turned to look at him as steadily as I could manage. "One, I forgot they were coming," I said. "Two, I wasn't aware I was cooking for four people, you neglected to mention I was cooking for four people. Three, I couldn't leave work early on account of the company plying me with presents, *leaving* presents." I took the Rating department's bottle of Jack Daniels out of a carrier bag, whipped out a glass, and poured myself a good slug. "On account of it being my *last day*."

"Oh great!" Gary cried in a high-pitched voice, which meant he really wanted to shout to the rafters but couldn't on account of our 'guests'. "You come home late and drunk and drink some more!"

"I have to say, you're not being very supportive, Gary." I slurped back the finger of whisky and poured myself another - reality held no particular interest for me now. "I am no longer employed at Richard Sovereign & Co. I am no longer employed *anywhere*."

"And is that *my* fault? Is it *their* fault?" he seethed, throwing an arm back towards the living room, "They're not getting fed because you're officially unemployed?"

"Look, I work full time, just like you! Well, I did, and I'm supposed to come home and whip up a dinner for four people? What planet are you on, Gary!"

"I told you *days* ago that Mike and Rhona were coming. You had *plenty* of time to prepare something. This is important to me; Mike's been offered a promotion and he'll be in a position to promote me too if we treat him right. This isn't treating him right, Suzanne!"

"Maybe I should offer to sleep with him instead," I said, draining my glass for the second time, mainly to annoy him.

"I doubt that would help," Gary snapped.

Silence while I tried to steady my eyeballs enough to glare at him.

"I'm taking them out," he finally said. "Some fancy restaurant to hopefully make up for this *fiasco*."

"Which restaurant?" I put down my empty glass, wondering if I could get away with work clothes to save me the bother of changing, or if it was going to be a 'posh' restaurant, in which case I could wear –

"You're not coming!" Gary looked surprised, horrified.

"You're drunk! Don't you think you've screwed up enough already without making matters worse?" He huffed and shook his head. "You know, Suzanne, you're a bloody liability."

He stormed off down the hallway to the living room, where I heard him saying, as cheerful as anything, "Right, let's go, restaurant of your choice, my treat. No, no, Suzanne's not coming, she doesn't feel up to it, bit of a headache."

I stood in the kitchen, fuming intoxicatedly. Then I heard Rhona say, "I'll just take the glasses into the kitchen," and braced myself. She appeared in the doorway and stared at me, slowly putting the glasses down on the counter between us. I said, "You don't like me very much, do you?", because, you know, I was drunk and didn't care.

She looked me dead in the eye and replied, "It's not that I don't like you, Suzanne, I just think you're an idiot if you don't know what's going on." And then she turned and left.

There was some murmuring and scuffling in the hallway, before they all trooped out the front door for their delicious meal, Gary's treat.

Leaving me alone. Again.

I shuffled into the living room with Jack and a glass and threw myself down across the sofa. I was aware that I should utilise this time to my best advantage and have some serious thoughts about my life and my future, but all I could think of was a variety of excruciating tortures I wished to inflict on Gary at that moment. I poured myself another drink. Bugger him, bugger everyone. Jack was all I needed.

Except, I suddenly didn't want any more to drink. Instead, I stood up and stared at myself in the mirror above the fireplace. "Is it me?" I said out loud, "Am I to blame for all this?" Then I recalled what people had said to me at my leaving do, nice things, surprising things, things that had made me feel good about myself for the first time in a long time. Was it me?

Was it?

I went into the kitchen and put the kettle on. I started drinking a lot of strong coffee.

And started thinking.

Really thinking.

Rhona had called me an idiot for not knowing what was going on, so what *was* going on? It was like all the doubts and concerns I'd buried in the back of my mind had been released, the tethers broken by alcohol and fear, and all of them crying out to be heard. Did he really work late most nights? Was he really going out for a drink with mates several times a week? All those 'poker nights with the lads', too drunk to drive home afterwards and sleeping on mates' sofas. All those 'lads fishing weekends' where 'someone was going to lend him the gear' because he had none of his own. Weekends away for football matches or golf tournaments or stag parties or training courses or conferences. Gary was hardly ever here, and when he was, he was detached and uninterested, always making excuses to break away again.

Something was definitely going on. I couldn't just ignore it any more. It was time to find out what it was.

I had nothing left to lose.

* * *

Gary actually came home in the early hours of the morning. I was still awake and now stone-cold sober, curled up on the sofa, coffee mug in hand, staring blindly into space, thinking. Gary wandered into the living room.

"You're still up then?" he said.

"Yes. Did you have a good time?" My voice was deadpan.

"It was okay." He sat on the edge of the sofa. "Listen, Suze, I might have ... overreacted a little earlier."

"A lot."

"Yes." Apologetic? Surely not.

"So, you had a good time then?"

"Yes, I just said."

"A *really* good time?"

Gary tutted and rolled his eyes. "What's up with you now? Are you in one of your moods again? Have you had too much to drink, *again*?"

"No." A long silence. "Where have you been?"

"You know where I've been! Out for a meal with Mike and Rhona."

"Until this time?"

"Yes. We ... we went on to a nightclub, that's why I'm so late."

Silence. It didn't make sense, and if it didn't make sense it wasn't true. "Who is she, Gary?"

"Oh, let's not go into all that again."

"Who is she, Gary?"

"For god's sake!"

"It's three in the morning."

"I know what bloody time it is." He was standing now, not apologetic any more, indignant again. "It's too late to have this argument, that's what time it is. Too late to start accusing me of all sorts of imaginary – "

"Don't lie to me. I know something's going on. I've known for a long time." Kind of, somewhere, in the back of my head, trying to speak up, and me too busy to listen, to pay attention. I was listening now.

Silence again. Neither of us spoke or moved. I could hear my own heartbeat pounding in my chest. I couldn't ignore this any longer, there was something seriously wrong between us and I had to face it, I had to know. It felt like the end of days, the end of everything.

"There's nothing going on," Gary said. "It's all in your head, Suzanne. I think you might need help. Maybe you ought to go and see the doctor. I've done nothing wrong. It's not me, it's you."

Maybe it *was* me, maybe everything was my fault. I didn't know, couldn't tell, I was so very tired. I stood up slowly, walked out of the room and went to bed. But I couldn't sleep, couldn't stand the thought of lying next to Gary like cold, angry strangers. Then I couldn't sleep because Gary didn't come to bed, he stayed downstairs. I began imagining him on the phone to this 'other woman', whispering words to her that he'd stopped whispering to me a long time ago. I imagined him with her, giving her all the love and attention that I so craved. I lay in bed, fighting with so many waves of emotions, until I could stand it no longer. This had to end, things had to change. I couldn't live like this any more, always on edge, always afraid and alone, never feeling good enough.

I leapt off the mattress and threw open Gary's wardrobe doors. He came into the bedroom just as I was throwing his underwear into a suitcase.

"What are you doing?" he asked.

"Well, I'm not packing for a holiday, am I!"

"I'm not leaving!"

"Aren't you?" I snapped the suitcase shut and hauled it off the bed, jolting when I realised how heavy it was. "I think you are."

"I pay for this bloody house and if you think – "

"Just go!"

"No, I won't!"

"You have two choices." I couldn't believe how calm my voice sounded when a tornado was raging inside me. I was glad we were in the bedroom surrounded by soft furnishings and not in the garage where there were sharp and heavy objects to hand. "You can either leave now, or you can wake up in the morning with a knife embedded in your chest, because, believe me, Gary, that's exactly what I want to do to you right now. I'm unstable, you've said so yourself, many times, can you be sure I won't stab you in your sleep?" He didn't answer. His eyes were wide. "Go or stay, make your choice, but I won't be fobbed off any more. I know there's something wrong and I don't think it's me. I need to know, Gary. Tell me what's going on."

He made a kind of strangled noise, and then slumped like a sack of potatoes onto the edge of the bed. Looking at the floor, he eventually said, "I didn't mean it to happen."

"What?" I hadn't expected this, I thought he'd just keep denying it and blaming it all on me. But here it was, the truth, the massive, heavy, dirty truth.

"It started off as a laugh," he said, "You know, just a bit of a giggle. Then she started taking it seriously, taking it a bit too – "

"I don't want to hear about it, I just want you to go."

He looked up at me with desperate, frantic eyes. "I never meant to hurt you, Suze."

"I'm not interested."

"It wasn't intentional, I didn't *plan* – "

"Write it down, Gary, I'm sure some women's magazine will feature it."

"How can you be so harsh?"

"Harsh?" I gasped. "You've been screwing another woman! I'm disappointed, I'm hurt and I'm bloody angry. For your own safety I think it's best if you leave."

"I didn't know she was like that, did I!" He was up on his feet now, pacing up and down the tiny space at the side of the bed, one and a half steps left, one and a half steps right. I wondered if he was getting dizzy. "Mike said she was a bit of a flirt, and when she came on to me – "

"Mike?" The word fell out of my mouth. I wasn't interested, but what had Gary's workmate got to do with anything?

And then I got it, everything suddenly clicked neatly into place, like the last piece of a jigsaw puzzle. "Your secretary!" I cried, "You're having it off with your bloody secretary! Christ, could you not be more *original*?"

"Oh right, next time I'll have it off with the Managing Director's missus, shall I, just to make it more *original*. Or perhaps you'd prefer it if I shagged the barmaid, just to make the stereotypes work a bit better for you."

"I'd have preferred it," I roared, "if you'd kept your bloody cock in your bloody trousers! And what do you mean, *next time*?"

The front door banged downstairs.

"I'm not going," Gary hissed, his face set like puckered concrete. "I live here. This is *my* home. I've *paid* for this house, and I'm not bloody leaving."

I stared at him, at my husband of 19 years. He used to be

funny, he used to be nice and kind and thoughtful. He used to love me. Now he'd lowered me to the position of 'wronged wife' while he bonked his secretary – his secretary! It all seemed so pointless, so extraordinarily clichéd, like a bad soap opera.

Downstairs, the fridge door banged shut.

"Burglars are raiding our fridge," Gary joked weakly.

Elliot thudded up the stairs. Gary suddenly looked uncomfortable and agitated. "I'm not arguing about this in front of him," he said.

"Why not? Don't you want your son to know you've cheated on his mother? Not something to be proud of really, is it."

Elliot appeared in the open doorway, his mouth full, his hands holding at least half a loaf of sandwiches. He took one look at us, standing like statues in the bedroom, and stopped chewing. "What's up?" he asked, alarmed. "Nobody's died, have they?"

"Not yet," I said.

"Shut up, Suzanne."

"Are you two arguing *again*?" Elliot huffed, already striding off to his room. "Can't you give it a rest? You're like a couple of kids squabbling all the time, it's very boring and very annoying."

His door slammed shut. Gary and I remained facing each other. I said, "If you don't leave, I *will* kill you."

He huffed and snatched up the suitcase. "You're going to regret this," he hissed, and went.

CHAPTER 6

I didn't sleep. How could I sleep when my world was crashing down all around me. I tossed and turned in bed all night. At 7am I was staring at the alarm clock feeling sick and ill, and not just with a hangover. I felt like I'd been mown down by a truck. Everything hurt, my head, my body, every individual internal organ. I needed to talk to someone, tell someone. I reached for my mobile phone and called my big sister.

I didn't call Katie very often, she was always so busy with her business and I was always so busy with life, and Gary always complained about the mobile phone bill, even though I was the one who paid it. Katie lived in Toronto with her adorable and adoring accountant husband, Aiden, and owned several thriving hairdressing-slash-beauty salons. Katie was beautiful and confident, everything I wasn't, but she had a good and wise soul. We'd been close growing up but had drifted apart as we grew older, especially since she'd moved to Canada 10 years ago, but she was still my sister and my best friend.

"Jesus, Suze, its 2 o'clock in the morning!" Katie croaked, when she eventually answered, and then her voice filled with panic. "It's not mom or dad, is it, or the boys? Has something happened? Should I book flights to the UK? I can be there by– "

"Mom and dad are fine," I said quickly, "But something *has* happened."

"What?"

"I've kicked Gary out."

I could sense Katie struggling with this, to find the right words. She'd never liked Gary, called him a miserable control freak, usually to his face, which didn't help relations much. I knew she was dying to say "Good!" Instead, she said, "Oh?" in a mildly curious way.

"He's been shagging his secretary."

"God, what a cliché. Couldn't he be more original than that?"

"That's what I said."

"Oh Suze, you poor thing, you must be devastated."

I lay back on the bed and stared up at the ceiling. "I'm not sure how I feel. I haven't had much sleep and, of course, it's all been very upsetting, but I think what I feel most of all is ... relief actually."

"You're probably in shock. Your emotions are in turmoil."

"No, I feel kind of ... released, you know? Like I've been carrying this massive weight around for the longest time and now I've finally put it down. It's not like Gary shagging his secretary came as much of a surprise, really. I knew something was wrong but I didn't question it, I was – "

"Too busy looking after everyone?"

"Yes." My sister knew me so well. Catch Katie running after husband and teenagers like I did, she had far more sense.

"Do you want me to fly over?" she asked. "I might be able to spare some time away from the business."

"No. Thank you, but no. I need some time to get my head together, to figure out what I want. I'm not sure I want to talk about it yet, I just wanted to hear your voice."

"I'm here for you, Suze. Any time, day or night. When you're ready to talk, call me. Whenever you want, to rant, to scream, to cry, to call him all the names under the sun or to plan his death, you call me, okay? I have a few fatal suggestions of my own."

I laughed. "Okay, I will. Love you, Katie"

"Love you too, Suze."

I lay in bed, staring at the ceiling, wondering why I wasn't sobbing my eyes out or dramatically shaking my fists at the ceiling and screaming, 'Why? Why me?' Maybe Katie was right, I was probably in shock.

I sighed. What to do, where to start, how to make things better, or at least more tolerable? Coffee, I eventually decided, and padded downstairs. Just as I was stirring dried milk – there was no 'real' milk left – into my coffee, my mobile rang and Gary's name came up on my screen. He'd be wanting to come home, get showered, get changed, and pretend that none of this had happened, just carry on as normal. My freedom had been brief. I felt disappointed.

I sipped my coffee as I considered not answering it, letting it go to voicemail, but every time it stopped it immediately started back up again. I imagined Gary's growing impatience. Eventually I snatched it up, aware of the bowling ball in my stomach.

"Mom?"

"Alex! How lovely to hear from you, and so early. What's wrong?"

"Nothing. I didn't wake you, did I? Only I have a bit of an emergency." His voice certainly sounded breathless and excited. I was instantly filled with panic.

"Oh God, your girlfriend isn't pregnant, is she?" I gasped.

"No, no, I – "

"You haven't got yourself married after some drunken binge, have you?"

"No! It's about our electricity bill."

"Oh. Well, I don't understand your excitement, but then I've had a lot of electricity bills in my time and I guess the novelty kind of wears off after a while."

"Its massive!" he cried.

"You must be so proud."

"Mom! We've had a text saying they're coming to cut us off today unless we pay. Can you lend me the money?"

"Ah."

"Please, mom, I'm desperate. If they cut us off we'll have no internet!" He said it like you might announce the beginning of the apocalypse.

"No!" I gasped.

"So you'll pay it for me?"

"No."

"Why not?"

"You'll have to ask your dad."

"Can't you ask him for me?"

It was a familiar routine – I wanted to give (my heart, my soul, my very life blood), but Gary was a stingy bugger and he didn't give anything, ever. I briefly imagined the conversation. 'Oh hi, Gary. I know I've thrown you out and our marriage is over and I hate you and all that, but you couldn't pay Alex's electricity for him, could you?'

"No, I can't ask him," I said.

"Why not?"

"Because … " Because I threw your father out, because your father's having an affair with his secretary and I can't stand his guts right now, because your father's always been extremely 'frugal' and the last thing I want to do at this moment is beg him for money. "He's out, you'll have to ring him on his mobile."

"Oh mom, can't you ring him?"

"Sorry, Alex, you know your dad handles all the money." Ever since we'd first been married, in fact. If any of us needed money, myself included, we had to ask Gary; or rather, I did the asking while the boys hid in their rooms with their fingers crossed. Gary would rant and rave a bit before miserably peeling notes out of his wallet.

"But this is an emergency," Alex persevered. "Just transfer some money to my bank account."

"Ask your dad, Alex." I was getting a bit peeved now. I had my own problems to think about.

"But you have your own bank account, don't you, mom?" Alex persisted. "If you transferred from that dad wouldn't have to know about it at all."

"There's twenty-five pounds and seventy-five pence in my bank account, Alex." I'd been saving up for a new bathroom suite. I'd been saving for two years now. "It's all I have."

"Can I have that, then?"

"No," I said.

Alex was dumbstruck. In the silence that followed, I hung up. I had nothing to give, financially or emotionally. I was empty.

I sat and stared out of the kitchen window, a million thoughts running through my head; divorce, work, my boys, poverty. I sat like that for a long time, trying to put it all into some kind of order, but it was like untangling a giant ball of elastic bands. And then the phone rang again.

It was Gary.

"You didn't tell him!" he bawled.

"Tell who?"

"Alex! That you'd thrown me out!"

"He rang you then."

"Asking for money, as usual. You all think I'm some kind of cash machine. Why didn't you tell him?"

"It's only been five hours, I haven't had the chance to have the announcement cards printed yet. I was thinking, 'Mrs Suzanne Philips is devastated to announce that her low life husband, Mr Gary Philips, has been shagging his secretary, and she's decided to call it a day', but I thought I'd better check with you first."

"You can make jokes at a time like this?"

"It's all I have left, my sense of humour, or I'd go completely bonkers."

"You lost your grip on sanity a long time ago," he snapped.

"I didn't lose it," I retorted, "It was taken from me piece by piece!"

"You think you're the only one who's suffering? I'm bloody stuck with my mother."

"My deepest sympathy," I drawled. "Has she asked for housekeeping money yet?"

"No, not yet. Probably. Oh, I don't know." I could almost see him running his hands over his head in agitation. "She won't stop *talking*! I stopped listening about 20 minutes after I arrived."

"Yes, you're good at that."

A pause. Then, "I'm coming home."

"You're not."

"I bloody well am."

"You've slept with another woman, Gary! You've cheated on me! Don't you understand, I don't trust you any more, I can't stand to look at you, I *hate* you."

"I've broken it off with her, the affair's over, believe me – "

"Believe you? Are you kidding? You've been lying to me for God knows how long, you're clearly very good at it. What do you want me to say, 'Okay, if you say it's over then it must be true, why don't you come home and we'll pretend it never happened'? In your dreams!"

"You're obviously still a bit upset."

"Oh, you *think*?"

"I'll ring later when you've calmed down," he said. "But don't leave it too long, Suze, my bloody mother's driving me round the bend."

"I tell you what, Gaz, I have a better idea. Why don't we just assume that we're done, the marriage is finished, the relationship has come to a final, bitter end, and move on. It's over, Gary, it's been over for a long time."

And for the second time in less than an hour I hung up.

"You and dad still arguing, then?" Elliot said, wandering into the kitchen.

"Whatever gave you that impression?"

Elliot pulled a knife out of the wooden block and swished it through the air in front of him. "Oh look," he cried, "I'm cutting the atmosphere."

"You think that's bad," I said, filling the kettle for another cup of coffee. "There's worse to come. We have to go shopping."

"We?" Elliot gasped. "As in, you and *me*?"

"That's right."

"I'm sorry," he laughed, shaking his head, "I *don't* shop."

"You do now."

"I can't, I promised Kelly I'd take her to her … her aunts. Where's dad, away?"

I hesitated for just the briefest moment. "I threw him out."

"What?"

I didn't want to go into details. "We have problems," I said.

"You're grown-ups," Elliot said, tossing bread into the toaster. "All grown-ups have problems. You should be more like me, free and easy-going."

"Just FYI, at eighteen you *are* a grown up, and it's about time you started behaving like one. And secondly, it's us hard-working, stressed-out grown-ups that finance your free and easy-going lifestyle."

Elliot just shrugged. I wandered into the living room with my mug of coffee and my phone. I normally asked Gary for food money, but he wasn't here, I'd have to use the joint debit card, even though I wasn't supposed to. I rang the bank to find out the balance, as I did often – only Gary had online access to the account. The automated voice told me how much there was, and I froze. There was hardly anything in it, and there was another week to go until we got paid.

Elliot wandered in eating toast without a plate. "Good news," I told him, "Looks like we won't be going shopping after all."

"How come?"

"It appears we're broke."

"Guess there's no point asking you for money, then. Only I promised Kelly – "

"No point at all," I cut in.

Elliot wandered back to his room. I sat there, thinking again. We were always so broke. Why were we always so broke? Gary earned a good salary as a Senior Operations Manager, although I didn't know exactly how much as he never told me and I never really thought to ask. My salary was pretty decent, and both were paid into the joint account, so why was there never anything in there, why was Gary always telling me to 'not use

83

the joint account'?

Our mortgage was comfortable after 19 years, our bills were normal for a family of four. We weren't extravagant, except for Gary's BMW, we didn't have holidays abroad more than once a year (and even then we went all-inclusive to keep cost down). So why was I always scrimping?

Why?

There was a small computer desk in the corner of the dining area where Gary sometimes did work expenses on his laptop. Underneath it was a mini filing cabinet, just two drawers, where he kept all his 'important papers', including, I knew, a list of all his internet passwords because he could never remember them. The cabinet was always locked, always. Only Gary had a key.

I stared at the cabinet now. I wandered over and gave the top drawer an exploratory tug. It didn't give. I sat on a dining chair, staring at it. All Gary's important stuff, including the log-in details for the joint bank account, were in there. I'd only caught brief glimpses of folders in the bottom drawer, pens and staplers in the top drawer.

I spoke into my phone, "How do I open a locked filing cabinet?" My screen gave me pictures. First, I needed a paperclip to fashion into a make-shift key. It took me 25 minutes of searching every drawer and crevice in the entire house before I found one down the side of an armchair. I twisted it as described and thrust it into the lock, twiddled it around a bit. Nothing. I twisted some more, twiddled some more. Nothing seemed to be happening. I felt like a bank robber failing to break into a vault.

I considered calling Elliot, but decided this probably wasn't role model material, his mother breaking into his father's personal belongings. I dug out my makeup bag, pulled out a nail file, and jabbed that into the keyhole, twisting and turning. I felt the bolt that held the drawers locked move a little. I pulled on the top drawer. It was open.

I rifled among the stash of pens and Post-It notes and the detritus of a top drawer. There, right at the bottom, hidden underneath The Complete Idiot's Guide to Microsoft Word 2000, was a familiar looking notebook, Gary's book of passwords.

"Elliot!" I yelled, "I need to use your laptop."

* * *

"*What?*" Katie bawled down the phone. "He did *what?*"

"His salary doesn't get paid into the joint bank account, he deposits a lump sum from his personal account into it every month." And I never knew, never suspected. "Just a few hundred pounds to top up my salary so it was enough to pay the bills."

"What about food and personal items?" she asked.

"I had to ask him for the money. He gave me cash."

"But … why?"

"I think … I think it was his way of controlling things," I said, still trying to figure it out, "Making sure I didn't overspend."

"Overspend! You never bought anything! I always wondered why you were so broke when you were both working. I said to Aiden – didn't I, Aiden? – I said you must be very bad with money to have none so consistently. I even asked Aiden to have a word with you about it, didn't I, Aiden, what with him being an accountant and all."

"His mother used to overspend," I said. "His childhood was full of people pounding on the door demanding money and his mother never had it because she'd spent it all."

"You're defending him, Suze. Stop it or I'll vomit. The man was depriving you of what was rightfully yours and keeping you and your boys in perpetual poverty, the scumbag. How much did he keep for himself? What's his salary?"

"I never knew," I said, almost to myself. "He never told me and I never asked, but there was a folder in the cabinet where he kept all his payslips. I looked. I saw. I mean, I knew he claimed expenses, like car allowance and petrol and stuff, but … but he gets bonuses too."

"What's his monthly salary, including expenses and bonus?" Katie asked abruptly. I told her. She sucked in breath. "And how much did he put in the joint account every month?" I told her. She sucked in more air. "And how long has this been going on for?"

"I ... I don't know, I only went so far into the statement be-fore ... before ... "

The silence from Katie seemed to last a very long time, I thought we'd been cut off. I eventually heard her say, "I'll ask around, see if I can find someone to bump him off. Aiden, you mix with some dodgy types, do you know anyone who owes you a favour for fiddling their tax returns? No, darling, of course I didn't mean 'fiddling', I meant ... whatever it is you do. Could you ask around for me, darling?"

"Katie, I don't think that's the answer."

"Of course it is," she hissed. "If he dies it'll all come to you anyway."

"Katie!"

"Okay, okay, but think about it at least. I know I will."

"And ... there's something else."

"Right, that's it! He's cheated on you, lied to you, kept you in poverty, and now there's *something else*? Can't you get your hands on a shotgun, Suze. Don't you just want to club the son of a bitch to death?"

"He ... he used the joint account to pay for ... for his personal expenses too."

"What kind of personal expenses?"

"Jewellery." And not from Argos either, where he'd bought me something once, but from proper jewellery shops with names I recognised. "And meals at expensive restaurants." So many meals! What did this secretary have, some kind of com-pulsive eating disorder? "And hotel rooms in Cornwall when he was supposed to be on fishing trips with his mates in Scotland, hotels in Wales when he was supposed to be at conferences in London, hotels all over the country! And flowers, and *clothes*," I cried, tears now streaming down my face, "He bought her clothes from *designer stores*. I get mine from Asda."

"Suze," she said quietly, "Suze, I'm going to have to phone you back. I need to go and scream into a cushion and swear a lot and maybe throw things around a bit, and then I'll call you right back."

And the phone went dead.

I pinched the skin on my arm. It hurt. I was definitely awake, and this, despite it having distinctly nightmarish qualities, was definitely happening. This was real. This was now my life. It was horrible. I felt afraid.

I sat at the desk in the corner of the room with my head in my hands, occasionally looking up to scroll through the online statement. Every roll of the mouse brought up new horrors; monthly payments to a golf club, a gym, a couple of online porn sites (!), car payments, car insurance, and shop purchases, so many shops. He'd had a good old time buying all the stuff he wanted, whenever he wanted, while I shuffled around in a bobbled office suit being told Not Use the Joint Account!

Furious, I scribbled down all the payments and withdrawals for the last month, added them up. Gary took out more than he paid in. I was basically paying for all the expensive gifts to his secretary! He was using *my* money to woo his mistress!

I screamed and pounded my fists down on the desk. How could he steal from his family like that? He galivanted about doing whatever the hell he wanted, whenever the hell he wanted, without a care in the world. How could he do that to us? Did he not care about us at all?

Elliot poked his head round the living room door. "Is now not a good time?" he asked quietly.

"No, no," I said, taking deep breaths to calm myself, "It's fine."

He sat in a chair at the dining table. "Dad's not coming back, is he," he said.

I glanced at the computer screen, still displaying the statement. I pulled the lid down. "No," I told him.

"Are you going to tell me what's going on?"

"No."

"Is it really bad?"

"It is for me, but I doubt your dad would agree."

"I think I can guess." Elliot was quiet for a moment. Then he said, "Come on, let's go shopping."

"But we don't have any – "

"I fixed a mate's car yesterday. I've got money."

"You're offering *me* money?" I gasped.

"Don't get too excited," Elliot said, going into the hallway for his jacket, "It's not going to be a regular thing or anything. And there *is* an ulterior motive."

"Oh yes?" I said, following him. "And what's that?"

"There's no teabags in the house! You can't have a crisis with no teabags."

Despite everything I actually laughed, although it came out sounding quite maniacal. Elliot was visibly relieved and I was touched by his concern. "Right," he said, holding the front door open for me, "Let's go get teabags."

I lifted up the arms of my dressing gown. "It might be a good idea for me to get dressed first, don't you think?"

Katie rang back on my mobile while we were discovering the cheap delights of Aldi supermarket. "Suze," she said, "Every time I think about *him* I want to scream and smash more things." In the background, I could hear the sound of a glass being swept up. "In fact," she added, "I'll have to call you back later, I'm still in killer mode."

Elliot was taking things out of my hands, putting them back on the shelves and picking up a cheaper option. "We're poor," he kept saying, "We can't afford the brand names any more." He was brilliant, even refusing his usual type of tea in favour of a plain white box.

"Probably grass cuttings," I warned him.

"Bit of sugar and milk, never know the difference."

At the till, Elliot unpacked the trolley, packed it all into bags, and paid. "Mom," he said, "Your jaw's gone slack again."

Driving home in his car I suddenly saw him for the man he was, the man he'd become. My child no more but an adult, going out of his way to look after his mom. I felt very proud, and very old.

"I'm not stupid, you know," he said at length.

"I know you're not. You could have gone to university, too, you know."

"I know, but … well, I wanted to get out there, not be stuck in classrooms for another three or four years."

"Well, it's never too late if you change your mind. I'm sure I could sell a kidney or something." I gave him a wink.

"I know you'd only throw dad out if he'd done something really bad, like cheat on you. I bet it was some secretary from the warehouse as well."

"Elliot!"

He glanced over at me, grinning. "I'm right though, aren't I."

I didn't answer.

"I knew it," he said, punching the steering wheel. "You two arguing and you crying all the time and ringing Aunty Katie, I *knew* something was going on."

"Sorry," I said, "About all the crying and stuff, I tried to hide it."

"I may act like a child sometimes, mom, but only because you let me."

"Ah, my fault." Of course.

"No, you're great." He glanced over at me. "Really, the best. So how – ?" He careered round a corner, engine revving, tyres screeching. I gripped onto my seat and gasped out loud. Totally unfazed, Elliot straightened up again and rammed it into top gear. "So, how long has dad been diddling another woman?"

"Diddling?"

"Would you like me to use another word?"

"No, I wouldn't."

"So, how long?"

"I think this is something you should talk to your dad about."

"Do you know?"

"No."

"Do you know who she is?"

"His secretary."

"Ethel?" Elliot cried, "Ancient Ethel who smells of cat pee?"

"No, Ethel retired last year. This is Ethel's replacement. I've spoken to her on the phone a few times but I've never met her. Your dad said she was very plain."

"Yeah, I'll bet he did." He didn't say anything for a few moments, and then, "Shall we go and take a peek at this plain secretary dad's having it off with?"

"What?" Elliot skidded around another bend in the road, and I suddenly noticed we weren't on the way home, we were on our way to Gary's warehouse. "Elliot, I don't think – "

"Don't think, mom, just do. Aren't you curious?"

"I haven't really thought about it." I hadn't had time, everything had happened so quickly I wasn't even sure if I was capable of thinking any more. "Anyway, its Saturday, there's probably nobody there."

"They're stocktaking," Elliot grinned. "Everyone's in this morning."

"How do you know?"

"I heard dad talking about it on the phone yesterday, just before Mike and his horrible wife turned up expecting to be fed."

Was that only yesterday? It seemed like a lifetime ago.

"I still don't think it's a good idea."

"Come on, mom, let's see what the old slapper looks like."

As I was in his car and he was driving, I didn't really have much choice in the matter.

* * *

Gary worked at a large warehouse, a concrete box in a landscape of concrete boxes. The car park was half empty. I thought we were just going to sit there for a while to see if Gary and his 'plain secretary' came out arm in arm or not, but Elliot unclipped his seatbelt and said, "Come on."

"Where are we going?"

"Where do you think? To eyeball the enemy."

"But – "

Elliot got out and opened up the boot, pondered for a moment, then picked a bottle of (non-brand) lemonade and a bag of (special offer) apples from our bags of shopping. "Poor dad probably left without lunch this morning. Let's surprise him with these."

He opened up the door for me and I nervously got out. "I'm not sure I want to – "

"Let's see what we're up against, mom. Come on, you haven't done anything wrong."

With my heart firmly in my mouth and my stomach hanging somewhere passed my intestines, we entered the building where Gary worked. There was no one on reception on a Saturday, so we made our way straight up the stairs to the area above the warehouse.

I felt sick as Elliot opened the doors to the large, open-plan office. A few people I recognised from social gatherings glanced over at me and waved or nodded. Elliot began to move towards Mike and Gary's separate offices at the far end, outside of which sat their secretary at a desk, the 'other woman'. As soon as I saw her I froze. Elliot held onto my elbow but didn't speak. We both just stood there, staring.

She was young. That was the first thing I noticed about the woman getting up and moving to the filing cabinets outside Gary's office, how surprisingly young she was. Early twenties perhaps, not much older than Alex. And she wasn't the least bit 'plain', she was very pretty, petite, delicate, like a china doll, but then, who *isn't* pretty at that age, youth is very attractive. She wasn't blonde like I'd expected – stereotyping, Gary would say, because I couldn't form my own opinion – she was brunette, with large dark eyes and one of those mouths that look as if they were swollen from a bee sting or from too much kissing.

She was very smart looking, in her short skirt and matching jacket, silk blouse and expensive looking jewellery, but then she would do, having had it all bought for her by Gary, from shops I couldn't afford, with *my* money. I knew the price of everything she was wearing, including the gold necklace and bracelet, I'd seen them all on the bank statement. I struggled to remember what Gary had got me for my last birthday; it was a book and a bottle of Prosecco from Asda.

Elliot and I both stood there, in the middle of the office, glaring at her. She must have sensed it, because she suddenly turned, saw us, and immediately broke into a huge smile. Of course, it was a *perfect* smile with perfect teeth.

"Can I help you?" she beamed.

I stepped closer, Elliot by my side. "What's your name?" I asked.

"I'm Poppi, with an 'i'", she said, and actually pointed up at her eye.

Elliot gave a sharp laugh. "Pop-eye!"

"Who are you?" The pretty smile was gone now and her face was starting to form a frown – a pretty frown, not a wrinkle in sight on her perfectly made-up face.

"I'm Suzanne Philips," I said. "I'm Gary's wife."

"Oh." Her eyes went wide and she suddenly seemed awkward and flustered, not quite knowing what to do next.

"Suze!" Gary appeared at his office door with a face that wouldn't have looked out of place on a horror film – Alien, perhaps, where the man you know is going to die spots the monster for the first time. With eyes bulging, he looked at me, at Elliot, then at Poppi-with-an-i, who was no longer frowning but seemed ready to burst into tears at any minute. "Suze!" he gasped again, "What are you doing here?"

Elliot promptly held up the bottle of lemonade and the bag of apples. "We've been shopping," he said, "We brought you some supplies?"

"Have you? That's nice. Why?"

"You know why, dad."

All this seemed to be happening in slow motion. I could barely tear my eyes away from the young girl. Did she *have* to be so slim? Did even *have* to look so prettily distressed. I would have preferred her to be some blonde bimbo with big boobs, it would have been easier to handle somehow. I suddenly thought,

'I bet he loves her'. That was something I'd not considered before.

"Do you love her?" I said out loud.

"What?" Gary gasped, glancing around at all the people in the office.

"Gary?" Poppi whined.

Gary looked at Poppi, then at me, then back at Poppi again, his mouth moving all the time but no sound coming out. I thought I'd gone deaf, especially since the whole office had gone deathly quiet as everyone sat there watching us. But then I heard my own voice repeating, "Do you, Gary?"

Gary bounded out of the office doorway towards me, pushing Elliot out of the way as he took hold of my arm, spun me round, and began marching me towards the exit doors.

"Let's talk about it somewhere else, shall we?" he said irritably. "Let's go home and talk about it *in private.*"

"Dad!"

Gary continued to hiss in my ear like a snake. "Don't you think things are bad enough without you turning up at work and embarrassing me like – "

"*Dad!*" Elliot was in front of us now, pushing Gary out of the way and putting a protective hand on my arm. "Don't talk to mom like that."

"Stay out of this, Elliot. This is grown-up stuff, nothing to do with you."

"No, dad, leave her alone. You've done enough."

Was that *my* son, talking to his father like that, sticking up for *me*? I might have felt proud, had I not felt so stupefied.

"This isn't any of your business, Elliot."

"It *is* my business, dad. You've hurt my mom. You're a bit of an arsehole really, aren't you."

"Don't speak to me like – "

"Do you?" I said in the middle of all this. "Do you love her, Gary?"

Gary spluttered a bit, glanced behind me at Poppi, then said, "No."

"Gary!" Poppi cried.

"That makes it worse," I said. "That you'd cause this much pain when you don't even love her. Elliot, I want to go home now."

"Okay, mom, we'll go."

"We need to talk about this, Suze."

"I think we're beyond words now, Gary. I found out about the joint account, by the way, how little you put into it and how much you took out, buying things for *her*. That's very ... " I couldn't think of a word, my brain was like goo rolling round in my head. It was all so horrible. Everything was horrible. "... *despicable* of you," I eventually said.

"I don't know what you're talking about."

"Dad?"

"She's not thinking straight," Gary said to him. "She's imaging things, making all this up. She's off her head, Elliot, you should know this about your mother. She's a few sandwiches short of a – "

I'm not quite sure what happened then. One minute Gary was pleading his innocence, saying I was hysterical and delusional, and I was standing there, watching him and listening without hearing. Then my arm, entirely of its own accord, moved behind me, came round in a fast arc, and punched Gary right in the middle of his face. He stopped talking. I was glad.

"You have no right to talk about me or to me like that," I said calmly, "Not any more, not ever again." I stared at him, holding a hand to his face with a look of horror. Then I turned and stared back at her, at all the people silently watching us. I hated them all.

Elliot guided me around Gary, who was spluttering and spitting blood, and led me out of the building. He put me in his car and drove home.

CHAPTER 7

The rest of Saturday was a blur. In a huge reversal of roles, Elliot put me straight to bed and I slept – slipped into a coma would be a more accurate description. I fell into a black hole of unconsciousness, grateful to not have to think any more.

When I woke it was mid-morning on Sunday. I had slept solidly for 18 hours. I hauled myself out of bed and padded downstairs feeling thick headed. Elliot was in the living room watching TV. As I pushed the door open to say hello I saw he wasn't alone. His arm was around an extremely pretty girl sitting next to him on the sofa.

"Hi there," I croaked, and they both sat up straight on the sofa, pulling away from each other like opposite ends of a magnet. I smiled. "You must be Kelly." She nodded. "I'm very pleased to meet you, Kelly."

"I'm very pleased to meet you, too, Mrs Philips."

"Oh, call me Suzanne. Mrs Philips makes me feel so old. I *am* old, of course, and to be perfectly honest I've never felt so old in my life, but you can call me Suzanne. Or Suze."

"Kelly stayed the night," Elliot said. "I didn't want to leave you on your own, so she came round, is that alright?"

"Yes, it's fine." I gave Kelly a huge smile as if to prove I wasn't some terrible ogre that chased husbands into the arms of other women – I figured Elliot must have told her something about what was going on, so I overcompensated by turning into one of those seriously excitable women who was just so *terribly* happy about *everything*.

"You okay, mom?" Elliot asked.

"Yes, I'm fine," I said, struggling to notch my insane smile down a bit without it looking obvious. "I need a coffee, though."

"I'll get it." Elliot was already on his feet and racing towards the kitchen.

"You don't have to wait on me," I cried, following him. "I'm not ill or anything. You go and keep Kelly company, I'm okay."

"Are you? Are you really?"

"Yes. I know I looked like the Cheshire cat on speed just now, but really, I feel okay, better than I should be under the circumstances, but then your dad always said I was a bit odd."

"He's a twat," Elliot suddenly said, without any emotion in his voice at all.

"Elliot! Don't talk about your father that!" I moved quickly towards the kettle. "He's just …. human. We've been married a long time, it happens, a lot."

"He's still a twat for hurting you like that."

"People get hurt all the time, Elliot. I think I've done quite well reaching this age without being hurt too much, but then, I may have been too busy or too stupid to notice."

"You're not stupid, mom."

"I guess life was just saving it all up for one big hurt, but it's really not that bad. I'm tougher than I thought I was, or else I'm in serious denial."

To my surprise, Elliot came over and gave me a hug. It was a proper hug, not one of those quick hugs he gave me when I asked for one or when he wanted something. "Oh Elliot," I said. "Don't worry, everything will work itself out, you'll see."

"I'll look after you, mom."

"I know you will."

He moved away, leaning against the counter as I filled the kettle and spooned coffee into three mugs. "He shouldn't have done it," he said, watching me. "He shouldn't have gone off with someone else like that. You're better than that skinny bird at the warehouse anyway. What *was* he thinking?"

"She was skinny, wasn't she," I sighed. "Like a baby bird, all tiny and fragile underneath her silk blouse, like you could *crush* her little neck with just the *tiniest* squeeze.

"She's just some woman dad has a crush on," Elliot said, and I looked at him, at his face, at his eyes that were now avoiding mine.

"You knew, didn't you."

Elliot huffed. "I ... I thought he was up to something, I was home all the time, wasn't I. I heard some of the phonecalls he made when he didn't think I was in. They were really embarrassing, I thought he was making a right fool of himself."

"How long have you known?"

He crossed his arms over his chest, still avoiding my eye. "A few months."

A few months, and I hadn't had a clue, not even a suspicion, just a vague feeling that things weren't right but I would deal with them later when I had more time, except I *never* had more time. "How many months, Elliot?"

"Three," he said, staring straight at me now. "That's how long I knew about it, so he must have been seeing her for longer. Like I say, mom, he's a twat."

I poured hot water into the coffee mugs and sipped mine slowly. "Elliot," I said at length, "I want you to remember something. I want you to remember that he's your father, no matter what happens between him and me he will always be your father."

"Doesn't mean I have to like him though, does it."

"Doesn't mean he doesn't love you either. It's me he's fallen out with, not you boys."

While Elliot and Kelly watched a video downstairs, I ran myself a bath, poured nearly a whole bottle of bubble bath into it, and lay in the hot water, soaking and thinking.

How come I wasn't devastated, howling and wailing and beating my chest and stuff? Isn't that what wives did when they found out their husband was cheating? I inspected my emotions carefully, as if I'd been involved in a car accident and was checking for injuries. I was upset, of course I was, but really things were no different now than they were before; Gary wasn't here now, he wasn't here before, certainly not physically and definitely not emotionally. So it wasn't like I *missed* him or anything, you can't miss something you never had, not really.

I turned on the hot tap to warm up the water. Not only did I *not* miss him, I actually felt a bit relieved that he wasn't around. Whether it was the affair with *her* or not (and was she the first?), but Gary had, at some time, quite a while ago, turned into a right old selfish sod. And he moaned, *constantly*. His endless whinging was like an irritable background noise, like a fly buzzing round your head or a toddler forever pulling on your clothes for attention. He moaned pretty much about everything; about the central heating setting, the food I bought, the food I cooked, the cleanliness of the house, the behaviour of the boys.

And since it was plainly obvious that Gary no longer loved me, I wondered if I loved him, still, after all these years of slowly drifting apart. That one needed serious consideration, so I let more hot water run into the bath and sank deeper beneath the bubbles. I lay watching the steam rising up to the damp-blotched ceiling and thought about the man he *used* to be – fun, spontaneous, easy going, affectionate, considerate, loving. Then I thought about how he was now – miserable, sarcastic, tyrannical, and mostly absent.

No, I didn't love him, I hadn't for a long time. It was quite a shocking revelation. I wasn't even sure if I *liked* him any more.

So, what was I going to do now? What should I be doing? Where should I start?

Before I could think about it further there was a knock on the bathroom door.

"Mom," Elliot said, "Dad's at the door, what should I do?"

I bolted upright in the bath. A tidal wave splashed from the full tub onto the floor. "Let him in," I said, "And then could you and Kelly leave us alone for a while?"

"Are you going to be okay? I can stay in my room if you

want, in case you need me."

"That's okay, Elliot, it's your dad, not Jack the Ripper. I can handle this."

Maybe Elliot should remove all the sharp objects from the house, for Gary's sake, but I didn't like to ask.

Wrinkled and water sodden, I got out of the bath and made my way into the bedroom.

It was time for some home truths.

* * *

"I didn't come here for an argument," Gary said straight away, when I found him sitting alone in the living room.

"What did you come for then?"

"To sort you out."

"I can sort myself out, thank you very much."

I lowered myself into an armchair opposite Gary, who was sitting stiffly on the edge of the sofa. I was wearing my best summer dress usually reserved for special outings (hence it had lasted, untouched, a good five years).

"I mean, us" he said. "I came to talk about us."

"There is no 'us', not any more, not since you started sleeping with your secretary. All solemn vows are null and void once you start doing that."

"We can sort this out, Suze. I told you, I'm not seeing her any more."

"You told me that before I came to the warehouse yesterday, and I have to say she didn't look the least bit like a woman who'd just been dumped by her married lover-slash-boss."

"I ... I told her last night."

"Over a candlelit meal, no doubt. For such a skinny bint she sure does like her restaurant food, doesn't she."

"Can you cut the sarcasm and talk about this properly?"

"It's my way of coping," I said.

"I know. I don't like it. I've never liked it."

"What, you don't like my sense of humour? Seems you're in

a minority, Gary, most people *do* seem to like it." I'd only recently discovered this, and it gave me strength. I thought about the secretaries at Richard & Sovereign telling me how 'great' I was at my leaving do, and Sarah saying, 'People like you, Suze, they really do.'

"Well I don't," Gary said.

"I think that says more about you than it does about me."

He huffed. "Listen, we've both got work tomorrow. Well," he laughed, "I have anyway. It's too far for me to travel from my mother's house every day so … I've got my things in the car." His voice suddenly became very bossy, very 'this is the way things are going to be'. "I'll bring them in and we can end all this nonsense and get back to normal."

"I don't think so, Gary."

"Don't be such a drama queen!" Annoyance now. Anger would be next. "You can't hold this against me forever, so I might as well move back now and save all the inconvenience. I certainly can't stay at my mother's for much longer."

"You're assuming I want you back. I don't, I really don't."

He gave a nasty little laugh. "Well excuse me, but this isn't your house."

"No, it's *ours*, and I don't want you in it any more."

"It's not your decision to make, Suze. And if not now, then *when!*" Anger now. He was so predictable. "How long are you going to be so bloody unreasonable about this?"

"Unreasonable? On Friday I found out you'd been screwing around with your secretary. Yesterday I found out that you kept nearly all of your own salary and just topped mine up enough to pay all the bills."

"What?" he gasped, his eyes immediately darting to the computer desk in the corner of the room, "You've done what?"

"I looked at the joint account online, Gary. I know what you've spent and where you've spent it."

"You've been sneaking through my personal stuff?" He was up on his feet now and racing to the dining area, to his computer desk, to the tiny filing cabinet underneath. He pulled at the top drawer and it opened. He glared back at me, his eyes full of fury. "You've been prying into my private things?"

"Joint account, Gary. The clue is in the title."

"And what else of mine have you been snooping about in, eh?" He was pulling the password notebook out of the top drawer, opening the lower drawer and pulling out cardboard files, piling them all on the dining table. "This is *my stuff*," he growled, hurrying into the kitchen for a carrier bag and pushing all his paperwork into it, "How *dare* you touch my stuff!"

"Oh, I dared," I told him, "I dare to do a lot of things now that I know what's been going on. Lying, cheating, stealing our money – "

"I didn't *steal* it, I was ... I was filtering it out for our future!"

"Our *future* is currently hanging off the skinny body of the girl you're sleeping with. I've seen the purchases on the bank statement, Gary, the jewellers, the designer stores, the hotels, so don't even bother trying to deny it, it's all there in black and white. That necklace you bought her, I could have bought three good work suits with that money, but no, I'm *not* to use the joint account, I've got to walk around like a bobble monster and col-our in the scuffs on my shoes with a marker pen." I paused for breath. Gary was just staring at me. I stared back, waiting for my heartbeat to dip below thunderous level. "I've had enough," I finally said. "Tomorrow I'm going to see a solicitor about a di-vorce, because this marriage is well and truly over."

"What? You can't be serious? Because of one brief fling?"

"No, over a lot of things, the fling was just the final straw. We don't like each other any more, Gary. Life's too short to be this miserable all the time."

"You're *overreacting!*"

"And I want the money back that you took from us to buy her stuff, so I can carry on looking after the boys and their home."

"That's *my* money," he spat, "I earned it and it's *mine*." He was pacing frantically in front of the fireplace now, his blue carrier bag bouncing against his legs, and, yes, there it was, the agitated hand running through his thinning hair. "You've finally gone completely round the bend, Suze, demanding this, demanding that, keeping me away from my own home. You can't survive without me!"

"Watch me."

"I'm all you've ever known, you don't know how to do anything without me."

"Wow, you've certainly got an elevated opinion of yourself, haven't you! Of course I can manage without you, I've been doing it for *years*!"

"Not the finances, you haven't, I always took care of the finances."

"Yeah, and what a brilliant job you did too, for you, not for us. I don't trust you to take care of our family any more, I'm going it alone."

"You don't even have a job!" he spat back. "How are you going to be able to afford this house? If you think I'm paying all the bloody bills when I'm not even living here you've got another thing coming! I'm not standing by and watching this house – *my* house that *I've* paid for for the last 19 years – be repossessed because you can't keep up with the mortgage! You'll end up in some shitty council flat and the boys will hate you for it."

Gary was literally buzzing with fury, like he'd been plugged into the mains, and for the first time ever I wasn't the least bit bothered. Let him rant if he wanted to, it wasn't going to make the slightest bit of difference. He'd done the worst he could possibly do, he couldn't tell me what to do any more.

"You've got hour to finish packing the rest of your things, and then I'd like you to leave. Collect the rest of your stuff by Friday, or I'll take them to the charity shop or burn them in the garden. This isn't open to negotiation, Gary. We're finished. Over. For good."

* * *

"Oh my God, Katie, you would have been so proud of me. I

was bloody brilliant! I was *so* in control and it was such a *brilliant* feeling. Liberating, you know?"

"Good for you, sis. You've done it then, you've kicked him out for good?"

"Yes. I am *reborn*. I didn't realise how miserable I was until he went. It's been awful between us for *years*, it was like carrying a heavy weight around with me all the time and now I've put it down."

"You certainly sound different."

"Oh God, Katie, I can't stop smiling. Isn't it ridiculous? Maybe I am slightly bonkers. I know I should be angry and devastated and crying all the time, but I've never felt so *good*. I'm in control of my own life. I mean, it wasn't *all* bad, but the last few years have been really tough."

"For you, not him," Katie said. "So how did he take it? Did he just pack up and leave?"

I laughed. "He went totally ballistic, started ranting about me being incapable and inept and I'd end up in some grotty council flat and my boys would hate me and I'll end up all alone and broke and *old*."

What he'd actually said was, 'Who the hell will want *you*?' Things had deteriorated pretty bad by then, it was the nastiest thing he could think of to say. I'd stood up at that point, smoothed down my summer dress, shook back my newly washed hair and said to him, 'Look at me, Gary, take a *good* look at me.' And he did, and to my great satisfaction I saw something on his face change; recognition perhaps. He hadn't looked at me properly in years, I was just part of the furniture.

"And then what?" Katie asked.

"And then Elliot came home. Perfect timing. Elliot took one look at us and said to Gary, 'I think you'd better go now, dad.' It was like a scene from a cowboy film, they just stood there staring at each other. And then Gary went upstairs and we waited for him to finish packing. He left without saying goodbye, just stormed out the house, slamming the front door behind him, and was gone. Then Elliot took me and Kelly out to lunch and we had a great time, didn't mention Gary at all."

"So what now?" Katie asked, "What are your plans?"

I took a deep breath. "Well, first thing is to get a job. Things are pretty desperate on the financial front."

"Let me transfer some money to tide you over."

"No, really, it's very kind of you but – "

"I insist. You're my sister and I want to help."

"Thanks, but – "

"No buts, I can afford it. I run my own business, remember, and I'm married to a wealthy and very good looking accountant."

"I need to do this on my own, Katie. I need to prove to Gary that I can do it, and, more importantly, prove it to myself. I'll take anything the temping agencies offer, even reception work if I have to, then I'll start the divorce and see what I'm entitled to financially. I'll be fine, honestly. If things get really bad I'll ask you, okay?"

"Okay," she sighed, "But if you change your mind let me know."

"Thanks, Katie, I will."

"And are you absolutely sure you want to do this, Suze? You know I've never liked him, but are you really sure you want to end it?"

I paused to consider this. I'd never been so sure of anything in my life. Flogging a dead horse can be very exhausting, I was too tired to do it any more. "Do you remember when we were kids and we used to stick those plastic clothes pegs on our faces and pretend we were monsters?" I said at length.

"Yes," she laughed.

"Well, divorcing Gary feels like it did when we took the pegs off, it stopped hurting. It feels good, it feels *right*."

"Then do it," Katie said. "You need money, call me. You need an ear to cry into, call me. You want me to come over or send you tickets to Canada, call me. You want to go out on the town – my town or yours – to celebrate, call me, okay? I can whip up a posse of bitter women faster than you can say amputated testicles."

I laughed. "Thanks, Katie. I love you."

"Love you too, sis."

* * *

"Hi, this is Suzanne Philips, do you have any work for me today?" I'd decided to take the direct approach and be proactive. The girl at the agency told me to hold, forced me to endure a plinking rendition of Peer Gynt, then returned, her voice so flat and slow I thought she'd be better suited to working in a morgue somewhere. "Nothing at the moment," she said, "But you're marked up as available for work a week on Friday."

"Today," I said, "I'm available for work from today."

"That's not what it's got here on your form."

That was because the agency was clearly staffed by rejects from a lobotomy experiment. "No, I'm available immediately."

"We've got nothing for you. Try again tomorrow."

I rang TemPers.

"Ah, Suzanne," a bright voice cried, and I felt my optimism surge. "We've been looking for work for you but don't have anything available at the moment, I'm afraid."

"Not even reception work. I'd consider anything."

"No, sorry."

"Filing clerk? Office junior? Janitor?"

The girl laughed. "We'll let you know," she said.

Bugger!

I looked online for the name of a solicitors and chose one in the city centre, which would, hopefully, be close to where I would be working. I rang one, arranged an appointment for the end of the week during the lunch hour - again assuming I would be working around there somewhere. That done, I cleaned the house, rousing Elliot from his coma with the vacuum cleaner. Like a bear stirring from hibernation, he emerged from his room (I averted my eyes from the accumulated debris behind his door, no point worrying about anything else right now) and disappeared into the kitchen. Much clattering and sizzling later, he re-emerged, just as I was giving my bedroom a 'good going over', and went back to bed.

I got ready for my interview at Cromby & Crocket, the surveyors in the city. When I searched my wardrobe for something smart to wear I noticed that I didn't actually own anything smart any more, the smart stuff was all worn out. I had old jeans, old jumpers and work clothes that looked decidedly threadbare. Even the pin stripe suit I always thought made me look vaguely professional was, now that I looked at it properly instead of glancing quickly, a bit shabby. I vowed to go on a mad shopping spree at the earliest possible opportunity, hopefully some time this decade.

Me and my shabby pin stripe made our way into the city centre. It was strange to be travelling on the bus with young mothers of screaming children and pensioners instead of suits and smart office workers. I was no longer a 'city slicker' but 'one of the unemployed'. I'd only been without a job for 48 hours but it felt like an eternity – so much had happened. I was no longer the woman I'd been on Friday, the woman who had a job and a husband and now had neither. I was now a statistic, a single, unemployed mother.

As I entered the tall office building of Cromby & Crocket I felt like an imposter, an outsider, a very nervous and very desperate outsider. I tried to appear confident to the receptionist when I told her who I was and who I'd come to see, but my voice came out too high pitched and I was aware I smiling too much. I was treading the fine line between being professional and just falling to my knees and wailing, "Gissa job."

I sat down to wait and struggled to compose myself. I was a good secretary, I kept telling myself. Just because my last boss had hated me and I no longer had a husband shouldn't go against me. But I was acutely aware that I was a woman on her own who needed work and money because she had neither, and my self-confidence nosedived.

"Suzanne Philips?" said a woman, approaching me with her hand outstretched.

I jumped up out of my seat to shake her hand. My handbag fell out of my lap and, because it was old and the zip had broken, the contents spewed across the floor. I dithered between the handshake and my personal belongings, then fell to my knees to gather together my lipstick, hairbrush, purse, several photographs of my sons, a ton of receipts, house keys, a tattered notebook, 15 pens (courtesy of Richard Sovereign), mobile phone, spectacle case and a battered Tampax. By the time I stood up again, I was burning with embarrassment. The woman's hand was no longer extended and she was no longer smiling – not the sympathetic type then, I decided. This was going to be fun.

I followed the woman to a meeting room – very plush with a huge, shiny table in the middle; too posh for the sound of ringing mobiles, so I turned mine off. A man sat at the top end. He was so far away I wouldn't have recognised him in a line up. The woman sat next to him. They both stared at me, then down at the CV the agency had sent them.

The man started talking, about the company, the department, the work they did, the surveyors they had, more about the work they did, a bit more about the company, then more about the work. He talked solidly for 20 minutes, breaking the monotone only to say to the woman, "That's right, isn't it, Elaine?" and Elaine would nod and he'd be off again. Finally, just when I thought I was going to slip into a coma, he said, "Do you have any questions?"

My brain was numb. I'd completely lost the will to speak. "Er," I said, "No, I think you've pretty much covered everything." In excruciating detail.

"Where do you see yourself in five years time?" Elaine asked earnestly.

I felt my brain twitch inside my skull. Five years time? I didn't know what I'd be doing tomorrow! I hoped to be employed, I thought but didn't say. Not living in some grotty council flat was another. But I guessed she wanted a 'professional' answer, like 'I see myself as Head of Department, possibly running the company, maybe the country, in five years' time'. "In a nice secretarial job working in a nice surveying company," was all I could think of. They didn't look impressed.

"Do you have any ambitions?" the woman pushed.

"I've achieved my greatest ambition," I said, smiling, "I've raised two lovely sons. Having survived their teenage angst, and believe me," I laughed, "Their angst was *huge*, everything else is a piece of cake. I'm pretty much bomb-proof." No response. Not a smile, not a nod, nothing. My brain, or what was left of it, waved goodbye and shut down.

"We'll be in touch," they said.

I was led back out to reception and made my way out the building thinking 'I didn't want your grotty job anyway'.

It was now lunchtime and the city centre was heaving with people. I looked at all the 'workers' rushing passed me and wanted so much to be one of them again. But I wasn't, not any more. My few remaining particles of confidence shrivelled up and died right then.

I popped into both my temping agencies and, trying to hold back the tears of defeat and despondency, asked if they had anything. Neither did. I joined another agency further up the road, filling in yet another form and enduring yet another typing test – 79 words a minute now, I was losing my skills!

I went home feeling desolate. Elliot was out, the house was empty. I put down my (shabby) bag and slipped out of my (shabby) jacket, and remembered to turn my mobile back on in case any of the agencies tried to get in touch. Moments later it started beeping like a mad thing. I looked at the screen and saw that I had 15 missed calls, five voice messages and 32 texts. It must be the agencies, I told myself, they'd phoned, all of them, several times by the look of it, to offer me fantastic secretarial positions. I began to listen to the voicemail, allowing myself a smile.

"Suze, its Gary. How long are you going to keep this up for? You can't keep me out of my own house forever, I have rights you –"

Next message. Gary again, saying pretty much the same

thing. Then, Gary again, a bit more irate now, hissing, "For God's sake this has gone on long enough. I won't put up with this any —"

Gary. Gary. Gary again, this time blaming me for every-thing, that it was all my fault. A double glazing company, and then Gary. "Listen, it's over between me and Poppi, I *told* you it's over. It was just a little fling, there's no need for you to get all high and mighty about it, you're no saint yourself, you know."

"Probably not," I said out loud, as I flicked through the rest of the messages, "But I don't go round bonking other people or withholding funds from my family, do I?"

I caught sight of my reflection in the mirror above the fire-place. Okay, so I wasn't any great beauty, but my face didn't make babies cry or people wretch into brown paper bags. I had good bone structure, and my eyes weren't too bad, still big and dark (cow eyes, Gary used to call them, the old romantic). Maybe someone, some day, would love me? I pushed the thought from my head, it was too soon, I had hurdles to leap before I could even begin to consider a future like that, and did I even want another relationship?

My eyes fell to the monstrous wooden clock on the mantle-piece, the one Gary's mother ('she who must talk') had bought us as a wedding present. Bloody ugly thing, like some remnant from the Victorian era. I was tired of looking at it, but Gary in-sisted it stayed there, God forbid we should offend his mother in any way. But Gary wasn't here, was he, and I was free to do what-ever I wanted. I picked up the clock, carried it through the kit-chen like an unexploded bomb and out the back door. I lifted the lid on the dustbin and forcefully lobbed it in, where it shattered pleasingly at the bottom. "Good riddance," I said, slamming the lid shut, "To the clock, to Gary, and to his bloody mother."

When I went back into the house my mobile was ringing. I picked it up quickly, thinking it might be a job offer. It was Gary. Again.

"Have you seen a solicitor yet?" he snapped.

"No."

"Oh." A long pause, and then, "Does that mean – ?"

"It means I have an appointment to see them on Friday."

"Oh, right, okay." A pause, and then, "Listen, Suze, when are you going to stop all this silliness and let me come home? You can't keep me away forever, it is my house too, you know. I think I'm being very considerate, giving you the time to realise how *ridiculous* you're being – "

I pressed the 'end call' button. He immediately rang back. "You can't hang up on me like that! We have things to talk – "

I hung up again. He called back again. "Suze!" he implored, "Can't we just talk about this?"

"You said we didn't have anything else to talk about, remember?"

"We *have* to *talk*."

"No, we don't," I said, and turned off my mobile.

Later, after I'd trawled through my wardrobe and had filled three black bin liners (not even good enough for the charity shop, I decided), I wondered if Elliot was coming home for dinner and turned on my mobile to ring and ask. The beeping of text messages was relentless, all of them from Gary. The first few told me to pull myself together, to stop being so silly and to let him come home. Then he got annoyed that I wasn't responding and started name-calling, then he became *really* angry and *very* abusive, some of the words he used made me actually flinch at the coarseness. I suddenly wondered why I was reading them at all and just glanced at the taglines instead, which was more than enough to get the general idea. And still they came, message after message after message. The phone would not stop beeping. Eventually I just turned it off again and tossed it onto the coffee table. Five minutes later I turned it back on again in case the agencies rang, I couldn't afford to be out of contact. They didn't ring, but Gary did, constantly, and the messages just kept on coming.

* * *

I rang all three agencies the next morning. None of them had anything for me, and I did start to wonder if maybe Callum had given me a terrible reference and had warned potential employers against hiring me. I made another coffee, flicked through a magazine I'd read at least three times before, then decided to ring Alex to see how he was and how he'd taken the news of his parent's separation.

"What?" he said, deadpan.

"Your dad and I have separated," I repeated, "Didn't your dad tell you when you rang him about the electricity money?"

"No, he did not!"

"Oh. Well, me and your dad have split up. For a bit. Well, probably for good, actually."

"When?"

"Friday."

"Why?"

"We're incompatible," I said, rolling my eyes at the lameness of it.

"After 19 years?" Alex drawled. "And you've only just realised this, have you?"

"There are some grown-up reasons."

"I'm a grown-up!"

"And I'm your mother, I wouldn't be comfortable discussing my personal problems with you."

"Mom, just tell me. What's going on?"

I spluttered a bit, started sentences I couldn't finish, but couldn't find the right words to explain.

"I've got a lecture in an hour, mom. Could you compress it to ten words or less?"

"Not without pen and paper and some graphs," I stalled. "Oh! I have a call waiting, it might be an agency with a job offer – "

"Job offer? What happened to your old job?"

"I lost it."

"Christ, does nobody tell me anything?"

"Sorry, Alex, I have to go," and I hung up.

There wasn't actually a call waiting, I just wanted time to think of the best way to explain it all to Alex. I should have prepared myself beforehand. 'Dad's been sleeping with his secretary,' perhaps, or maybe, 'Your dad's been a very naughty boy so I kicked him out'? Too much detail, I wanted to be more delicate than that. 'We've drifted apart', I thought? That sounded kinder. I went to pick up the phone to call Alex back, but it rang right in my hand, making me jump about three feet in the air.

"Mrs Philips?" came a woman's voice.

"Speaking."

"Hi, its TemPers here. We have a legal secretary position for you." Halle-bloody-lujah! "Bit of a rush job, I'm afraid, they need someone straight away, can you get there within the hour?" I said I most certainly could.

It was only when I hung up that I began to panic. I knew nothing about working for solicitors, had no legal experience at all. And the location, I no idea where it was.

"Elliot!" I screamed up the stairs, "Elliot, I need your sat-nav. ELLIOT!"

I eventually had to run up the stairs, shake him from his coma, dash into my room to change into something vaguely smart whilst screaming his name with increasing decibels, race back into his room to shake him again, and then, eventually, I was forced to pull off his duvet and tip the half empty glass of water on his bedside table on his face.

"Whaaaa – ?"

"Sat-nav! Need! Quick!"

Quick is not a word I'd associate with Elliot first thing in the morning, I doubt it's even in his vocabulary. Sloths have more motivation. Elliot rolled slowly out of bed and shuffled, zombie-like, from his room, with me following behind trying to hurry him up without actually touching/slapping him. He meandered slowly down the stairs, paused at the bottom for a good yawn, then opened the front door.

"You're not going outside like that, are you?" I cried.

Elliot looked down at himself, naked apart from a tiny pair of pants a three year old would struggle to maintain its dignity in. He shrugged, turned, and headed back towards the stairs muttering, "I'll get my dressing gown."

I leapt up and grabbed him by his shoulders, spun him round using every fibre of muscle I possessed, and catapulted him out the front door. "I need it now!" I hissed, "Employers are waiting for me!"

Elliot tip-toed out to his car, tried the door, found it locked, and tip-toed back into the house again. At this point I was bouncing up and down with frustration, trying very hard not to swear at him. Elliot stared at the empty hallway table for what seemed like an eternity, before wandering into the living room. "You seen my car keys?" he asked.

I raced to the coat stand and began searching through various pockets. No keys, only a pair of tiny, frilly knickers. Kelly's? I looked at the coat stand. They hadn't come from Elliot's jacket, they'd come from Gary's. I tossed them aside and chomped down a few expletives.

Elliot meandered up the stairs, yawning so hard I thought the top of his head would fall back like a lid. I raced passed him to the bathroom, where I washed my hands three times and raced back down the stairs again. Elliot still hadn't returned. I waited and waited. I waited so long I thought he must have fallen back into bed and gone back to sleep.

"ELLIOT!" I howled.

He came into view at the top of the stairs, dressing gown on. I grabbed my coat and bag and impatiently waited for him to reach the bottom of the stairs. He *eventually* made it back out to his car, where he spent forever sifting through the interior debris to locate his sat-nav. He straightened up and handed it to me. I snatched it off him and asked, "How do I turn it on? How do I use it?"

"You'd be better off using the maps app on your phone," he said.

I hadn't thought of that. "Thanks," I said, and started running to the nearest bus stop, managing to miss one by three seconds – I swear the bus driver was laughing as he roared passed. I managed to locate the maps app on my phone whilst waiting for the next one, and located the solicitor's office – right on the other side of the city centre.

Bollocks!

I ran down the road to another bus stop, which I hoped would take me where I needed to go. Three different buses arrived and three different drivers told me they went nowhere near there, the last one telling me I needed to catch a number 76 to Harborne, then a 21 into town, and finally a 90 or a 94 to Millennium Point. It sounded like a takeaway order. I almost turned round and went back home, only the thought of abject poverty spurred me on, but catching three buses was going to take forever. I rang Elliot.

"Emergency," I told him, "Can you drop me off at Millennium Point on the other side of town?"

He mumbled that he could. I waited. Fifteen minutes can seem like an awful long time when you're trying to get somewhere. Eventually, I heard his engine roaring and his music thumping and, a couple of minutes later, he pulled up in front of me.

"Taxi?" he screamed above the crescendo of noise as he threw the passenger door open for me.

The journey through the city centre and out the other side was enough to send a saint into a frenzy. Elliot crashed gears, revved his engine to just this side of explosion, zig-zagged through traffic until I thought I was going to throw up, and wailed along to the music.

"Don't you have any Katy Perry?" I screamed.

"What?"

"Katy Perry, or Beyonce?"

"Who?"

I gave up, allowing my ears to be assaulted and my nerves shredded. It was a huge relief to finally get out, unscathed but deaf. I handed him a tenner to cover petrol money, and started walking off in what I hope was the right direction, staring down at my maps app. The road was one of those 100-mile affairs and I must have walked at least ten looking for the solicitor's office. There wasn't a soul around to ask, so I rang my agency, who gave me the telephone number for the solicitors, who I rang and who gave me directions.

Almost two hours after the agency had called, I arrived at my very first temping assignment.

CHAPTER 8

My first day as a temping secretary was *dire*. I tried to see it as my initiation of fire and that things could only get better, but that didn't stop me crying buckets every time I visited the toilet. The solicitors were based in what used to be somebody's home, a house converted into two downstairs offices and three upstairs ones for the solicitors, and they were *tiny*. It was also incredibly run down, with peeling paintwork, stained wallpaper and dirty windows. The people that worked there were equally run down, obviously weren't being paid enough and seemed too demoralised to even smile at me – not a good sign.

A woman in a pin stripe suit even shabbier than mine complained that I was late, that they'd been waiting for me, that they'd been expecting me first thing this morning.

"But the agency didn't phone me until 11 o'clock and I've had to come from the other side of – "

The woman wasn't interested. She spun on her heels and began to stride down the narrow hallway. I assumed she wanted me to follow her but, when I did, she stopped abruptly, spun round and glared at me.

"In there!" she snapped, pointing at a door I'd just walked past. When I didn't move because I was already confused and disorientated, she huffed, rolled her eyes (a characteristic of the company I was soon to discover) and pushed passed me to open the door. I looked inside. The room beyond had, at one time, been either a small living room or a small dining room. Now it was an office crammed with six desks, printers and boxes of files. There were people in there too, five of them, all staring at me.

I stepped inside. My heart was hanging in my guts and a plethora of thoughts exploded inside my panic-stricken head; what was it going to be like, what work would they expect me to do, would I be able to do it, were the people nice, would they like me, where's the coffee and (importantly, as it later turned out) where were the toilets?

The woman, I assumed she was some sort of Head Secretary although, in her enthusiasm to bawl me out for being late, hadn't actually introduced herself, pointed to a desk in the far corner of the living/dining room near the window. To reach it I had to wriggle my way past five occupied desks lined up along the walls, gasping, "Sorry, sorry," with every step I took. I smiled fanatically, but nobody smiled back; only two women even bothered to look up from their terminals and none of them acknowledged me.

It was going to be one of *those* jobs, I could tell, but even working for Callum Redfern hadn't prepared me for what was to follow.

"There's a red book on your desk," the bossy woman shouted over the heads of the others. "Inside is a list of people we need to attend a very important meeting next week. Do you understand?" she snapped, and I jumped in my seat, feeling like I was back at school being reprimanded by the teacher. "This meeting needs to be organised *post haste* and without any *further* delay."

She spun on her heels and left, slamming the door closed behind her and imprisoning me in the claustrophobic room. I looked at the people around me, three depressed-looking women along one wall and two miserable-looking men along the other, but none of them even glanced in my direction.

I looked at the red book. It was an address book and there were about a million people and companies scrawled in it, most of them incomplete; 'Andrew ?? MacUlpine, Newcastle. Phone number, [unintelligible] 3419'. Who exactly was I supposed to invite to this supposedly important meeting?

I called out to my work colleagues to ask if they knew anything about it. After they'd huffed and puffed and rolled their eyes at me for much longer than was necessary, they were no longer my work colleagues but sworn enemies who deserved to die long, lingering deaths. I didn't have a clue what I was supposed to do and nobody would tell me, so I sat there like a bloody great lemon trying to figure out the computer system – it was DOS! Purely by accident I came across a memo about a meeting, but it didn't mention a date and it certainly didn't list who should be attending.

It was an impossible task. I felt the first flush of tears about 30 minutes after I'd arrived but held them back for another 10, until one of my sworn enemies (a woman who epitomised the saying 'bulldog sucking a wasp') snarled, "Are you actually going to *do* any work today?"

I hurriedly bumped through my enemies in my race for the loo, where I burst into tears. I did this on the hour, every hour, until 5.30pm, when the bossy woman suddenly materialised like the Wicked Witch of the West.

"Did you organise the meeting?" she growled.

Everyone else had vacated the premises at a speed I'd never witnessed in an office before, so there was just me left. "I couldn't find any details about the meeting," I told her, feeling more tears stinging at my eyes. I blinked rapidly to hold them back. "Nobody would tell me anything."

"So you'll be back tomorrow to finish what you've started then." It wasn't a question, more of an order.

"Yes," I said, lying through my back teeth.

I let myself out of the shabby house on the wrong side of the city and shuffled miserably to a bus stop, vowing *never* to return there again for as long as I lived. I felt deflated and useless. Had I been kidding myself all this time, believing I was a good secretary when I patently wasn't, just like Callum always said? I was a rubbish wife, too, why else would my husband leap so enthusiastically into the arms of another woman? I was jobless, moneyless and would probably soon be homeless soon too, and my boys would realise I was rubbish at everything and hate me, just like Gary said.

The bus came. I snivelled silently on each bus I caught until I simply couldn't snivel any more.

* * *

"How was it?" Elliot shouted from the kitchen, when I stumbled into the house nearly two hours later.

I caught a glance at my face in the hallway mirror. My eyes were red and puffy and completely bereft of makeup. I looked old and knackered, which brought on a fresh bout of tears.

"Fabulous," I sniffed, shuffling into the kitchen. "It was … " My voice trailed off. I blinked the tears from my eyes and Elliot came into focus. He was standing at the cooker. There were three saucepans steaming in front of him.

"Mom!" he gasped, "What happened to your face?" He suddenly rushed over to hug me.

"The life of a single woman is hard," I said in a mock Irish accent, then, peering over his shoulder at the cooker, I added, "Is it my birthday?" Had I forgotten my own birthday?

"Nope."

"*Your* birthday?"

He laughed, handed me a wad of paper towels to mop up my face, and returned to his stirring.

"It's not … it's not *Christmas*, is it?"

"There's no occasion," he said, "I just thought you could do with a meal when you got in."

"I need a chair. And a glass of water. And possibly a fan."

"I've cooked before," he said defensively.

"Beans on toast," I said, "You've attempted scrambled eggs and baked potatoes, but never anything on this scale."

"Kelly helped me. Well, she started the process off and left me detailed instructions." He snatched a piece of paper off the counter and diligently moved his wooden spoon to another saucepan.

"I ... I don't ... I ... "

"It's okay, mom, I know what you mean."

"Can I do anything to help?" I asked.

"Yep, open the wine I bought, then go and chill out before I dish up."

Still in shock, I did as I was told, opened up a bottle of wine, poured us both a glass and went to take mine into the living room for a good sit down. At the kitchen doorway I paused.

"Thanks, Elliot," I said.

"No probs, mom."

I sat and watched him lay out the dining table feeling guilty, but he refused to let me get up. The meal my son had cooked was delicious. As we both sat there talking about normal things, I allowed all the tension and the misery to seep out of my body.

"Don't let them get you down," Elliot said, when I told him about my first temping assignment. "It's just a job. Nobody's going to die if you don't do it properly."

"That's not strictly true," I told him. "We might die of starvation if I don't work or get paid."

"Come on, mom," Elliot urged, "You can do it, you know you can. You're a good secretary."

"How do you know?"

"Because you've been telling us for the last six years that your boss doesn't deserve you. Plus," he added, "you're a brilliant mom, so it stands to reason you must be a brilliant secretary too."

"Oh Elliot." Tears welled up in my eyes for about the fiftieth time that day.

"Don't go all mushy on me."

"You're right," I said. "I've raised good men, I can't be that bad."

Elliot grinned, just as the front door slammed shut. We both froze in our seats, hardly daring to breathe. Someone had invaded our house. If they'd come for money or valuables they were going to be very disappointed.

Gary appeared in the living room doorway, looking sheepish

with a bunch of flowers in his hands.

"Hi, dad," Elliot said, immediately jumping to his feet to clear the plates from the table (another first!).

"Son," said Gary, who never in his whole life referred to either of the boys as 'son'. "If you could just give me and your mother – "

"Panic not, I'm outta here, don't want to be caught in the crossfire." He was almost out the door, plates in hand, when he caught sight of Gary's bunch of flowers. "Dad, those just ain't gonna hack it."

Elliot promptly disappeared into the kitchen, where I heard the sounds of washing up taking place. Which left just me and Gary, staring at each other. He held the flowers out.

"Ah," I said, surveying them from the table, "Tesco special offer blooms, reduced to half price. You certainly know how to make a girl feel special."

"How did you – ?"

"It's on the label, Gary."

He slumped into an armchair. "You're not a girl, Suze, you're my wife."

"Which accounts for the half price flowers." I briefly recalled seeing several Interflora purchases on the bank statement, but didn't have the energy to bring it up.

"How long are you going to keep this up for?" he asked wearily. "My mother is driving me round the bloody bend."

"Move in with one of your mates, then."

"I've asked."

"Don't trust you with their wives, eh?"

"No, it's not that! I'm sure it's not that."

"You could always get yourself a flat or something."

"A flat! Why? How long are you intending to keep me away from my own home."

"You no longer live here, Gaz. There is no coming back."

He pounded the arm of the chair, hissing, "This has gone too far now, you're taking it too far!" He was all high pitched and furious. I was really too tired for this. "We're married, Suze. I'm your husband, you're my wife, and this is our home, *my* home. You have no right to – "

"I have every right after what you did."

"But that's over now, can't you just forget about it?"

"Oh, okay, Gaz, I'll just let it slide shall I? And next time you go sleeping around I'll just shrug and tut and say, 'Oops, another little indiscretion, he's such a incorrigible philanderer, that husband of mine'."

Gary leapt up from the armchair. "Are you going to let me come home or not?" he bawled, the half price flowers now abandoned on the floor where, I noticed, most of the petals had fallen off.

"Not!" I bawled back.

"Right, that's it! If you want to play this *stupid* game you can do it on your own, *completely* on your own. Don't expect *any* help from me from now on."

"Fine," I shrugged, "I'm used to doing things on my own anyway, I've had *years* of practice."

He was heading for the living room door in a wild fury. "Well, we'll just see about that, won't we. You'll soon come crawling back, mark my words."

The front door slammed shut. "Bye, dad," Elliot shouted from the kitchen. He came and sat down next to me at the table. "Always good to see the old man," he said, "He brings such joy to the house."

"Sorry, Elliot." And suddenly I was crying again and Elliot was hugging me. "I've made such a mess of everything."

"No, you haven't."

"I'm completely useless."

"No, you're not."

"I wish I'd never bawled out my boss or found out my husband was having an affair or – "

"Mom," Elliot interrupted me with a weak smile, "I love you and all that, but I'm out of my depth here. Why don't you give Katie a ring?" And then he promptly excused himself and went out, which made me feel bad, that I'd driven him away – driven everyone away. I really was rubbish at everything.

"Katie!" I wailed into my mobile.

* * *

The following morning I got up at 5.30 to get ready for work. I walked to the first bus stop with grim determination, Katie's words of wisdom and expletive-strewn battle tactics still swimming around in my head.

"Don't let the bastards get you down," she'd raged the night before, "They're just cretins by the sounds of it. It's a job, and you need the money, so don't let them scare you off, show them what you're made of."

"Okay," I sobbed, opening up a second box of tissues and thinking I was made of snot and tears, "I will."

"Go for it, Suze. You've a whole new life ahead of you, grab it with both hands and shake it by the neck until its eyeballs pop out."

So, this was it. I was going back to the tiny solicitor's office on the other side of the city to show them what snot and tears was capable of.

I entered the converted house with gusto – The Temp Has Arrived! Someone came out of the kitchen stirring a mug of something hot. She looked at me, and yes, there was a slight hesitation, but she almost had a hint of a smile on her face.

"You're back then," she said.

"I am."

"They don't usually come back."

"I can't imagine why."

We entered the tiny office. It was ten-past 9 but there was nobody else there yet. I sat at my desk by the window, already feeling the gut-wrenching desolation dragging me down once more. 'Think positive!' Katie has insisted, 'Think Rambo, think Russell Crowe in Gladiator ... yeah, let's think about him for a while.'. Despite the pep talk, my resolve was waning fast and I could feel the tears rising to the surface again. And then the woman I'd met in the hallway said, "Fancy a drink?" And I felt so relieved I could have hugged her.

Her name was Julie and she introduced me to everyone else as they came through the office door, huffing and puffing and cursing public transport. They all nodded and, yes, actually smiled at me.

Maybe it wasn't going to be so bad after all.

"Wrong day for you to show up yesterday," said the man called Bill, who was extremely large and extremely pale, like a giant baby with a cute face. "We all had a *serious* dressing down from Annabel just before you turned up."

"Annabel?"

"The supervisor," Julie said, "You know, the woman in the pin stripe suit."

"Watch out for her," said the other man, called Jeff, who was tall and slim and almost handsome if you looked at him in just the right way, "She can be a mean old ... oh hi, Annabel."

And there she was, standing like the Wicked Witch in the doorway, her painted mouth already tight and her small eyes flashing. "Right, you lot," she snapped, "Remember what I told you yesterday. *No* slacking, *no* cock-ups and *definitely* no telling the clients to eff themselves."

"I didn't know it was a client, did I," Jeff muttered.

"You've got work to do," Annabel said, "So get on with it."

I leapt up out of my seat, almost raising a hand to attract attention. "I'd love to get on with some work," I said, feeling like a pupil sucking up to the teacher, "If only someone would tell me what it is I'm supposed to be doing."

"The meeting," Annabel sighed wearily, "I told you yesterday."

"Yes, but – " I snatched up the red book and made my way through the various chairs and desks as quickly as I could without tripping up, holding the open book in front of me. "*Who* do I invite? Who needs to attend the meeting? What's the meeting about and where is it being held?"

Annabel rolled her eyes. I waited for her to send me to the

headmaster's office for a good telling off. Instead, she flicked to the back of the book, took out a wad of loose papers, unfolded a particularly grubby page, and held it out to me. "People," she drawled, "Date, time and place for the meeting."

"Right, thanks." I had a job to do, and now I knew how to do it.

Piece of cake.

An hour later, eight people from various companies around the Midlands had confirmed their attendance at the meeting the following week. I enjoyed a few brief moments of intense satisfaction as I emailed Annabel to let her know it had all been sorted, before boredom gripped me again.

"Anyone need any help?" I said out loud.

Five faces turned towards me, three with their mouths open. "Well," said Jeff dubiously, "I have a document to amend if you – ?"

"Great." I contorted my way over to him and took the red scribbled pages from his outstretched hand.

"Thanks," he gasped, raising his eyebrows at the others, who all raised their eyebrows in response.

"What?" I said.

"Nothing," Jeff said, "It's just … we're not used to temps actually doing any work."

"No, we usually just watch them run to the toilet to cry," a girl called Claire said.

"You didn't do too bad," said Muriel, noticing my burning face. "Only seven times in one afternoon."

"Maybe if you were a bit nicer to them," I dared to say.

"Oh, we used to be nice," Bill said, tipping the remains of a crisp packet into his open mouth.

"But then Annabel started working here," Muriel sighed, "And that *really* changed everything."

"Why?" I asked.

"Because she's a vindictive, sadistic, power-crazed tyrant," Jeff snarled.

"Calm down, mate," Bill said, patting Jeff's shoulder, "Think of your ulcer."

Later, after I'd amended a few more documents for Jeff (who's desk was awash with seemingly blood-stained documents) and typed up some letters for Muriel (who was drowning in dictation tapes, actual tapes), Annabel came into the room. Tension fell like a heavy blanket and I was almost afraid to breathe – her animosity seemed barely contained within her pin striped suit. Without a word, she gathered folders of work from each of our desks and took them upstairs, where the solicitors resided. There followed the muffled sound of raised voices, and then one of the solicitors – short, extraordinarily round, with a face that indicated high blood pressure – burst into the room.

"Who did these?" he bawled, looking straight at Muriel, who seemed to sink into her seat.

I recognised the folder and said, "Me."

The solicitor cut a swathe through the chairs like Moses parting the Red Sea, and furiously tossed the folder down on my desk. "You haven't spelled my name right on these letters!" he boomed.

I looked up at him, at his red face that definitely required medical investigation, and frowned. His name was Robert Smith. How many variations can there be in the spelling of Robert Smith? "I'm sorry," I said, "I didn't know."

"Didn't know, didn't *know*?" he raged, "It's Smyth, S-M-Y-T-H!" I was suddenly reminded of Callum, arrogant, bullying Callum, and of Gary, perpetually angry.

"Give me a break!" I found myself saying, "I just got here!"

"What?"

"She's a *temp*," sneered Annabel.

The solicitor huffed loudly and glared at me. I glared back, thinking he was just a fat man with a heart problem, whereas I was a woman of indeterminate age who'd raised children and lost husbands.

"It won't happen again," I said, calmly but firmly.

"See that it doesn't," he said. All his anger dissipated, and I briefly wondered if he was about to clutch his chest and have a heart attack (that would go well on my CV, I thought, 'Bawled out one boss, killed another'). Instead of keeling, he turned and left the room. Annabel briskly followed him.

"Wow!" Jeff gasped.

"Way to go," said Bill.

"Cup of tea?" beamed Muriel.

Having earned myself about a million brownie points for standing up for myself (when it had previously only earned me unemployment), the rest of the day passed pleasantly, with endless cups of tea appearing on my desk at regular intervals. At lunch, because this wasn't the city centre and there were no nearby shops or bars to go to, we all sat around chatting. By the end of lunch my once sworn enemies became possibly the nicest people I'd ever known.

In the afternoon, in the midst of our keyboard tapping, Claire suddenly shouted, "Oh bloody bollocking hell!" I was the only one who seemed surprised at this outburst, nobody else bothered looking up from their work.

"What's up?" I asked, moving towards her.

She had a problem with Microsoft Word. It was simple problem that I'd come across about a billion times, so I fixed it for her. The way her large blue eyes looked at me I thought I must have inadvertently discovered time travel or something. "Thank you," she gushed.

"You don't happen to know how to fix this, do you?" Jeff said, nodding at his screen.

I did, and I did. Suddenly my self-esteem was flying through the stratosphere like Superman as my fingers flew over keyboards, fixing stuff.

"Where did you learn all this?" Muriel asked, as I installed a new printer driver onto her machine to stop it crashing all the time.

"I taught my boys how to use computers when they were little," I said. "Now they teach me. My eldest son is at university doing a degree in Computer Studies, he shows me things, and of course you pick things up along the way."

"You have a child at university?" Claire gasped.

"You don't look old enough," said Jeff.

"Oh please," I blushed, fanning a hand in front of my face.

When I got on the bus to go home that night I felt like a new woman. I *was* a good secretary. I'd been a good wife, too, if only Gary had realised it. I felt good. I had been challenged and I'd passed with flying colours. Things weren't so bad after all.

Or so I thought.

Until I got home.

CHAPTER 9

"Mom, don't panic!"

"Oh my God!"

"Mom, its nothing, really."

"What have you done?"

Elliot was lying on the sofa being tended to by Kelly. He had a deeply black eye, a sore gash across his chin and, worse, his right wrist was wrapped in a brace and hung in a sling across his chest.

"It's not broke," he said quickly, "It's just sprained."

"I had to drive him to hospital," Kelly said.

"Hospital?" I cried, rushing to his side and frantically stroking the hair off his forehead. "What happened, tell me what happened? Tell me where it hurts. Is your back okay? Your head?"

"He fell off a bike," Kelly said, with a disbelieving grin.

"A bike?" I was in shock. "What bike? He hasn't got a bike. A pushbike? Elliot?"

"My mate Darren's just bought a motorbike – "

"A *motorbike*?" I gasped, "You were involved in a traffic accident?"

"Not exactly." He winced. "Mom, if you don't stop pulling my hair back like that I'm going to be bald pretty soon."

"Tell me what happened!" The panic was coursing through my body like pulsing electricity. My child was injured!

"Darren let me have a go of his motorbike in a pub car park.

I pulled the throttle back a bit too much and – "

"He drove straight into a wall," Kelly finished. "It was quite spectacular, actually."

"Oh Elliot!"

"Don't fuss, mom. I'm a grown man, plus my girlfriend's here and you're embarrassing me. If you could just move that cushion a bit, and a cup of tea would be great."

"Are you sure you're alright?"

"Yeah," he grinned, "A sprain isn't usually fatal, but I've got to wear this wrist brace for a week."

"Did they check all your vital organs?"

"Yep, all the ones they could find anyway, they're still searching the pub car park for the rest."

"WHAT?"

"I'm joking, mom!"

"This is *not* a time for joking, Elliot."

He grinned, "So, about that tea then."

I made them both mugs. I cleared up the mess they'd left in the kitchen, then the mess they'd left in the hallway. Finally, I cleared away the mess they'd left on the dining room table so we could eat the meal I was cooking. There was a large vase of flowers in the middle of the table.

"That's nice of you, Kelly," I said, moving them to the sideboard. Boys didn't usually appreciate flowers when they were ill, computer games and car magazines were more their thing, but they were certainly lovely flowers.

"Dad sent them," Elliot said.

"Your dad?"

"No, somebody else's dad, what do you think?"

"Oh." I stared at them, dumbfounded. Lilies and roses and some other flowers I didn't recognise but which looked big and expensive. It was the best bouquet of flowers I'd ever had, I wanted get my phone and take photos so I could remember it for the rest of my life. Then I remembered the messages on my phone and why he'd sent them and took them into the kitchen. The attached card read, 'Please let me come home'. Nothing about love or regret, still just thinking about himself. The only reason I didn't throw them in the bin was because the bin wasn't big enough.

After dinner – during which Kelly fed Elliot like a baby and he soaked up the attention like a sponge – they went off to play loud music in his room. I sat down to watch TV for the first time in days, but then my mobile rang.

"Did you get the flowers?" Gary asked.

"Yes. Thank you."

"So, am I forgiven?"

"What, one bunch of flowers and I'm supposed to forgive you? How cheap do you think I am, Gary?"

"*Bouquet*," he said, "It was a *bouquet*, not a bunch, and they cost an arm and a leg."

"But nowhere near the amount you spent on flowers for her, I'll bet. I've seen the bank statement, Gary, I know how much you've spent on your mistress, and I'm supposed to be bowled over by a measly bunch of flowers?"

"Mistress?" he laughed, deflecting, "Quite a big word for a brief fling. Do you see how you're making this out to be a much bigger issue than it actually is, Suze?" A pause, and then, "I still can't believe you'd lower yourself to snoop through my stuff?"

"Not *your* stuff, *our* stuff, and what you don't like is me seeing all the evidence you left in your wake."

Silence. And then, quiet now, soft, "I want to come home, Suzanne. I miss you. I love you."

I rolled my eyes. Did he really think a bunch of flowers and a few insincere words would change everything back to the way it was before? I didn't want things back to the way they were before, I couldn't go back there again.

"It's over, Gary. Please try and accept it, we're over."

"But I love you, I miss you. Please, Suze, let me come home."

"I can't."

He huffed. "You've had *plenty* of time to think this through, Suze, you know you can't go it alone at your age, I'm what keeps this family together."

I laughed at that. Arrogant much?

"And while you stew in a hormonal fit over some minor in-discretion, I'm homeless and lonely and bloody fed up with the whole thing."

"Lonely?" I scoffed. "What, with your mother's constant at-tention and a young thing to pander to your every whim?"

"I told you, I don't see her any more, I ended it. Let me come home, Suze, *please*?"

"I can't. I'm sorry."

"Yeah, you sound sorry. You sound pretty smug actually, Miss Indignant punishing her naughty husband. Well, you drove me to it, this is all *your* fault."

I didn't want to be dragged into yet another pointless argu-ment where I was to blame for everything, so I said nothing.

"This is your last chance, Suzanne," he growled. "I'm not grovelling to my own wife any more. You let me come home right now or its over between us."

"Okay," I said, "It's over between us." And I hung up.

He immediately rang back. "I mean it, Suze," he hissed, "You either let me come home and we'll sort this out together, or – "

I hung up. It rang again. "Suze, you can't just throw our marriage away like this!"

"I didn't throw it away, you did!"

"You can't seriously prefer to be on your own than be with me!"

"I'm used to being on my own, Gary, I've barely noticed any difference since you've been gone."

I stabbed the red 'end call' button, feeling agitated now. Did he really think he could just waltz back in and we'd forget all about the cheating and the absences and general lack of atten-tion while he waltzed off with some young girl he'd enticed with expensive gifts that *I'd* paid for? Wasn't going to happen, not a chance.

The phone rang again. I turned it off and tossed it onto the coffee table. I would not be bullied into doing something I didn't want to do, Gary was good at that, wheedling and manipulating until he got what he wanted. He wanted to come home, I couldn't think of anything worse. Could I actually live with him again knowing everything I knew now? Trust him again? Was I, as the dutiful wife, supposed to just carry on as if nothing had happened?

No, I couldn't. I just couldn't.

I snatched up the phone, turned it on and rang Gary's number. Time to end this, I was tired of all the calls and all the messages.

His mother answered his phone. "Is Gary there?" I asked.

"No, he's not," she said, her voice dripping with revulsion.

"But he just called me."

"You'll be lucky to get him back after all the fuss you've made over one tiny indiscretion," she hissed. "A man doesn't stray unless he's desperate for love and affections, Suzanne. You drove him to it!"

Oh god, my fault again. I was sick of hearing it. "Where is he, Philippa, I just want a quick word."

"He's done everything he can for you, worked hard, bought you everything any of you could have ever wanted –" news to me "– and you've thrown it all back in his face because he made one tiny mistake."

"Look, Philippa, I just wanted –"

"Women today treat relationships like disposable commodities," she continued, really getting into her stride now, "You just toss them aside when you're tired of them, when it seems like too much hard work. You're so selfish, Suzanne, you don't deserve someone like Gary". I was in agreement with her there. "You don't know how to treat a man properly, don't know how to commit –"

"Where is he, Philippa?"

"He's a broken man. You've reduced him to a nervous wreck and it's *all your fault!*"

"He's the one who had the affair," I said, "How, exactly, is that my fault, Philippa?"

"You obviously didn't make him happy," she sneered, "Your

coldness pushed him into the arms of another woman. You're the reason – "

Stuff this for a game of soldiers. "Is Gary there or not? He must be there because his phone is, and he called me just a few minutes ago."

"He's upstairs, packing," she sniffed, "He's … he's going to stay with a friend to save his poor mother the agony of watching his dreadful decline into – "

I knew all of Gary's mates were married, with kids. He wouldn't be staying with any of them. So that meant –

"He's moving in with her," I said, laughing bitterly, feeling foolish, feeling like an idiot again. "So much for wanting us to get back together. Well, if that's what he wants, she can have him."

I stabbed the 'end call' button with a ferocity that made it crash to the floor at my feet, and screamed out loud at the unfairness of it all. Elliot immediately thumped to the top of the stairs. "You okay, mom?" he yelled down.

"I'm fine," I yelled back, "Just been talking to your grandmother."

"Oh God, that's enough to make anyone scream," he laughed, and returned to the blaring music in his room.

* * *

"How goes it, Suze?" Jeff greeted me when I entered the office the following morning.

"It goes pretty crap, actually, Jeff, but thanks for asking."

Jeff was immediately at my desk, a huge arm round my shoulders. Claire came into the room at that moment and, seeing us together, almost hugging, jumped to all the wrong conclusions. "Oh, I'm sorry," she said, backing out again, "I didn't mean to interrupt."

"Don't be stupid," Jeff said, "Suzanne's upset."

"Why?" she asked, coming over.

"Why?" Jeff asked me.

"My husband," I said.

"Say no more," Claire said, "You can't tell me *anything* about husbands I don't already know."

"What's he done?" Jeff asked sympathetically.

"I don't really want to talk about it," I told him. "I just want to get on with my work."

And I did. Furiously. Maniacally. I did all of Muriel's tapes, practically snatched red stained documents out of Jeff's hand, and lingered menacingly around Bill's desk until he gave me his pile of filing. By lunchtime I was exhausted but still frothing at the mouth every time I thought about Gary and *her*, which was roughly every five seconds.

To get away from all the concerned faces, I went out at lunchtime for a walk – it was raining, of course it was. I sat in a covered bus stop and took out my mobile. Today was end of the month, pay day, and I would finally have some money. I checked the balance on the joint account. It was empty. Zero balance. My salary had been gobbled up by the overdraft and the bills. I was totally broke.

Overwhelmed with the kind of panic I'd never before experienced, I flicked through 'situations vacant' on my phone, tears trickling down my face. There was only one even remotely suitable position being advertised.

"Hello, I'm calling after the secretarial vacancy." My own voice sounded desperate and a bit phlegmy.

"We need someone experienced and suitably qualified," a woman told me.

"That's me," I said, forcing myself to smile so I'd at least sound cheerful. A bus roared past, followed by a lorry, then another bus. "What are the duties, and what's the salary?" I yelled, one finger in my ear.

"I'm sorry, I can't hear you."

"What's the salary?"

"You'll have to speak up. Where are you calling from, the middle of a motorway?"

"I'll call you back," I yelled, and walked up a side road, sitting morosely on a garden wall. Just as I was pressing 'redial', an old man wielding a walking stick came charging out the house behind me. "Get off my wall," he roared, "I'm fed up of telling people to stay off my wall."

I moved on, trying to get the woman on the other end to hear me. The traffic was relentless, the howling wind and torrential rain adding to the cacophony. In the end, we both gave up. It obviously wasn't meant to be, I told myself, wandering back to the office.

The solicitors didn't know what had hit it that afternoon. First, knowing there was no way I was going to be able to afford it, I cancelled the appointment to start divorce proceedings the following day. When they asked if I would like to make an alternative appointment, I snarled, "No, but if you know the telephone number of a good hit man, I'd be grateful." I immediately regretted saying such a thing to lawyers and fervently hoped nothing happened to Gary in the immediate future.

Not wanting to think about my wretched husband a second longer, I set about keeping my mind fully occupied. I typed like a machine gun, I ran folders upstairs and brought work back down again, all of which I kept for myself. Mugs of tea kept appearing on my desk at increasingly rapid intervals – I'm sure one had a hefty splash of something alcoholic in it in an attempt to calm me down.

"Are you alright?" Claire asked, which elicited more sympathy from Muriel's pitying face and Julie's concerned eyes.

"No," I said, as nicely as I could considering the rage that was bubbling inside me. "I'm not alright, but I will be."

Work got done and I raced upstairs again. None of the three solicitors sitting up there like Gods in their offices had any tapes that needed transcribing, any filing, or any other work for me to do. I was horrified, I had to keep busy or I'd crumble into a sobbing heap. Beneath the stairs was a cupboard. I threw it open. Cleaning equipment. I pulled out an upright vacuum cleaner and began pushing it with urgent gusto down the hallway. Annabel appeared.

"What's going on?" she yelled above the noise.

"Man trouble," said Claire, who was standing at the office door watching me. Beside her, Muriel nodded and Julie sadly shook her head.

"Suzanne, turn that off!"

I did, almost jumping from foot to foot with nervous tension. I needed something to do, I had to keep working to take my mind off all the horrors of my life.

"We have cleaners to do that," Annabel said.

"Well, they're not doing a very good job," I said, and we all stared down at the threadbare carpet with its dust encrusted edges. "I don't mind doing it."

I went to turn the vacuum back on again, but Annabel stopped me by saying, "It's too noisy, the bosses won't like it."

"Okay," I said, hastily pulling out the plug, rolling up the chord and pushing it back into the cupboard. "I'll clean the windows instead."

I reached down for a bucket, but Annabel took me gently by the arm and, waving the other women back into the office, led me into her room next door, which was equally tiny but only had one desk in it. "Sit down," she said.

I did as I was told, itching to be doing something, anything. A glass was placed in my hand and a bottle upended into it. Brandy.

"Drink," she said, not unkindly.

I took a gulp, felt it burning down into my stomach, and burst into tears. I was amazed I had that much fluid inside me, it felt like I had been crying for days.

"Tell me," Annabel said, and her voice was so gentle I did. At the end of which, she left the room, came back with my coat, and said, "Go home."

"I can't!" I gasped. "I need this job, I need the money."

"Come back tomorrow when you feel better. We'll pay you for the rest of the day."

"You will? Why?"

"You're not the only one who's had to go through something

like this, Suzanne."

"You too?"

"Yes. Broke my heart."

"I'm ... I'm sorry, Annabel."

"Don't be sorry," she said with a smile. "It made me stronger. This will make you stronger too. Now go home, I insist."

On the long journey home I rang all three employment agencies on my mobile and they all told me they would probably have assignments for me next week. I tried to ring Gary, feeling desperate enough to maybe beg him for some money to tide me over, but his mobile was still switched off. I called his works number and a woman's voice I didn't recognise, certainly not Poppi-with-an-eye, told me he wasn't in today. He was probably at her place, drinking champagne and laughing at me. I hated him.

* * *

"You're home early," Elliot said, when I fell into the house after surviving public transport. "Cup of tea?"

"Please, no more tea! I'm tea'd up to the eyeballs." I collapsed at the kitchen table. "We have a problem," I told him, "Or rather, I have a problem which will probably affect you too."

"Dad?"

"Money."

"Dad," Elliot said again. "What's he done now?"

"He hasn't put anything into the bank account and my salary got eaten by the overdraft and direct debits. We're broke, Elliot, I mean *really* broke. I don't know how I'm going to buy food or anything else we might need. Sorry to dump this on you, but I don't know what I'm going to do."

"I can eat at Kelly's."

"That's not a solution, Elliot."

"No." He bowed his head, then jerked it back up again. "Have to make a call," he said, and raced up the stairs.

"You're not phoning your dad, are you?" I shouted after him,

"I don't want you getting caught up in all this nasty – "

"No, not dad," he yelled back,

Ten minutes later he leapt back into the kitchen, smiling broadly. "Got a job," he said.

"I probably do tomorrow, but I don't know about next week."

"No, me," he said, "I've got a job?"

I looked up at him. "You've got a job?" I gasped, "How?"

"My mate works in a garage."

"Not the mate with the motorbike?"

"No, another mate. His dad runs a garage, been asking me to work with him for ages, fixing cars and stuff, he knows I'm good." He paused to raise a proud eyebrow. "Just rang him to say I'm available. I start Monday."

"Elliot, that's marvellous!" I stood up to hug him. "But what about your wrist, can you work with it in a sling like that?"

"Mom, if you can carry on working after what dad did, I'm sure I can work with a wrist brace on for a few days."

I hugged him again.

"So," he said, embarrassed, "What's for dinner?"

We ate beans on toast, then Kelly came in her little red mini with a union jack on the roof and took him out for a drink to celebrate his new employed status.

"Want to come?" Elliot asked at the door.

"Nah, you're alright. You two go and have fun."

"You're allowed to have fun too, mom."

"I'll have fun knowing you two are having fun."

"God," he gasped, "Parents are weird. See you later. Call if you need anything."

What I needed was to get off this hamster wheel for a while, I needed to slow life down a bit so I could get to grips with it. So much had happened in just a short space of time, I felt I was reeling from one major catastrophe to another. When would it all end, or was it going to be like this for the rest of my life, struggling and fighting just to survive? I didn't even know where the next loaf of bread or next carton of milk was coming from.

Despite this sense of impending doom, I still felt better off without Gary. Poverty was waving at me like an excited new acquaintance, but I'd rather starve than have him back in my life. I was used to being on my own, I would just have to learn how to be better at it.

* * *

My phone pinged with a text message late afternoon. 'You'll get no help from me until you come to your senses and let me come home.'

'They're your sons too, will you let them starve?'

'Don't be so dramatic! Your problem is you didn't know when you were well off, you had it all, but only because I gave it to you.'

'Get stuffed.'

'Let's see how long you can last without me, eh? You'll soon come crawling back, begging me to come home. Don't leave it too long though or it might be too late, I might have changed my mind.'

'Why are you texting me instead of playing with your girlfriend? Bored already? Leave me alone.'

'This is your last chance, Suze. I come home tonight or not at all, ever."

'Not. At. All.' In a separate text I wrote, 'Ever!'

There followed long texts describing all my faults, some horrible things about my character, some worse things about the way I looked and the way I behaved, and a lot of swear words, but I merely glanced through them and replied 'OK' to every single one.

'You'll lose the house and the boys will hate you', was his last one. Enraged, I tossed the mobile across the room. It hit the wall and pretty much exploded. Great, I thought, as the pieces settled, I'd just broken my phone and my only contact with the temping agencies.

Could things get any worse?

Of course they could.

And they did.

CHAPTER 10

After a restless, sleepless night, bouncing between vitriolic rage and hysterical but muffled sobbing, I clawed my way out of bed and hauled my carcass into the bathroom. The vision that greeted me in the mirror told me I shouldn't inflict myself on people today, but I had no choice. I showered, pulled on clothes, and endured an hour and a half of travelling through a clogged-up city to the solicitors' offices.

My last day.

"Cheer up, it might never happen?" Bill quipped when I shuffled to my desk. "I see you're going for the ultra-casual look today then."

"What?" I looked down at myself. Without thinking I had put on my gardening clothes, which were my old office clothes only covered in splatters of mud. I was beyond caring.

"It's okay," he chuckled, turning back to his computer screen, "If we get any visiting clients I'll tell them you're the cleaner."

"Cheers."

"You're welcome, always happy to help."

My outfit elicited comments from Claire, Julie and Muriel, before I put up a hand when Jeff arrived and said, "I look like shit, I know I look like shit, you don't have to tell me I look like shit."

"Quite pretty shit, though," Jeff grinned.

I laughed. "Thanks!"

"Any time, gorgeous."

We all began to work. I was sure one of the solicitor's had stayed up to dictate his way through the night, there was so much of it, but I was glad to keep busy. Annabel appeared, no longer looking like the Wicked Witch of the West. "Can I have a word?" she said to me.

I staggered through the chairs into the corridor. She beckoned me into her tiny office next door.

"We're very pleased with your work," Annabel began, sitting behind her desk with her hands tightly clasped in front of her. "You're fast, efficient, and you seem to know what you're doing. I know you have some personal problems at the moment, who doesn't, but I've talked it over with the partners and we'd like to offer you a permanent position here." Annabel was beaming at me now. "The partners are aware you don't have much legal experience, but you learn fast and we'll give you training."

"That's so nice of you, thank you."

"Same job you're doing now at a starting salary of ... "

And there was the catch. The Gods above were just teasing me, promising me much and coughing up little. The salary was, as I'd suspected, pitifully low. I'd never be able to survive on it, and the commute to get here was too expensive and time consuming.

"I'm sorry," I said, meaning it. "I've really enjoyed working here, but the salary's a bit on the low side."

"Oh." She looked surprised. "Well, I know we can't hope to compete with city centre salaries, but we don't want to lose you, so I'm sure I could persuade the bosses to increase the salary a little."

"It's not just that," I said, knowing that a little more wasn't going to be enough. "It's the travelling time as well. I live on the other side of the city and it takes so long to get here."

"Would you like time to think about it?"

"There's no point," I said, "But thank you for trying to help."

When I went back into the office all five faces turned to me expectantly, and I realised that they all knew. "Sorry," I said, "I can't."

They all groaned. I felt really sad.

At lunch time they dragged me out to a pub down a back street, and we all had diet Coke and a plate of chips with mayonnaise (the cheapest thing on the menu). They were a lovely bunch of people, I liked them a lot, but I couldn't stay. Back at the office I used my desk phone to call the agencies about work the following week.

"We've been trying to contact you," said the woman at Office Fairies, sounding quite irate.

"My mobile's broke, but you could have rung the office," I replied, holding my throbbing head, "You must know the number, you got me the assignment."

"We haven't found you any assignments yet," she said. Too late, I remembered it was TemPers who'd found me the solicitors' job. The girl continued, even more irately, "It's not our policy to accept people who are signed on at other agencies."

"It's not my policy to be unemployed for any length of time," I countered. "I've been with your agency over a week now and you haven't found me any work yet."

"Well, we have something for you now, starting first thing Monday. Receptionist at – "

"Not reception work," I groaned. Then, realising I was in no position to be picky, I quickly added, "Okay, where?"

She told me. Dead end road in a grotty part of the city, but it was a job and it was paying decent money. I should be grateful.

I'd no sooner hung up when the desk phone rang. It was TemPers. "Alison here," she enthused wildly. "I've got an assignment for you next week."

"Ah, well, actually – "

"It's only two days' work I'm afraid," the girl continued regardless. "Monday and Tuesday."

"Oh, I need a full week's work," I said, glad of the excuse to turn it down.

"Okay, we have another position. Receptionist." The details were exactly the same as the assignment I'd had from the other agency. "How much are they paying?" I dared to ask. It was the same hourly rate, so I told her I didn't fancy it. She promised to keep looking for me.

Just before 5 o'clock I got up from my seat for the last time. Julie and Muriel immediately ran from the room – overcome with grief I thought – then returned with a big bunch of flowers and a card.

"You shouldn't have!" I gasped, "I've only been here a few days!"

"You've been great," Muriel said, dabbing her eyes.

"A real breath of fresh air," Julie added.

"Thanks," I said, looking at them all. "You've made me feel really good about myself for the first time in ages. I've really enjoyed working here, you've all been brilliant."

Claire laughed. "First time a temp's ever said that."

"First time *anyone's* ever said that," Jeff laughed, and then he leaned forward and kissed me tenderly on the cheek. It was the nicest kiss I'd had for the longest time. I looked at him. He looked back at me and winked.

Shouting final farewells, I left the small solicitors office on the wrong side of the city clutching my flowers and still feeling the kiss on my cheek. Even the rain and the arduous journey through rush hour traffic didn't dampen my spirits.

* * *

"Yo, mom!" Elliot cried.

"Yo, son," I cried back, grinning as I walked into the living room feeling like I was 'down with the kids'.

"How was your day?" Elliot was slumped across the sofa like a line of crumpled clothes, watching TV.

"Pretty good, actually."

"Wow, flowers. They must have really liked you."

"Of course." I still felt warm and fuzzy inside.

"I've performed some magic." He sprinted over to the dining table and pointed at the pile of plastic that was once my mobile phone. "From this, to this," he cried, and whipped a tea towel off the table. Underneath was another mobile phone, still in its box.

"Where did you get that from? Oh Elliot, I can't afford – "

"Fear not, mother, it's a freebie. My mate just brought it round, he's had an upgrade and doesn't need it any more. It's an old model but it works. We just take out your sim card ... " He rooted round in the pile of plastic pieces and pulled out a tiny white card. " ... and pop it into your new phone."

The phone immediately began to beep with messages. I tried to snatch it from him but he held it above his head, about a foot and a half above mine, laughing. "What do have we here, messages from a secret lover, eh?"

"Elliot, give it to me."

"No, wait, let's look." He was pressing buttons as I struggled to get it out of his hands. And then his face fell. He looked at me. "Mom," he said, "These are all from dad."

"We were having a text argument, its quieter that way."

Elliot snatched it away from my grasping hands and looked at the phone again, repeatedly pressing buttons.

"Please, Elliot, don't take it out of context. We were fighting."

"Oh my God." His eyes grew wide as he read one text after another. "This is not out of context, mom, this is out of order."

He thrust the phone into my hands and headed for the door.

"Where are you going?"

"To see dad."

"Elliot," I cried, chasing him down the hallway, "Don't! You'll make it worse. It's not your fight. He didn't mean it, any of it."

He stopped at the door and turned to look at me, his young face twisted with rage. "He shouldn't say things like that to you, mom!"

"Please," I said, "Let me deal with it my own way. Please, Elliot."

He stood there, his jaw clenching and unclenching. Then he huffed loudly and bounded up the stairs in three strides.

I went into the kitchen and made dinner – chips, Aldi's own brand beans and eggs reduced because they had to be eaten today at the very latest before salmonella set it. Elliot's jaw was still twitching when he came down to eat it.

"It's not right, mom," he said, brooding.

"I've thrown him out of his own home, Elliot, he's bound to feel a bit upset."

"A bit? He's acting like a raving lunatic. He shouldn't text you stuff like that."

"It's not your fight, Elliot. Don't get caught up in it."

Kelly came shortly afterwards and they went out in her Mini again. "You promise you won't say anything to your dad?" I whispered to Elliot before they disappeared.

He hesitated, then rolled his eyes. "I promise."

I closed the door behind them and headed for the kitchen. My mobile rang on the counter. It was probably Gary, calling for another rant, or it could be Katie, calling from Canada.

"Mom!"

"Alex! How are you?"

"Desperate," he replied.

"Aren't we all."

"Dad says he's not picking me up."

"Up from where?"

"From university?"

"They've kicked you out?" I gasped.

"Mom!" he cried, exasperated, "I'm coming home."

"Why?"

"Because I live there!"

"Only during holidays, Alex."

"Mom, it's the end of the academic year. It's the summer holidays! And dad's refusing to pick me up, says something about you wanting to do everything on your own from now on. So, what's happening, mom?"

"I don't know. I'll phone you back as soon as I think of something."

I rang Elliot. "Problem," I said.

"Dad?"

"Alex."

"Alex is a problem?"

"Not normally, no. He wants to come home for the summer holidays."

"Cool. When?"

"Tomorrow."

"Don't panic, mom, I know Alex eats like a swarm of locusts but I'm sure we can make the food situation spread to three people if we ration a bit."

"That's not the problem. He needs to get home and your dad won't fetch him."

"Why not?"

"Something about me doing everything myself."

"Leave it with me, mom. I'll sort something."

When the phone rang again a short while later, I snatched it up without looking at the caller, thinking it was either Alex or Elliot. It was neither.

"How did you get on at the solicitors?" Gary asked straight away.

"I didn't go."

"Oh? Why not? Have you changed your mind?" His voice suddenly took on a whole new tone, victorious and smug. "I knew you'd come to your senses eventually, though you certainly took your time about it. Still, better late than never. Discovered you can't live without me, eh?"

"Actually, Gaz, I like living without you, it's very ... peaceful. I cancelled the appointment because – " I didn't want to admit I couldn't afford it. " – we're really busy at work and I couldn't take time off, so I've rescheduled."

"Oh. So you're still going ahead with it then?"

"Yes, Gary, I still want a divorce."

"Oh." A pause, and then, "Right, we'll see about that."

* * *

"I have it all under control," Elliot said, bursting through the front door a short while later with Kelly in tow. "Borrowed a van off my mate, but he needs it back by tomorrow night."

"Exactly how many mates have you got, Elliot?" I asked, amazed.

"Oh, loads, mom, but I promise not to invite them all round to dinner at the same time. Kelly said she'll drive up to Manchester." He lifted up his sprained hand, still in a brace and sling.

Kelly looked terrified and was biting furiously at her fingernails. "Are you sure?" I asked her.

She shook her head. "No, not really. I drive a Mini, I've never driven a van before."

"But you said – " Elliot began.

"That's okay," I told them, "I can drive."

"You can't drive, mom."

"I can, I have a full licence."

"No, I mean you *can't* drive. You're rubbish."

"I am not! I've never had a single accident."

"But you've seen loads," he quipped, and they both burst out laughing.

"I'm driving," I said. "Final word."

* * *

The next morning, after Elliot had arranged one-day insurance cover for me online, Kelly drove us in her Mini to a breaker's yard a few miles away, where a battered, rusting, barely roadworthy van awaited us.

"It's great," Elliot enthused to a bloke who, at first glance, appeared to be at least middle aged but, on closer inspection, turned out to be a young man about Elliot's age wearing old, oil smeared clothes.

"Ar, she's a goodun," the boy said. "Get you there and back, no trouble."

"Are you sure?" I asked, looking at the van again. "Does it have an MOT?"

Elliot and the boy just looked at each other and laughed. I nervously got in the driver's seat – or what was left of the driver's seat. There were no 'instruments' in the dashboard, just holes where they used to be.

"How will I know how fast I'm going?"

"Oh, you won't have to worry about going too fast," the boy said. "Just watch it in third gear."

"Why, what happens in third gear?"

"It ain't there, gearbox is knackered."

Fabulous!

"How much petrol is in the tank?" I asked, looking pointlessly at the dashboard holes.

"Dunno. Just keep it topped up, to be safe."

Safe wasn't a word that immediately sprung to mind.

Elliot said a passionate farewell to Kelly as though he was about to go off to fight in a war instead of travelling to Manchester and back, while I tried to start the engine. It sounded like an old man with severe bronchitis, coughing and spluttering a lot before finally admitting defeat and churning into lethargic life. The clutch was almost non-existent and getting it into first gear took two hands.

"This will never get us to Manchester and back," I shouted above the banging and the rattling as we kangarooed off down the road.

"Have faith, mom. Have faith."

* * *

We got as far as a petrol station near the Spaghetti Junction before it broke down the first time. Elliot got out and, one-armed, fiddled under the bonnet for a while. We filled the tank with petrol and Elliot, when he went to pay, rather alarmingly bought two large containers of oil back with him.

"Try it now," he said.

Those three words were to haunt me for the rest of the day as the van spluttered up the M6, cutting out for no apparent and forcing us to roll into Hilton Park Services, Stafford, Keele, Bartholomew, Sandbach, and Knutsford. It was like our mantra: try it now, try it now.

"What's the matter with it?" I asked, when Elliot got back into the van after another fiddle under the rusting bonnet somewhere around Crewe.

"It's old," he said, "It just needs a bit of attention, but it'll get us there, don't worry."

I worried.

The steering was about as responsive as jelly, the gears so stiff my left arm was screaming in pain, and the indicators didn't work. Not only did I have to contend with this, but also Elliot, who, car driver extraordinaire, made for a terrible passenger.

"Easy on the clutch," he instructed. "Don't turn the wheel so fast, *ease* it slowly." Presumably so it didn't come off in my hands. "You're going too fast, mom. You're going too slow, mom. Watch that car! You just cut him up! You're in the wrong lane!"

We whizzed past the exit for Manchester, staring at the sign as it flew passed. I got off at the next junction and doubled back. The van cut out again as we bounced down streets towards Alex's student house, and I'm sure it was only the power of my rage and frustration that got it started again.

Finally, we made it. It had taken four and a half hours to get there, and I was so stiff as I hauled myself out of the driver's seat I thought my bones had set and my bottom had dropped off.

Alex was, we discovered, still in bed, but his four flatmates gleefully offered to wake him up. Like excited puppies, they filled a bucket with cold water and raced into his room, whooping and laughing. Seconds later I could hear the dulcet tones of my eldest son screaming profanities, and they all raced out again, still whooping and laughing.

Once he was awake (also clean, thanks to his flatmates), we dared to enter the sanctified domains of Alex's student room. Or at least we tried to. There was a 12 inch gap in the door that we had to squeeze ourselves through because there was so much junk piled up on the other side and, once inside the room, there was nowhere to go because there wasn't a single inch of space anywhere. Empty takeaway cartons, overflowing ashtrays (Alex smoked?), piles and piles of clothes, CD's, computer parts, videos, empty bottles and colourful array of magazines strewn around like the final flamboyant touches of an interior designer.

Alex lay in a soaking wet bed on sheets that didn't look as if they'd been washed since the dawn of time. He raised a weary hand at us but didn't lift his fuzz covered face off the grimy pillows.

"Nice pad," Elliot said, nodding his head in approval.

"You've not packed!" I gasped.

"Didn't think you were coming until later," he croaked.

"This *is* later, Alex. It's two o'clock in the afternoon."

"S'early."

"Alex!"

"Okay, okay, I'm moving." It was like watching a film in slow motion as Alex gently eased himself out of bed, his face muscles grimacing, his hair ruffled like a black candyfloss. He went to the loo down the hallway. I sat perched on the edge of the bed, trying not to touch anything. Elliot went in search of bin bags.

While Alex stood in the doorway rubbing his face awake, Elliot tossed rubbish into a bags, while I tentatively picked at the piles of clothes, wishing I'd thought to bring rubber gloves and a mask. "I don't know whether to pack it or burn it," I said. "I'm not washing all this, Alex, you'll have to go to the laundrette."

"Yeah, every day for about a month," Elliot laughed.

Alex continued to stand in the doorway, rubbing his face, rubbing his head and his manly parts. It was only when he slowly flopped against the wall that I realised he'd actually fallen asleep again.

"What time did you get to bed last night?" I asked.

"Hmph? 'Bout an hour ago."

"Celebrating the end of the academic year, eh?" Elliot grinned.

"Um."

"How long were you out celebrating?"

"'Bout a week."

"A week!" I gasped, thinking of his poor kidneys.

Alex began to slither down the wall at that point. Elliot jumped up and slapped his brother across the face with some considerable glee. His brother looked startled for a moment, then began to close his eyes again. Elliot enthusiastically slapped him again. I wormed my way between them and took control.

"Elliot, take out the rubbish, if you can identify it. Alex, you … Alex!" I reached up and shook him vigorously by the shoulders, rattling his head against the wall. "Get showered and *get dressed.*"

Alex shrugged and shuffled oh-so-slowly to the bathroom. I surveyed the room and shook my head. I turned and yelled down the hallway, "John! Barry! Robert! Steve! We need a hand!"

Four incredibly tall flat mates trooped down the hallway, punching each other and laughing. Teenagers weren't all that different from toddlers, I thought, except they were a lot taller. I stared up at them and pointed behind me, "We need to be packed and gone within the hour, do you think you can do it?"

They nodded earnestly. Half an hour later the room was cleared of Alex's belongings and the van outside was packed to capacity, the rusty exhaust hanging mere millimetres from the ground. I went in search of Alex and found him fast asleep in the bath with the shower still on. With a loud cheer and much jostling, his four flatmates manhandled him into jeans and t-shirt, and carried him out to the van.

"Thanks," I shouted through the cracked window.

"See you September, Al," they yelled, but Alex didn't respond, he was asleep with half his face contorted against the passenger window. Elliot was in the back, wedged between a giant computer screen and fifteen solidly packed bags of clothes.

"You okay, Elliot?"

"It bloody stinks back here. Why couldn't Alex get in the

back, he's used to the stench?"

"Alex, get in the back."

"Hmph?"

"Get in the back."

"Wha'?"

"Just throw him out," Elliot sighed. "See if he's got the intelligence and ability to find his own way home."

We eventually prodded Alex into the back of the van, where he promptly fell asleep again. I attempted to start the engine. It coughed and spluttered and belched out some blue smoke, but positively refused to turn over. The four flatmates cheered and ran up behind the van to push it. Halfway down the long road it eventually churned into life, and I waved out the window at the four boys all gasping and leaning on their knees in the road behind me.

We were off. For a good five minutes. Then we had to stop because other motorists were flashing their lights and waving their arms out of windows at us, screaming, "Exhaust! Your exhaust!" I peered in the driver's mirror and saw sparks flying out behind us. Elliot got out and performed emergency roadside repairs with the aid of one of Alex's belts and a couple of wire coat hangers.

We broke down just outside Manchester, where we filled up with petrol, and again at Knutsford. It broke down another five times after that – it would have been quicker to walk, dragging Alex and his belongings behind us. Then, just when I thought we might possibly make it home by Wednesday, if we were lucky, a tyre blew out and we skidded onto the hard shoulder of the motorway.

"Bollocks!" Elliot cried.

"Language," I tutted.

"Oh dear," he squeaked, "We appear to have a flat tyre, what jolly bad luck."

Above us, a dark sky thundered ominously and, thirty seconds later, it began to lash down with rain so hard we couldn't see out of the windows. Elliot looked at me. I shrugged – what did I know about changing a tyre (in the pouring rain), I was but a mere woman. We both turned to look at Alex, still fast asleep in the back, sprawled out like a broken marionette. We eventually woke him up by dragging him out of the van and lying him face up on the ground. He opened his eyes, stared up at the sky and said, "Oh, it's raining, we must be nearly in Birmingham."

Half an hour later we were all totally drenched to the skin, standing at the side of the motorway with a thunderstorm raging overhead, still trying to change a tyre.

"Turn the bloody thing!" Elliot screamed, cradling his slinged arm as he watched Alex attempting to get a wheel nut off.

"I am bloody turning the bloody thing!" Alex screamed back. "It won't bloody budge."

"Well bloody well try harder then!"

"I bloody am!"

"You are turning lefty-loosey, not righty-tighty, aren't you, Alex?"

"Yes, of course I bloody – ah bollocks!"

"Is the excessive use of expletives really necessary?" I asked.

Elliot, who's hands were visibly itching to do it himself, lashed out a leg and hammered his Timberland boot down against the wheel wrench. It spun round like a helicopter blade and caught Alex hard on the back of his hand. He leapt up, gripping it to his chest, hissing "Fffff – "

"Wait!" Elliot screamed, holding a hand out to Alex and spinning round to me, "Mom, go stand right the way over there by those trees, go now!"

Alex was jumping from foot to foot, still going "Fffff – " like a rapidly deflating balloon.

"Why?" I asked.

"Just go! *Quick!*"

I hurriedly moved off towards the trees on the side bank, thinking the van was going to explode or something. But it wasn't the van that exploded, it was Alex – I watched his mouth moving and his eyes bulging as a crack of thunder thankfully drowned out his rage. I stood underneath a tree watching my sons wallop each other in the lashing rain, shouting and bickering over the flat tyre.

After two more fiddles under the bonnet by a drowned-looking Elliot, we finally made it home, beyond exhausted, soaking wet, and barely able to move. It was 11pm.

"I'll take the van back in the morning," Elliot said, as we weakly began emptying the van into the house. The boys carried all the electrical equipment up to Alex's room and filled the hallway with his sports equipment, but, when it came to the bags of clothes, we were all so tired we simply piled them up on the driveway next to the front door.

And then we all fell into bed.

CHAPTER 11

My second temping assignment was in a high-rise office block in Five Ways. I had to get there early for a quick run through the switchboard system, which sounded ominous. The lift took me up to the nineteenth floor and opened up onto a massive reception area with a panoramic, floor-to-ceiling window that gave a great view over Birmingham city centre. A curved reception desk made out of glass and chrome sat next to it. The carpet was as thick as my overgrown lawn. Very posh.

As I got out of the lift, wondering if my battered shoes would pass muster (or if I would get sent home to change), I spotted a very frantic woman behind reception who was trying to stop buzzers from buzzing. When I introduced myself she almost burst into tears with relief and dragged me round the desk, pushing me into the chair and wriggling a headset into my hair.

"Press this to answer," she said, pointing vaguely at the keyboard. "I think that one's to hold, that one's to transfer calls, this one's to call back, and I'm just looking for the key that stops all the buzzing."

"What is all the buzzing?" I said.

"Incoming calls," she said, pressing a key marked SILENT. Up on the computer screen numerous boxes quietly flashed on and off.

The woman began to move away. "Sorry I can't stop, but I guess you've worked a switchboard before otherwise the agency wouldn't have sent you."

What? The woman was halfway across the reception area by now. I jumped up. "How do I answer incoming calls?" I cried after her.

"You say, 'Good morning, Stepps & Partners Legal Company Limited, can I help you?'" She was still moving away down an adjoining corridor, and fast. "Don't leave reception unattended. There's a partners' meeting this morning and I have to organise the coffee and biscuits. If you need any help just ask – "

She disappeared through a door in the corridor and was gone. I lowered myself into the seat and stared at the flashing boxes on the screen. I pressed the 'answer' key. "Good morning, Stepps & Partners Legal Company Limited, can I help you?" The sentence seemed to last forever, and every word sounded alien on my lips.

"Marcia Bannister please."

"One moment, I'll just connect you." I only knew how to say that because I'd seen it in films, and I could barely recognise my own short-vowelled voice. I almost felt quite proud of myself, except I didn't know who Marcia Bannister was or how I could get the call through to her. I was going to kill my agency for doing this to me.

There was a search box at the top of the screen. I quickly typed in 'Marcia Bannister' and it came up highlighted. I pressed the 'transfer' button as it seemed the most logical thing to do. Nothing happened. Stress level was around 8 at this point, and rising.

Suddenly, a different voice came through my headphones. "Marcia Bannister here."

"Er, its reception," I spluttered, "I have a caller on the line for you."

"Who is it?" The voice of Marcia Bannister sounded very abrupt and impatient, probably a partner or above.

"Erm," I spluttered, "I don't know, they didn't say."

"Well find out who it is and what they want?"

"Okay." I pressed a few buttons trying to get the caller back into my headphones. I might have muttered 'bugger!' a couple of times because, suddenly, Marcia Bannister's voice said, "Are you still there?"

"Yes." But I wished I wasn't, oh how I wished I wasn't. "I'm sorry, I'll just put the call through to you now."

"But who is it?"

I pressed the 'transfer' button half a dozen times, wondering what the hell it did if not transfer, and suddenly everything went silent. I wasn't sure if I'd cut them off or put them though, but there were now six flashing boxes screaming for attention on my computer screen. Tears prickled my eyes. I was *so* out of my depth.

By the time I'd cut off three callers, put one on hold for so long he'd gone by the time I found him again, and put seven calls through to the wrong people (who all asked, "Who is it?" before I cottoned on to the fact that I should probably ask), I'd pretty much got the hang of the buttons. Almost. I'd worked out the switchboard buttons but, because I was panicking about it all, my brain just collapsed in on itself and I couldn't remember anyone's name.

"Rupert MacDonald please," a caller said, and I typed the name into the search box on screen whilst asking, "Who shall I say is calling?" While they were telling me their name, I'd forget what name I was typing, then I'd get flustered about scribbling down the caller's name before I forgot it, then I'd have to ask who they wanted to speak to again because I'd forgotten that too. By the time I put the call through and they asked who it was, I couldn't remember. Eventually I stopped introducing callers to the people they wanted to talk to and just put them straight through – let them sort out the details themselves, I thought.

I had thirty seconds of flashless peace and quiet to gather what remained of my senses and survey my surroundings. It was 9 o'clock and people began drifting though reception, and every single one of them smiled at me and said, 'Morning'. I don't think any of them actually noticed I wasn't the usual receptionist, but it *was* first thing Monday morning and it *was* nice to have my presence acknowledged.

Young women began appearing, all chatty and lively. A group immediately rushed up to me and cried, "Oh hello! You're new, are you the temp? I'm Anita/Jean/Rhianna/Pat/Jackie and I'm on extension 3674/3645/3676/3634/3665 if you need anything."

What a friendly place, I thought, allowing my stress levels to sink to about 6. Reception work wasn't so bad after all. Bit of a doddle, actually, once you got the hang of it.

The 'bosses' arrived. I could tell they were bosses because they wore expensive suits, carried expensive briefcases and were far too busy/important to glance in my direction. Except for one, who might as well have had 'predator' tattooed across his forehead. He strode out of the lift wearing an immaculate suit, with immaculate hair and an immaculate face that wore a 'Look at me, aren't I drop-dead gorgeous' expression.

"Well hel-lo," he leered, leaning on the reception desk and giving me a good looking over. I pulled my jacket tighter in front of me. "And what's *your* name?"

Caught off guard by a man who looked as if he could eat me alive as a starter, I instinctively went on the defensive. Which is why I introduced myself as Pauline.

"Nice to meet you, Pauline," he said, his voice so heavy with innuendo I wondered if he should be let out on his own without a police escort. "My name's Adam, Adam Palmer, and I'm in Equity."

I didn't know what Equity was or if I was supposed to be impressed or not, so simply nodded and eagerly answered an incoming call.

"Good morning, Stepps & Partners Legal Company Limited, can I help you?"

To my relief, Adam Palmer winked, looked me over once more, and sauntered off – or rather, slinked off like a prowling panther. I shuddered.

"You want to watch him," said a young girl appearing at reception.

"Yes, I figured."

"Thinks he's God's gift. Undoubtedly handsome, but rumour has it he's only got – " She wiggled her little finger and I laughed. "Want a drink?" she asked.

"Love one."

Every single person who came through the reception area towards the kitchen asked me the same question, so I overdosed on tea and coffee and, in between flashing boxes, indulged in a bit of light gossip about the people I was now working with. They all seemed lovely.

By mid-morning the corporate world had obviously woken up, had had a good cough and a strong coffee and was *raring* to go. Incoming calls piled one on top of the other, and there were so many boxes flashing on my screen it was like playing some kind of computer game. I struggled to put them all through but lost a few and misdirected others. Clients came in for meetings and needed to be directed to meeting rooms I'd never seen, delivery men wanted signatures and, in the midst of it all, my mobile started ringing. It was Sarah from Richard Sovereign. I answered quickly, blurted, "Busy, call you back," and returned to my ceaseless battle with the switchboard.

An hour later I was still being swamped with calls and, after all those drinks, was absolutely bursting for the loo. I dialled a random extension number and cried, "Help!" A young girl came racing out of one of the offices.

"I'm so sorry," she cried, "I was told to keep an eye on you and help out, but the partners meeting fell into disarray and two people have threatened to hand in their notice because of it, and quite honestly it's been complete chaos."

"I need the loo," I gasped, wriggling in my seat.

"Sorry," she said again.

"Where is it?" I asked.

"Down that corridor, through the double doors, first left."

I began to run in a knees-together kind of way. The double doors wouldn't open when I pushed them. With a cry of desperation I noticed a swipe card security box on the wall next to it. I raced back to reception and screeched, "Card?"

She threw hers across to me. It flew through the air, seemingly in slow motion. I reached out a hand and saw the card brush past my fingers and fall onto the floor behind me. I turned and bent and picked it up like a sprinter in a relay race, breathing, "Bugger! Bugger! Bugger!" to try and take my mind off my grossly swollen bladder.

Afterwards, as I sauntered back to reception, the girl laughed and said, "I thought you were going to burst. You look much better now."

"Bit of a close call," I grinned. Then I stopped mid-step, halfway to the reception desk and sucked in air. I was standing right next to the floor-to-ceiling window and, for the first time since I'd arrived, realised how high up I was, higher than I've ever been in my entire life, and all that stood between me and all that highness was a thin sheet of glass. For a terrifying moment I imagined I was going to trip and fall, crash through the window and plummet to the ground far, far below. The floor beneath my feet seemed flimsy, the walls insubstantial. My heartbeat pounded throughout my entire body and I simply couldn't move.

"It's strengthened glass," said the girl, rushing towards me and guiding me like a blind person passed The Window to the reception desk. "We get this a lot, but you soon get used to it."

"Never," I breathed, unable to tear my eyes off the sheer drop outside.

The girl laughed. "We had a client in once, went to get one of those leaflets over there." She pointed to a leaflet holder on the wall right next to the window. "He froze, just like you did, only we couldn't get him to move, he just gripped onto the leaflet holder and wouldn't budge. We eventually had to call security to prise him away. He went with another firm of solicitors after that, refused to return even to the lobby downstairs. We get people freaking out about it all the time."

"Then they should brick it over," I hissed fiercely. "You don't want glass on the nineteenth floor, you want a *proper wall* so people don't visualise their own deaths.

"It's reinforced glass," the girl said again, laughing, as if falling to your death was funny.

"I don't care," I told her, "I don't want to see what's out there, I want to be enclosed and safe within solid brick walls."

She laughed again. "Call me if you need anything. I'll have the security guards on standby if you require further assistance."

As I sat in my chair, my heartbeat slowly returning to normal and visions of my blood splattered demise receding, I returned to my work. An hour later, there were no more flashing boxes left to answer and I took the opportunity to ring Sarah back.

"It's me."

"Busy," she gasped, "Place manic. Lunch. When?"

"Today? Tomorrow? I'm easy."

"I've heard. Today. 1 o'clock. Old Joint Stock."

"I'm in Five Ways, Nando's on Broad Street is closer."

"Closer for you, Mail Box, better for me."

"O'Neill's, and that's my final offer."

"The Rep bar and we'll call it quits."

"Done."

* * *

It was great to see Sarah again. She looked positively radiant and, as always, turned every male head in the bar when we walked in.

"So, how are things with you?" she asked, ordering diet Cokes.

"Fine," I said automatically.

"Hello," she beamed, shaking my hand, "My name is Sarah and I'm your best friend. 'Fine' is not an answer, I want details. Come on, spill the dirt, what's happening with you?"

So I told her about Gary and the secretary – it sounded like the title of a grubby book. She was suitably sympathetic but, like

Katie, a little restrained.

"You didn't like him either, did you," I said.

"Total retard," she sniffed. "The way he spoke to you at the office barbecue last summer, well, I was ready to punch his lights out."

"I'm not getting much positive feedback about him."

"Nor will you. You're better off without him, Suze, honestly. How are you coping?"

"Oh, up and down, you know? It still feels strange at the moment, being on my own, but then I've always been on my own really. Gary was never around much, but it's still quite daunting." I forced a smile to lighten the atmosphere. "Can one adult and two teenagers with gargantuan appetites survive without the alpha male? Watch this space."

We talked about it a bit more, then I told her about my two agency assignments, which had her howling with laughter, and she told me about her job in the Management department; "Hormone hell," she said, "Ten women and four men who get *extremely* nervous once a month." Eventually, when she hadn't mentioned it and I could hold back no more, I blurted, "And how's James?"

She grinned and sighed.

"That good, eh?"

"Better than good, Suze."

"Have you kissed yet?"

"You've only been gone three weeks!" she cried. "Give us a chance."

Three weeks, was that all it was? It seemed longer than that – I'd half expected Sarah to be married with kids by now.

"There's definitely an attraction there," she continued eagerly, "But nothing's official yet. I mean, he hasn't asked me out on a proper date or anything. I think he's a bit concerned about mixing business with pleasure."

"Well, keep me posted on developments."

"Oh, don't worry," she winked, "I will."

All too soon lunch was over and we were hugging each other

out in the street. "We must do this again soon," she said.

"How about Wednesday."

"Can't, lunch with James."

"Thursday then?"

She shook her head. "Lunch with James."

"Friday?"

She shrugged.

"I thought you two weren't officially dating yet?"

"Lunch isn't dating, Suze, lunch is sustenance so you don't die of starvation in the afternoon."

"What's a proper date then?"

"A fancy meal in a fancy restaurant with candlelight, walking home hand in hand and making passionate love on the living room floor."

"On a first date?"

She grinned. "I live in hope."

* * *

Later that afternoon Alex rang me on my mobile. It sounded like he'd just woken up. I briefly wondered how anyone could sleep that much without it being a medical condition, then remembered he was a teenager.

"Mom, you know you were nagging me all day yesterday about moving those bags of clothes off the driveway?"

"I have a vague recollection of beating you with a newspaper about it, yes."

"Well, where did you put them?"

"I haven't touched them."

"You must have 'cos they're not there."

"Maybe Elliot moved them."

"Nah, I rang him and asked. Couldn't get much sense out of him about it actually."

"Why, what did he say?"

"He didn't really say anything, he just kept laughing every time I asked about the bin liners."

"Oh *shit!*" I suddenly gasped.

An elderly suit waiting in reception peered over the top of The Times at me.

"Shitzsu," I said, smiling sweetly, "Yes, lovely breed of dog, very loyal." And then I couldn't help myself. I lowered my head beneath the reception counter and desperately tried to stifle a mad fit of giggles.

"Mom! Is this like a private joke between you and Elliot?"

"You should have moved the bags when I told you to," I spluttered.

"I will, as soon as I find them."

"You won't find them, Alex."

"Why? Have you burned all my clothes or something?"

"No." Tears were streaming down my face.

"Mom!"

"I'm sorry, Alex, but they're gone."

"Gone where?"

"The bin men," I wheezed. "They collect on Monday."

* * *

Alex was still fretting about the lost bags when I got home that night. I was just grateful he was awake for once.

"All my clothes!" he wailed. "You'll have to lend me some money, mom."

"No can do, I'm afraid."

"But I've got nothing to wear!"

"And I've got nothing to give. You'll have to get a job or something."

"A job?" His face was like that famous picture of The Scream. "Get a job how? Where?"

"I don't know, but you've got three months to figure it out before you go back to uni, haven't you."

Alex was still digesting this piece of news when Elliot burst through the front door. My son, the worker. I noticed he'd taken off his sling, but he still wore the wrist brace, now covered in oil.

"How was your first day at your first job?" I asked, as he loped into the living room.

Elliot shrugged. "Okay."

I waited. Nothing more was forthcoming. "And?" I urged.

"And what?" He threw himself into an armchair, snatched the remote control off Alex, who was lounged across the full length of the sofa, and began flicking through channels on the TV. "Had this bloke come in," he said. "Fan belt had come off so I fixed it for him, only took a couple of minutes. When he asked how much it was I told him just a drink, you know?" He looked up at me then and started laughing. "He gets back in his car and drives off, which I thought was a bit rude, didn't give me anything. Five minutes later he comes back and gives me a can of lager."

Both Elliot and Alex were howling now, throwing cushions at each other. I smiled. My family. I wallowed in a sudden waft of acute pride, before going into the kitchen to feed them with the aid of three eggs, a tin of own-brand beans, and some very green looking potatoes.

"What's the matter with these baked beans?" Alex asked, when we sat eating.

"Why?"

"All the sauce has fallen off." He prodded them with his fork, "There's just this orange goo spreading across the plate with rock-hard beans sitting on top."

Elliot began inspecting his beans. "Yuk," he said, "I'm not eating that."

"Then starve," I told them both. "We're poor. We can't afford luxury items like proper baked beans anymore."

"The mashed potatoes are green, mom."

"It's the light."

"Are these eggs off?"

Gary rang just after I'd cleared away three almost untouched plates of food. I tried to be civilised and not get worked up, but it was difficult when he immediately began ranting about *his* house and potentially unpaid bills and the unfairness of my behaviour again.

"Aren't you with Poppi-with-an-i now?" I asked in the middle of his lecture. Speaking her name didn't send shivers up and down my spine, nor elicit any particularly violent thoughts.

"Yes," he snapped, "So what? You threw me out, she took me in. Your loss, I think."

I let it pass. "But if you're with her now, why are you bothering me?"

"To try and sort this out!"

"Sort what out?"

From Gary's end I heard a door open and close, and a woman's voice – *her* voice – asking, "Who are you talking to, darling?"

"Just a minute, love." And then his voice went all quiet and muffled. "*Us*," he hissed, "Sort *us* out."

"There is no *us*, Gary." I was amazed he still thought there was. Talk about having your cake and eating it! He didn't get to screw around *and* hassle me too, there had to be some benefit for me somewhere. "You bonked the secretary," I said calmly, "You're now *living* with the secretary. Where is '*us*' in that equation, Gary?"

"I can't talk now," he whispered.

"No, I'll bet you can't. But listen, Gary, just so we're both absolutely clear about this, we're finished, over, kaput. There is no '*us*' and there is nothing to sort out. It's over. Do you understand?"

He didn't answer. Silent, for once.

"Right then," I said, "You'd better get back to mistress, hadn't you. You don't want her getting suspicious about you talking to your soon-to-be-ex wife."

He ended the call without saying anything else. I stared at my phone while inspecting my emotions. Nothing, nothing at all. Well, a bit of sadness for the way we'd once been, but not for what we'd become. He was with her now, he'd made his choice, and I just had to learn how to live with it. I imagined him with her and felt a slight twinge, but that was all, just a twinge. How 'over' was a marriage when you didn't feel anything when you imagined your husband with another woman?

* * *

Work the next day wasn't quite as traumatic as the first since I knew what to expect. I avoided looking at The Window, thinking about The Window or going anywhere near The Window, and managed to somehow retain my sanity as I fought with the switchboard. I braced myself for the onslaught of phonecalls, then unbraced myself when someone came to relieve me for my lunch break, which I took in a small meeting room with my home-made sandwiches. After lunch there was a flurry of phonecalls, delivery men, offers of tea and coffee, and visitors. One visitor in particular.

A man stepped out of the lift in front of me. I glanced up and my eyes widened, my heart gave one big beat and then stopped altogether. Everything went into slow motion as he strode across the reception area. I'm sure I heard music somewhere in the background, but that could have been my blood pressure singing through my head.

He was very tall, very handsome, and walked with a casual confidence. When he looked at me to speak I saw that his eyes were incredibly blue and bright, like diamonds, lit by the sunlight streaming through the panoramic window. I think I forgot to breathe.

"Hi there, I'm Alan Talbot," he said, and I literally had to stop myself from swooning at the sound of his voice, like warm syrup washing over me. His smile was broad and genuine. "I'm here to see Richard Cavanagh."

I opened my mouth to speak but nothing came out, not a thing. I coughed and tried again, squeaking, "Please, take a ... " Oh god, what was it called? "... seat. I'll let ..." Who did he want to see? "... them know you're here."

What ... the hell ... was wrong ... with me? Well loads, actually, none of it helped by this gorgeous man looking at me with those startling blue eyes and smiling – or was he laughing?

I called Richard Cavanagh and said he had a visitor, and took more calls, acutely aware that I had this incredible man sitting close by who was emanating charisma like a radiator giving off heat. I suddenly found I had all these marbles in my mouth when I spoke, "Yars, I'll just co-nnect you. Wun mo-ment please." I kept snatching a look at him from the corner of my eye, once or twice I caught him looking back at me, probably wondering what was wrong with the receptionist. I really had to pull myself together ... but *kwoar*.

Alan Talbot was eventually taken away from me by a secretary, but as he was led through the reception area towards the meeting rooms and out of my life forever, he turned to face me with those riveting blue eyes and said, "Thank you." Never have two words sounded so delectable. I nearly passed out.

I was so shaken that I immediately had to ring for assistance and splash cold water on my face in the toilets. I stared at my reflection in the mirror. "Daft old bat," I told it, making a mental note to visit my GP at the earliest possible opportunity to check for iron deficiency, stress, or dementia. It was the only explanation. I was not prone to 'episodes' like that.

An hour later, when he was leaving, he again glanced over at me and I turned into a puddle of goo. "Bye," he said.

"B-bye," I said.

Wow. Just wow.

Seems I wasn't completely dead inside after all.

On Wednesday a visitor came into reception, blurted his name and who he'd come to see, then threw himself into one of the waiting chairs and began to read The Times. "Do you have any leaflets on Private Equity?" he asked.

"Yes, just on the wall over there," I said with a huge, glad-to-help smile, whilst studiously keeping my eyes firmly away from The Window.

"Could you get it for me please?" It was more of an order than a question and, because he seemed like a very important client who was used to being obeyed, I slowly stood up with my back to The Window. Firmly averting my eyes from it, I sidled sideways for a bit and, when I thought I'd covered enough area (but didn't know for sure since I wasn't looking where I was going), reached out a hand to fumble for the leaflet stand. I was acutely aware that the 'important visitor' was now watching my crab impersonation with a stunned expression on his face, but I didn't care. As long as I got his leaflet and didn't start screaming all would be fine.

Except my outstretched hand was waving in thin air. I couldn't feel the leaflet holder on the wall right next to The Window at all. There must be more window left to cover, which meant that I was, at that very moment, standing right in the middle of The Window with only thin glass separating me from certain death. My feet refused to move – one wrong step and I'd slip and fall backwards. Abject panic began to build up inside me. I couldn't breathe, I couldn't move.

"Are you okay?" the man suddenly asked.

"V-v-vertigo," I gasped, desperately trying to smile and appear professional. "I … I appear to be a bit stuck."

The man jumped up and raced towards me. The urge to scream was strong as I imagined him tripping and crashing into me, pushing me through the glass. I could almost hear the sound of it shattering all around me. I threw both hands out in front of me, my mouth hanging open, my eyes pleading for him not to come any closer. The man stopped instantly, thought for a few moments, then leaned forward as far as he could without moving his feet and stretched out a hand.

"Try to reach me," he said, "Don't worry, I won't let you go. It's okay. Come on, you can do it."

Our fingertips touched. The man lunged forward, grabbed my lower arm and pulled me away from the window as if he were snatching me from the path of an oncoming train. I fell onto one of the visitors' chairs, vibrating in terror and relief.

"T-t-thank you," I gasped.

"Wife has it," he said, "Terrible thing."

One of the secretaries took me into the kitchen for a strong coffee (and, I suspect, a sneaky shot of brandy) until I'd calmed down again.

My relationship with The Window became very distant after that. The secretaries did their best to make me feel more comfortable. One taped brown paper across half the window nearest to the reception desk, while I sat and watched, hands clasped to my face, gasping, "Be careful, please be careful." The paper was ripped down when a partner complained that it was lowering the tone of the company.

Another secretary kindly piled box files at the end of the reception counter so I couldn't actually see The Window, whilst another suggested I Sellotaped cardboard to the sides of my head like horse blinkers (I didn't). When window cleaners hung like rock climbers on the outside of the building later that afternoon, several secretaries came running out of their offices and hurried me away before I got to the screaming stage. They were very good.

On Friday afternoon, in between a surge of incoming calls, I managed to call TemPers and Office Fairies about work the following week.

"Receptionist," they kept saying.

"Secretary," I kept replying.

Eventually TemPers came back with a secretarial assignment at another legal company in the city centre.

"Which floor?" I asked.

They didn't know. I told them to find out and get back to me.

"Top floor," they said.

"Top floor of how big a building?" I asked.

They didn't know. They got back to me. "Five floors."

"Fine," I said, "I'll take it."

At the end of the day, just before I was about to leave, secretaries came pouring out of their offices, one holding a big bunch of flowers.

"I'm really sad to leave," I told them, "You've all been so lovely."

"Come back any time," they said.

172

But I knew I wouldn't. Not until they'd bricked up The Window anyway.

CHAPTER 12

When I got home that Friday night something truly miraculous happened. My bus had been late (when it had *eventually* turned up it was so packed with passengers it was positively dangerous), so I arrived home after Elliot.

I found him in the hallway. Shouting. Up the stairs. At Alex. So loudly he didn't hear me come through the front door. Where I stood, transfixed, wide-eyed and amazed.

"Come and clear up, you utter slob!" he was yelling, "Mom will be home in a minute and she won't want to see all this crap everywhere, will she!"

"Bugger off," came Alex's muffled voice, "I'm busy".

"Busy doing what? Playing games on your computer? Alex!"

"What?"

"What do you think!" Elliot's voice had reached a high pitch of frustration, almost soprano. "Get down here and tidy up!"

"I'm dreaming," I gasped. "I've died and gone to heaven. My slob of a son is telling my other slob of a son to tidy up. This can't be happening."

"Oh, hi mom," Elliot beamed. "I'm trying to get the genius to tidy up after himself. I've got more chance of splitting the atom with a plastic spoon."

"I know *exactly* how you feel," I grinned, heading off towards the kitchen, "These teenagers, don't know when they've got it made, do they? Treat the place like a hotel, give no respect and no thanks."

"I know," Elliot sighed, shaking his head, "I know."

"So, teenager number two, what do you want for dinner?"

"Well, me and Einstein have decided that we couldn't eat another plate of green chips, spoiled eggs and bullet beans if our lives depended on it, so Einstein very generously agreed to let me pay for a takeaway. And," he said, swinging open the fridge door with a flourish, "I got you a bottle of wine on the way home."

"Wow, Elliot!"

"I'm trying to become the favourite son," he said, flicking an imaginary fringe off his forehead, "I don't hold out much hope for the opposition."

The opposition wandered into the kitchen with a computer coding book in his hands. "Right," he said, "Mom's home, where's the grub?"

"Tidy up first," Elliot demanded.

I couldn't help laughing at the irony of it.

While we waited for the curry to be delivered, Elliot forced Alex to clear his things away while I checked the online account on my phone. It wasn't good. I was now overdrawn again and getting more overdrawn every day.

"I know I keep saying it," I said, wandering back into the kitchen, where (unless my eyes were deceiving me) Alex was washing up, "But we're broke, impoverished, beyond poverty-stricken."

"Don't beat about the bush, mom, just tell us straight, why don't you."

"Broke?" Alex gasped, clattering a plate along the draining board. "You mean, there's no available money?"

"That's generally what it means," I sighed. "In fact, we're broker than broke, we're in debt to the bank."

Alex groaned. Elliot reached into the back pocket of his jeans and pulled out a wad of notes. "Here," he said, "I got paid today. I drew some out of the cashpoint on the way home. Take this."

"I can't."

"I'll have it," Alex cried.

"Take it, mom. We need to eat. Besides, we're a family, a team. Which reminds me," he said, turning to Alex, "How's the job hunting going?"

"Okay."

"You haven't looked, have you."

"I have!"

"Where? When? What for?"

Alex shrugged.

"You need to get a job," I told him gently. "I can't support you both on my own any more."

"Great!" he cried, "All gang up on me at once, why don't you? I'll get a job, okay?" And he resumed his washing up with increased vigour.

The curry was delicious, the wine more so. In the middle of this culinary feast, Alex suddenly said, "So, where's dad then?"

Both Elliot and I stared at him. He noticed us staring and said, "What? I'm just asking!"

"Do you remember me telling you that your dad and I had split up?" I said slowly.

"Yeah, but that was ages ago. I thought he'd be back by now."

"Alex," Elliot sighed, "For an academic genius you're a bit bloody slow, mate. Of course he's not coming back, not after what he did to mom."

Alex put his fork down. He'd stopped eating, a clear sign that he was upset. "Isn't he coming back at all?"

"No," I said as gently as I could, "We just sort of drifted apart."

"Helped by some bint in his office," Elliot blurted.

"These things happen sometimes, Alex, but you can still see your dad any time you want."

"Yeah, so long as you don't mind his strumpet being there," Elliot snapped.

"What, dad's living with this other woman now?"

"Try to keep up, Alex."

"These things happen," I said wearily.

"To dad though!"

"It can happen to anyone, Alex."

"Yeah, but *dad!*" He suddenly burst out laughing. "He's no oil painting and no slave to the gym either, that's for sure, *and* he's old."

"He's the same age as me, thank you very much."

"Yeah, but you've aged better, and you don't go round sleeping with other people."

"You don't know that," I sniffed indignantly. Both boys glared at me with wide eyes. I sighed and said, "Okay, I don't, but that doesn't mean I couldn't if I wanted to!"

"We don't even want to *go* there, mom."

"Why?" I teased, "Can't you see your mother with a new man? Think I'm too old and past it, eh?"

"Mom, it's too disgusting to think about. Parents ... well, parents don't do that sort of thing."

"Don't they? Seems your dad didn't get that memo. I try so hard to be hip and with it and 'down with the kids'." I indicated my ancient office suit and windswept hair.

"Nobody says 'hip and with it' any more, mom."

"Or 'down with the kids'. I mean, yuk."

"Anyway," I huffed, "I put up with your girlfriends, why couldn't you put up with mine?"

"What, *girlfriends?*" Alex laughed.

"You know what I mean. If I ... you know, started seeing someone." The thought seemed ludicrous even to me, but I wanted to test the water in case Chris Hemsworth ever broke down outside my house. Actually, if Chris Hemsworth found himself stranded outside my house I wouldn't care what the boys thought.

"What someone?" Elliot asked suspiciously.

"I don't know, *any* someone."

"No particular someone, then?"

"No, definitely not any particular someone."

"I suppose it would be alright, as long as you were discreet about it."

Now it was my turn to laugh. "And you two are discreet, are you? You think I don't hear all the giggling in your rooms or the banging of the headboard against the wall. I may be old but I'm not deaf yet."

Alex and Elliot both turned puce and started picking intently at their curries.

"Where is your girlfriend, anyway, Alex?" I asked into the ensuing silence. "I expected to meet her by now. Is she coming for the weekend any time soon?"

"Not until he's covered his headboard in bubble wrap," Elliot spluttered, "And soundproofed his room with egg boxes."

Alex pointedly ignored him and said, "She's backpacking round Europe for the summer."

"Oh. You didn't fancy going with her?"

"What!" cried Elliot, "Alex leave his computer *and* his bed! Come on, mom, be *serious!*"

Alex threw naan bread across the table at him. Elliot caught it. "Cheers, bro," he said, ripping it in half and dipping it in his curry. "So, with the girlfriend away all summer, you'll have plenty of time to find work and earn some money, then?"

"I said I would, didn't I?"

"Yeah, but you've been saying it all week and not doing much about it."

"I will!"

"He won't," Elliot said to me. "You know he won't. I doubt he's even left the house since he got back."

I briskly changed the subject and we talked about less controversial matters. Afterwards, Elliot made Alex clear up the plates, saying he needed the practice. Alex put his foot down at washing up again. "I did it last time," he whined like a four year old, "There's *three* of us living in this house, you know."

"Yes, but only two are contributing *financially*," Elliot said, "and I can't wash up with this brace on, and mom's not doing it, she's been out at work all day, like me!"

Later, after we'd had quite a skirmish round the kitchen sink, all of us washing and wiping and flicking tea towels at each other, we snuggled up together on the sofa, watching one of Alex's blood-thirsty films - the boys cheered, I hid my face behind a cushion.

When the film finished and we all began to stir, Elliot suddenly said, "Just make sure he's a nice man, mom."

"I'm not really thinking about another man quite yet."

"You should."

"Before it's too late, you mean," I said, nudging him.

"No, because it would be nice to see my mom happy for a change."

"I am happy." I threw my arms across the broad shoulders of my tall boys sitting either side of me. "Got you two, haven't I?"

"You need a man, mom," said Alex.

"No I don't."

"You know what I mean, someone to take you out, someone to have fun with."

I thought about it for a moment. "And you wouldn't mind?"

"We're not babies, mom."

"No, you're not." I felt tears stinging my eyes. "I miss you being babies."

"Take the wine off her," said Elliot, "She's going all mushy on us."

* * *

In the spirit of family unity, and after having hauled Alex's carcass out of bed and dragged him into the bathroom by his feet, we went to a supermarket that one of Elliot's mates assured us was 'the cheapest there is'. Alex drove, Elliot directed, I broke up the fights.

The supermarket was, indeed, cheap, but not very cheerful, with aisles of unpacked and still wrapped boxes that you had to dive into to get at the eggs, the potatoes, and pretty much everything else.

Alex lobbed items into the trolley with wild abandon, while Elliot methodically pulled them out again. "Shop brands," he kept saying, "Same stuff, only cheaper."

At least, that was his mantra until we came to the baked beans. Supermarket's own brand versus The Proper Beans. All three of us stood in front of the two towers of tins. I eventually made an executive decision and grabbed the more expensive ones.

"Mom!" Elliot gasped, "We're on a *very* tight budget!"

"I'm sorry," I said, putting them firmly in the trolley, "We may be poor, but there are some things in life you simply can't skimp on, and this is one of them."

"And Cadbury's chocolate gateaux," Alex cried, picking up three. Elliot made him put them back.

At the freezer cabinets I read the ingredients for a box of 12 beefburgers that were priced at less than a pound. "Never been anywhere near a cow," I declared. "They should have a label saying 'No cows were harmed in the making of this product'."

Elliot snatched them off me and tossed them into the trolley. "Bit of brown sauce and they'll be fine," he said.

"Bit of actual meat and they'd be even better," I muttered.

The bill for a week's worth of grocery for three people came to an astonishingly small amount.

"Let's go round again," Alex suggested.

We didn't.

Back at home the boys unpacked, tossing tins and packets at each other while I watched, wondering if I'd ever be able to find anything again. Then they made themselves lunch. Beans on toast, four rounds each. "Ah, proper beans," Elliot sighed dreamily.

"Pity about the toast," Alex said, sticking out his tongue in disgust.

We compiled a list and stuck it on the fridge door. 'Items of food not to scrimp on: Baked beans. Bread.' Later we added wine after the home-brand made me wretch.

Elliot put his arm across my shoulders as we stared at the list. "We're getting quite good at this poverty lark," he said, nodding his head. "It's not so bad after all. Of course," he added, unable to resist having another dig, "It would be even better if Einstein would get off his lazy bum and get a job."

I left them to fight it out in the kitchen.

* * *

My temping assignment the following week wasn't too bad - basic typing of memo's, letters and the occasional report. I was sat in a small office with a much older woman in a battered green cardigan, who hardly spoke to me for the first three days and spent most of the time simply glancing at me over the top of her glasses. Her name was Olive. On the fourth day, she deigned to speak.

"I collect teapots," she said, completely out of the blue.

"Oh? That's interesting," I said, desperate by now for conversation. "How long have you been collecting teapots for?"

"Eight years."

"And how many do you have?"

"Five," she said, and turned back to her computer. I had to push my fist into my mouth to stop myself from laughing.

On the last day Olive approached my desk. She did this nervously, as if she wasn't used to leaving the safety of her chair. "Just so you know," she said, avoiding all eye contact and staring at the wall behind me, "It's been nice working with you, I've really enjoyed having you here."

I was so touched by this I rushed out at lunchtime and splashed out on a tiny bunch of flowers from Tesco Direct. When I presented them to her, she burst into tears and said it was the nicest thing anyone had ever done for her. We hugged. I promised to keep in touch.

When I got home on Friday night I sensed an atmosphere in the house. There was a heavy bump from one of the upstairs rooms, followed by a muffled cry. I dropped my bags and raced up the stairs. Alex and Elliot were fighting, and fighting for real, in Alex's room. Swear words were hissed as they writhed like snakes from the bed to the floor. This was serious.

"What's going on?" I demanded.

They released their strangle holds and stood up, hot and sweaty and glaring fiercely at each other.

"He keeps taking my clothes," Elliot snarled.

"Only because I don't have any of my own," Alex snarled back.

"Well, you'd be able to bloody afford your own bloody clothes if you found yourself a bloody job, wouldn't you!"

"I've been looking!"

"No you haven't, you're *lying*."

Alex punched Elliot hard on the shoulder. Elliot pushed Alex backwards, and they fell onto the bed, punching and gasping like long distant runners.

"Stop that!" I cried, "You're too old to be fighting, and I'm not brave enough to try and break you up."

They pulled away from each other and sat on opposite sides of the bed, animosity sparking between them.

"He hasn't been out all week," Elliot said.

"I have!"

"No, he hasn't, mom. I checked. His shoes haven't been moved in the hallway. There's cobwebs inside them."

"Alex?"

"I've been busy," he said.

"Yeah, busy *stealing* my clothes! You don't even ask, you just *take* them. *And* he's eaten all the food in the house," he said to me, "There's no milk, no bread, nothing! We're out earning money all day while he's lounging at home doing bugger all and eating all the bloody food!"

It didn't seem that long ago that Elliot was doing the same, but I didn't say so. "Is this true, Alex?" I asked instead, "Have you looked for a job at all?"

"Yeah," he said, elbows on his knees and head hanging between them. "I've looked on the internet."

"That's not looking for a job!" Elliot snapped, "That's wasting time. The only way to get a job is to send out your CV, actually *phone* people, join an agency like mom."

"Oh, and you're the big expert, are you? You've only had a job, what is it now, *two* weeks. Before that you sponged off mom and dad just like I do."

"Yeah, but unlike you," Elliot hissed, turning and giving Alex a fierce jab in the back, "I could see how desperate mom was and how bloody *mean* dad was being."

Alex's head fell lower. "I will get a job," he mumbled.

"Okay," I said, "I wouldn't nag you if I didn't have to, Alex, but things are pretty desperate at the moment. We only really have Elliot's money to live on once all the bills are paid."

"Talking of which," Elliot said, standing up and forcing a hand into his jeans pocket, "Here's the housekeeping money, mom." He glared pointedly at Alex, who scowled back. "I got some tips, too."

"Keep some for yourself," I said.

"I don't need much, mom. I've … er … got some money in the bank."

"Have you?"

Elliot turned coy. "Well … " He ran his hand over his head, so reminiscent of his dad. "You know all the times I couldn't find my bank card and cadged money off you and dad?"

"Yes."

"Well, I never found my bank card, mostly because I didn't bother looking for it because it was easier to ask you for money instead."

"Oh Elliot."

"I know," he said, shrugging, "But I'm a changed man, a reformed character. Anyway, all the Jobseekers Allowance they paid into my account is still there, and – " He pulled something out of his back pocket, " – I finally found my bank card. So you keep all the cash, mom. There's just one condition."

"Condition?"

"Yeah. I'm not slaving away in a garage all day to earn money to feed *him*," he said, pointing but not looking at Alex. "He's like a swarm of locusts in the kitchen. *He* doesn't eat until *he* finds a job, that should give him enough incentive to get off his lazy backside."

"Mom!" cried Alex.

"I mean it, mom. He's dead wood."

"I can't see my own child *starve!*" I protested.

"He's not a child, mom, he's a man and perfectly capable of working and putting food on the table like we do. Until he does, I refuse to let him eat anything that *we've* bought."

While Alex gasped and spluttered, I leaned closer to Elliot and whispered, "You don't think you're being a bit ... harsh?"

He shook his head, lips pursed together.

I whispered, "Do you think it will work?"

He nodded his head, a tiny grin tugging at the corners of his mouth.

That night Elliot ordered curry whilst Alex sulked in his room. I felt terrible, but Elliot stood firm. I knew I'd crack within 24 hours. I was a mother who needed to feed and nurture, starving my children was against all my instincts.

The following morning I woke to the sounds of raised voices, punctuated by some very strong language. I leapt out of bed and raced downstairs. Elliot had Alex pinned up against the fridge. Alex had a chicken leg in his hand.

"I caught him eating!" Elliot said.

"This is ridiculous," I said, ignoring them and making myself a coffee. "We need to be pulling together, not fighting like this. Things are pretty tight around here and they're going to get tighter, so we need to make some changes, we need to cut down."

"Well we've found a cheap supermarket," Alex said, finishing off the chicken leg as Elliot glared at him.

"We have to do more than just buying cheap food, we need to cut down on the bills too. I've given it some thought and, I'm sorry, Alex, I'm going to have to cancel the broadband and the streaming services."

"No!" he screamed – literally, screamed.

"I can't afford it, and we don't use them much when you're not here."

"No internet? No Netflix or NOW or the Disney Channel?"

He looked horrified, his wide eyes rolling from left to right as if trying to imagine a world without broadband. He suddenly raced into the hallway. "Where's my shoes?" he cried.

"Break open the pupae under the hallway table," Elliot drawled, "You'll find them in there."

"Where are you going?" I called after him.

"Out!"

"Out where?"

Alex was already half way out the front door when he yelled, "To get a job!"

* * *

Three things happened that Saturday.

First, a delivery van pulled up outside our house and unloaded bags and bags of shopping into our hallway. Elliot and I looked at each other and shrugged as we hauled it all into the kitchen, drooling over the contents as we packed it into cupboards.

I rang Alex, who was out fixing a computer at a mate's house. "Did you place an order with Waitrose?"

He laughed. "Yeah, sure, mom. I tried to order from Harrods but they don't do home delivery."

Gary wouldn't have done this, we were his Aldi family, not his Waitrose girlfriend. That could only mean...

"You sneak!" I laughed into the phone five minutes later, when my kitchen cupboards were filled to bursting and Elliot was munching his way through a packet of fig biscuits. "I said I wanted to do this alone."

"Ah, you got the delivery then?" Katie said.

"You shouldn't have."

"It's the least I can do. I feel bad that I can't be there to hold your hand or offer you a shoulder to cry on because we're both so busy with work at the moment, but I can give you a bit of a boost, and I'm sure the boys will appreciate the food."

"I'll say. Elliot was salivating just reading the labels."

Katie laughed. "Can't have my nephews starving, can I."

"They're not starving! They're teenagers, they'll eat *anything*."

"Even bullet beans and beefless burgers, apparently," she said.

"Okay, who've you been talking to?"

"I was sworn to secrecy, Suze, his name will never pass my lips. All I'll say is it wasn't Elliot who had a right good moan about the food crisis in your house when I rang him the other day."

"He didn't!"

"Don't be too hard on him, the poor boy was in the final stages of malnourishment, almost delirious with it, he said, and it makes me feel better to do something practical to help. Don't be angry with me, if it was the other way round and Aiden left me – "

In the background I heard Aiden shouting, "Leave you? Darling, I'd *never* leave you."

"I know it's hard to imagine, but let's say it happened – "

"No, darling," he cried, "Let's not say that at all. Why are you saying these dreadful things?"

" – could you just stand by and do nothing, Suze? Wouldn't you want to help in any way you could?"

I had to admit she was right. "Thanks, Katie," I said, "You're a star."

"And the same goes for the tiny bit of funding I put into your bank account."

"What?"

"Just to tide you over for a bit. Oh, I have to go now, Aiden seems to be having some kind of panic attack."

Alex came crashing through the front door, "The student has returned!"

Elliot's eyes widened and he gripped my arm. "Don't tell him," he hissed, pushing jars and bottles to the back of the cupboards and trying to hide them with boxes of cereal. "One midnight feast and we'll be back to starving again."

"Alex!" I cried, when he burst into the kitchen, "Katie's sent posh food!"

Elliot groaned. Alex whooped and snatched up a packet of chocolate chip cookies. "Oh God!" he cried, spraying biscuit crumbs all over the place, "These are *fantastic*." He pushed another into his mouth. "I'll never eat another own-brand cookie again as long as I live." Another biscuit disappeared. "Mmmmmm-mmmm. UMMMMMMMMMM."

"See!" Elliot howled, "He's started already! Can't we get a Hannibal mask for him or something?"

"First son has an announcement," Alex finally said.

"You've developed a food intolerance and can only drink water from now on?" Elliot asked.

Alex laughed sarcastically. "Nope," he said. "I've got a job."

CHAPTER 13

Alex had actually got himself a job.

"So what is it?" Elliot asked.

"It's intellectually barren and obviously beneath my capabilities," Alex said.

"Doing what?"

"It's not what I'd imagined for myself and I certainly won't be making a career of it."

"What's the job, Alex?"

"It's demeaning work, but I do it for the good of the family."

"Alex!"

"What?"

"What's the bloody job?"

"Shelf packer. Sainsbury's."

"Five days a week?"

"Saturdays, but," he cried, holding a hand up to Elliot's rolling eyeballs, "I have a cunning plan."

"Which is?"

"Wait and see." And, with a huge grin, he raced up the stairs. Three hours later, he came racing down again. "Look!"

We looked at the postcards he'd printed, which read, 'Extremely good looking and highly intelligent IT and Computer Studies student offers his services for all your computer needs: problems installing, game playing (cheats available), upgrading, tuition in the comfort of your own home. Systems built to order, satisfaction guaranteed. No job too big or small.'

"Well?" he asked. "What do you think?"

"I think it's a good plan to skive all week," said Elliot. "You could have just put 'Skint computer nerd seeks money, phone with donations'."

"Funny! Not!"

"I like it," I said, "I'm not sure why it's necessary to mention your good looks, but it shows initiative. Who knows where it might lead?"

"It'll lead to him lounging in bed all day waiting for the phone to ring," Elliot sighed.

Alex, full of unbowed enthusiasm and raving about potential fortunes, rushed out to put them in local shop windows. He was gone for most of the afternoon. When he returned I was in the kitchen preparing dinner and singing away madly to Shania Twain on Alexa. I didn't hear him come in, and when he touched my shoulder I nearly shed skin.

"Alex!" I screamed. "You scared me half to death!"

"Sorry," he whispered, waving his arms to quieten me, "Just wanted to warn you, nan's here. I let her in. She's in the living room."

"Which nan?"

"Well, you know the nan who refuses to leave Bognor Regis even if a nuclear bomb fell on it, the one who plies us with sweets and presents when we visit and insists on kissing us at every opportunity?"

"Yes?" I beamed, wondering if my mother had, in fact, tore herself away from Bognor on my behalf.

"It's not that one."

"Oh." It was a heavy 'oh', full of disappointment and a growing sense of impending doom.

Gary's mother had deigned to visit.

"Hi, Philippa," I said as brightly as I could manage as I entered the living room and found her standing stiffly in front of the gas fire. Her eyes were roaming the room, collecting evidence to use against me, her eyebrows arched in disapproval.

"Suzanne," she drawled, "I've come to see my grandsons."

"Just off out mom," Alex cried, rushing past the open door and making a bolt down the hallway. I grabbed hold of his sweatshirt before he'd made it to the front door and hauled him into the living room with me, the smile on my face already starting to ache.

"Your nan's come to see you," I said sweetly.

"*Grandmother*," Philippa boomed. "I'm their *grandmother*."

"Hi na – grandma, nice to see you. Sorry, can't stop, just off out with –"

I pushed Alex down into an armchair. "I'll just get the other one. ELLIOT!"

Philippa grimaced as I bawled up at the ceiling.

"ELLIOT!"

A muffled voice. "What?"

"SOMEONE TO SEE YOU!"

"Who is it? Kelly?"

"IT'S A SURPRISE."

Philippa's whole face was a mass of pained revulsion, which, childish though it was, spurred me on all the more. After all, it was my house and I could bawl at the ceiling if I wanted. "COME AND SEE FOR YOURSELF!"

The thudding of feet down the stairs, the appearance of Elliot's expectant face in the doorway, a moment of deep disappointment, another moment thinking about potential escape routes, a glance at me, a glance at Alex (who shrugged helplessly), and finally, a forced smile. "Hi, nan ... I mean, grandma."

"Oh, my poor children," she howled dramatically, "You need looking after. How you must be suffering without your father!"

"They're fine," I said.

"We're okay," said Alex.

"We're chill, grandma."

"Chilled?" she gasped, "Is there no heating in this house?"

"Tea?" I asked through gritted teeth.

"I'll help!" Elliot cried.

"Let me!" Alex offered.

"No, you two stay and talk to your grandma. She's come to see you. Isn't that nice?"

"Yeah."

"Fabulous."

I put the kettle on, determined not to listen to the conversation in the other room but unable to resist pressing my ear against the wall. "Your poor father," I heard her say, along with, "You can always come and stop with your grandfather and I if you like." I waited for their responses, holding my hand over my mouth to stifle a laugh, but the boys just mumbled incoherently.

I hastily made a pot of tea. I automatically began to load up a tray with milk jug and sugar pot (bought specially for Philippa's visits on Gary's insistence), then decided I couldn't be bothered and poured out four mugs. I carried them into the living room just as Philippa was saying, "Your father is devastated, he misses you both so much. He wants to come back, you know, but your mother won't let him."

"Philippa!" I snapped.

"I'm just telling them the truth, Suzanne. They deserve to know the truth."

I bit my tongue. "Tea?"

"In a mug?"

"It's that or a soup bowl, all the teacups are broken."

"You were always so clumsy."

"It wasn't me," I said, struggling to reinstate my false smile, "It was Alex, using them as targets for his air pistol."

"I thought you were going to throw them away, mom," he protested, "You kept saying they were horrible and you were going to throw them away." I was surreptitiously shaking my head but Alex didn't appear to notice. "They were bloody ugly cups anyway, they deserved to be shot."

"I bought that tea set," Philippa said.

The silence throbbed in our ears. Philippa allowed a suitable period of remorse before saying, "Now, if you two boys need anything, I want you to know that your grandfather and I are always there for you. There's no need for you to stay here if you don't want to."

"But we live here," Alex said, frowning.

"It's our home," said Elliot.

"What is a home without a father?" Philippa sighed.

"It's a home with a mother in it," I told her. "They do still have a mother, you know."

"Yes, well." Philippa made a great show of picking her mug up off the coffee table, saying no more. Alex mouthed, 'Help!' at me, and Elliot slumped in his chair like a rag doll, his eyes glazed.

"Where's the antique timepiece I bought for your wedding?" she suddenly asked, glancing at the mantlepiece.

"Er … " I said, remembering the pleasing sound of it smashing in the dustbin.

"I broke it," Elliot said quickly, "Playing football."

"In the living room?" Aghast, she turned to me. "You have no control over them, Suzanne. That's why they need their father. Growing boys need their father."

"They're not boys, Philippa, they're *men*." I stood up, the pain of my teeth gnashing into my tongue now intense. "Just need to check on dinner," I beamed, trying not to actually run from the room.

"What are we having?" Elliot shouted after me.

"Quail eggs on French toast with organic garlic butter," I joked from the kitchen.

"Not again!"

"We've run out of caviar, I'm afraid." I tipped a bag of home-brand oven chips onto a tray. "Remind me to get some more from Marks & Spencer's tomorrow. How about fillet steak with organic petits pois and hand-crafted new potatoes tossed in butter and finely chopped herbs?"

"Third time we've had it this week, but I suppose if there's nothing else."

I pushed beefless burgers under the unlit grill and, bracing myself, returned to the living room. Philippa was whispering to the boys, "Now, don't tell your mother, this is just between you and me."

"Nan's given us 40 quid each," Elliot said.

Alex held the money in front of his wide-eyes and said, "Drugs!"

"Booze!" Elliot laughed, waving his in the air.

The look on Philippa's face was priceless. "They're joking," I told her, but she didn't look convinced.

Alex managed to extricate himself a short while later by saying he had an exam to study for. As he walked past me, sitting stiff and tense on the edge of the armchair, he put the money in my hands. Elliot immediately jumped up, did the same, then said, "See ya, nan. Gotta run, my girlfriend's expecting ... me."

"You're ruining them," Philippa said when they'd gone, "They're practically running wild without Gary around."

"No, they're not. They've both found themselves jobs."

"You're making Alex *work*? But he needs time to study!"

"He has plenty of time, Philippa. If you weren't so biased you could see they're both perfectly fine."

"They are most certainly not. They're eaten up with misery, you can see it on their poor faces. If you weren't so intent on destroying everyone's lives you'd be able to see it for yourself."

"Can I remind you that this situation is not of my making."

"Of course it is! You won't let Gary come back to the family home."

"Because he screwed and is still screwing his secretary, Philippa!"

"There's no need to be so crude."

"Okay, he was *fornicating* with his secretary, he was *bonking* her, *giving her one* on a regular basis, is that better?"

"There's no smoke without fire, Suzanne. If you didn't give him what he needed he was bound to – "

"Give him what *he* needed!" I was up on my feet now, all goodwill gone. "What about what *I* needed? Where was *my* fornicating and *my* bonking, my meals in posh restaurants and extravagant hotel stays, *my* expensive jewellery and – "

"You're so selfish, only thinking of yourself all the time."

"Get out!" I snapped. Philippa glared up at me. I glared right back. Nineteen years I had spent listening to her whingeing and interfering and making me feel small and insignificant. "I don't have to listen to you any more, Philippa. You're a very silly, small minded, bitter woman and I'd like you to leave this house. And take your money with you, it won't buy you anything here." I pushed the money into her hands. She stared at it for a while, then slowly stood up.

"You're making a grave mistake," she said.

"No, I'm doing what I should have done years ago. Now get out."

She strutted stiffly down the hallway. "You can't keep me from my own grandchildren," she said.

"My sons are free to see anyone they please. If they want to see you, Philippa, they know where you live."

"You'll keep them away, you'll turn them against me."

"No," I said, "I won't. I never have."

For the briefest moment we just stared at each other, and I could see a genuine sadness in her eyes. Suddenly she didn't look like the nasty old witch who'd tormented my life all these years, she just looked like a very sad old woman.

And then she left. And I actually felt a bit sorry for her.

But, on a personal level, I felt bloody marvellous.

* * *

The weeks that followed flashed by in a blur of work as the agencies kept me busy with assignments. I did a week at a solicitors' office in Digbeth that the agency promised was 'busy and challenging'. The company were *obsessed* with meetings, at least two hours a day was spent in a meeting room listening to someone drone on about something I wasn't the least bit interested in. The challenge, I soon discovered, was to stay awake.

The work was brain-numbingly dull, but the people were nice – I couldn't remember the last time I'd laughed so much or so often. I heard one secretary ask another secretary how her gardening skills were coming along.

"Oh, I've given up on that," she replied, "The window box was too labour intensive, so I had it crazy paved."

The secretary I sat next to in the open-plan office would often pick up a thick paperback and disappear, sometimes for more than an hour at a time.

"Where does she go?" I eventually asked someone.

"To the loo."

"Gastric problem?"

"Book problem, just can't leave them alone. If she's gone for too long we tend to go and get her before the bosses start complaining about her absence."

Then TemPers obviously began to have faith in my abilities and sent me on a 'long term' assignment. I had two whole weeks working for the Gambling Commission at the top of New Street, which was great. I really settled in, got to know the people, who to speak to, who to avoid like the plague, and the work was interesting. Then the 'proper' secretary returned from sick leave and I was 'surplus to requirements'. It was like being fired all over again. I was back out on the streets once more, jobless.

I went back to 'short term' assignments after that. Office Fairies promptly sent me to a hovel, and even 'hovel' doesn't portray how utterly *awful* it was. It was a tiny solicitor's 'shop' thing just outside the city centre, right next to the busy A38. On my way there on my first day my bus got stuck in a gridlock, so I arrived forty-five minutes late, which I thought was pretty good under the circumstances.

"You're late!" the female solicitor snapped at me as soon as I walked in the paint cracked door, and I knew right away this wasn't going to be a 'good one'.

The assignment was to update an office manual. It was possibly the most tedious thing I'd had to do in my life; the solicitor amended a paper copy in red pen, passed it over to me, and I amended the computer copy. At the end of the week, when I went to her to have my timesheet signed, she said, "You were late on your first day."

"Yes, but I made it up during my lunch break," I told her, for about the tenth time, thinking she was not only lucky I'd turned up at all but that I'd stayed for the whole week. She grudgingly signed my timesheet and I bolted.

I worked on antiquated computer systems and systems so new nobody knew how to use them. I struggled with temperamental faxes and photocopiers, and learned that miserable people created miserable working environments and that smiling didn't always help, it just made you look like a moron in an insane asylum. I worked with good bosses who asked nicely and acknowledged effort, and bosses like Callum who moaned constantly, if they deigned to speak to the temp at all, that is. I developed the skin of a rhinoceros.

I felt like I was on a hamster wheel of corporate slavery, only falling off at night to glance around like some rabbit caught in the headlights of an oncoming car to see where my life was. By some miracle, bills got paid, sons got fed, and everything in life was fine apart from the velocity at which it was passing.

Elliot, long out of his wrist brace, was taken on permanently at the garage owned by his mate's dad, who, by all accounts, thought he was a mechanical genius. He started giving me regular money.

Alex began work as a shelf stacker at Sainsbury's every Saturday and learned the fine art of 'getting up on time' – screaming and banging on the wall for him to turn off his alarm clock usually worked. His computer venture started off dubiously, with several calls from women requiring his 'good looking services'. At first he was shocked by their requests, then he became quite engrossed in the idea; I found him looking in the mirror above the fireplace a lot, combing back his hair and muttering, "How you doin'?". Finally, and rather alarmingly, he began to say things like, "A gigolo, a nice lying down job."

"Right up your street," Elliot drawled. "But I think they'll be expecting some Brad Pitt look-alike, not some creature from the pit with acne and an aversion to personal hygiene products."

"Acne!" Alex cried, rushing to the mirror again.

One night, when he answered a call on his mobile, I heard him cry, "You want me to do *what*?" I snatched the phone off him and yelled, "Stop badgering my son for sex!"

"Sex?" came a man's voice, which only enraged me further, until he added, "But I only wanted him to fit the cup holder on my computer."

"It's his CD drive," Alex explained, "He thinks it's a cup holder."

Then he started getting 'proper' jobs, teaching youngsters and old ladies how to use software and rescuing computers that had been doused in coffee/tea/beer. Huge mail order boxes from Bradford were delivered with increasing regularity as he began building computer systems for new customers, who were so pleased with the results they recommended him to others, who ordered more computer systems and, suddenly, Alex had a thriving business on his hands.

"I'd have still preferred the gigolo job," he'd sometimes say with a touch of melancholy.

Life increased to warp speed. I'd get up some mornings and not only wonder what day it was, but who I was and where I was supposed to be that day. The sat-nav app on my phone became my best friend as I trudged all over the city centre to locate my assignments. I regularly met Sarah for lunch, spoke to Katie a lot, managed somehow to pay the bills, made sure my sons were happy, and accepted assignment after assignment with no potential permanent jobs in sight.

I went on a couple of interviews where I dared to get my hopes up, only to have them savagely crushed. A firm of solicitors expected their secretaries to regularly work overtime without pay, including weekends. I turned it down on the grounds that I simply wasn't slave labour material. Office Fairies made the second job interview sound fabulous but only, I suspect, because everyone else on their books had turned it down. It was in the worst part of town, in a run-down building, staffed by people who had long given up the will to live. I turned it down on the grounds that my mental health was more important; also, the pay was terrible.

I religiously searched the internet for situations vacant every day, but it seemed there was a lack of decent jobs out there. I would have been despondent, if only I'd had time.

That Friday night, as we all sat watching a science fiction film that I couldn't fathom, Alex said, "I'm going back to university tomorrow, mom."

"Don't be silly, you've only just got here."

"I've been here three months, mom."

"No!"

"Oh yes," said Elliot, "Three long, arduous months of computer parts and strange people trooping through the house carrying boxes and monitors."

"Oh," I said, surprised and disappointed, "We've hardly spent any time together. I'd planned to do all these things and now it's too late."

"You were going to take us to the West Midlands Safari Park, weren't you," Elliot grinned.

"No," I said, lying, "I was going to take you to museums and stuff."

"Phew, lucky escape then."

"We're teenagers, mom, not toddlers."

"Shut up, Alex, you'll make her cry again."

"My babies!" I cried.

"See!"

"Worry not, mother, I'll be back every weekend to carry on the computer business. And there's more good news." He sat up from his prone position on the floor and beamed up at me. "I'm making enough money to pay my own way through university, so you won't have to pay me an allowance every month."

"Oh good." I gave a weak smile, then wailed, "You don't need me anymore!"

"I'll always need you, mom."

"We'll have to sort out a van, one that works properly this time," I said, glaring at Elliot, "to take you back."

"Sorted," Alex said, "Dad's taking me."

"Your dad?"

"Yep. He offered. I accepted."

I let out a fake scream. "You don't need me anymore!"

Both boys bombarded me with cushions before settling back down to watch the film, but I couldn't concentrate and eventually wandered into the kitchen to wash up. Gary was coming tomorrow and I suddenly felt nervous.

Apart from the endless texts and voice messages declaring his undying love or undying rage, I hadn't seen Gary in weeks.

CHAPTER 14

Gary arrived the next morning. I watched him through the window as he got out of the hire van. He looked older somehow, and he'd definitely put on some weight. I noticed his hair was longer than it should be and he seemed a bit *dishevelled* – even from a distance I could see his normally immaculate shirt was creased and his trousers had a tramline running down the front of them. *She* obviously wasn't taking proper care of him – I'd had twenty years of taking care of other people, I could do it in my sleep (and often did). How could she possibly compete with that?

Ah, but she didn't have to, did she. She was twenty years younger, twenty years prettier. She didn't have to compete at all, least of all with me.

"Hi," I said, when I let him in. I tried to sound casual and unemotional with that one word, but I felt like a nervous wreck inside.

"Hi."

"How are you?"

"Can't complain."

Really? Gary, not complaining?

"Coffee?"

"Love one."

He followed me into the kitchen. I hoped he noticed the new dress I'd splashed out on for a theatre trip with Sarah last month, and the way my long hair bounced with shine and vitality, just as the mobile hairdresser had promised. I busied myself with the coffee mugs.

"You look good," he said.

"Thanks."

An awkward silence, and then, as if he couldn't think of anything else to say, "Heard you destroyed my mother's china tea set."

"Yes. Well, not me, Alex."

"Ah." More silence. He looked around the kitchen. "The old place is looking good," he eventually said. "I miss it. I ... I miss you."

His hand came out towards mine across the kitchen counter, but I quickly moved away on the pretext of closing a cupboard door. "How's Poppi-with-an-i?" I asked.

"I don't know."

"Oh?"

"We broke up. It ... it wasn't quite how I imagined it was going to be."

"You imagined it was love." He looked down and nodded miserably. "And it wasn't." He slowly shook his head. "Oh, what a waste of misery that was then."

"I know. I'm sorry."

Repentance. Interesting, but worrying. Desperation was oozing off him like thick smoke, trying to smother me, choke me. "So," I said brightly, "Are you back at your mother's then?"

"No," he laughed. "I'm sofa surfing for a bit."

"Oh."

"It's very unsettling and very ... lonely."

"Loneliness can be a drag, but you get used to it." I'd gotten used to it a long time ago, way before he left.

"Oh Suzanne," he suddenly cried. "It doesn't have to be this way. Neither of us have to be alone. We can be together. I miss you."

I shook my head, surprised and alarmed. "You miss someone looking after you is all, taking care of your needs and not asking for anything in return. You miss having a wife. You don't miss me."

He suddenly stepped around the kitchen counter towards me. He looked like he was about to cry. "I miss *you*. I miss this house. I miss the boys and – "

"I don't miss the moaning, Gary. Or the poverty, or the deceit."

"No more lies," he gasped, standing in front of me. "I swear, no more mistakes, if you'll just – "

"No." I put up a hand to stop him coming any closer, to stop him touching me. "I don't want you back, Gary. I'm okay on my own. I ... I quite like it."

"You *like* it?"

"Yes, I've learned a lot about myself these last few weeks, I've learnt I'm stronger than I thought I was, and I haven't lost the house like you predicted. You must be very disappointed."

"I'm actually quite proud of you."

"I'm more capable than you gave me credit for, eh?"

"You're a lot of things I never gave you credit for, Suze."

I didn't know how to respond to this and, in the silence that followed, Gary stepped towards me again. I stepped back until I was pressed up against the kitchen sink. This wasn't what I wanted. I didn't like where this was going.

"Please, Suzanne, let me come home. We can make a go of it, I know we can."

"I'm sorry, Gary. I can't go back to the way it was before."

"Then we'll make a new way, a better way, a way that works for both of us."

"I don't trust you any more," I said. "You don't add anything to my life, you just take."

"I'll change, I swear. Things will be different, I promise."

"No."

"But I'm lonely," he breathed.

"Then find another Poppi."

"I don't want another Poppi, I want you."

"Well, you can't have me."

"You're my wife. You're still my wife."

"Gaz, you dumped me for a younger woman, left me destitute, and then, when you decide the younger woman wasn't all she was cracked up to be, you want to make do with the old wife again, just until you find something better. I'm sorry, it's not going to happen."

"I'll make it up to you, I swear I – "

"I like my life the way it is," I said. "For the first time in a long time I actually like my life and I like myself and I like everything I'm doing. I don't have to answer to you or anyone else, and that's a nice feeling. I'm my own person, I'm independent, and I want it to stay that way."

"You ... you won't take me back?"

"No."

"I'll give you anything you want. Freedom, money, a car of your own."

"It's too late, Gary."

"A conservatory! I'll build you that conservatory you always wanted."

"If I want a conservatory I can get it myself." I couldn't, but the price he was asking was too much.

"Can you?"

Not a chance. "Yes."

"But – "

The back door flew open at that moment and a total stranger walked into the kitchen carrying an extremely large cardboard box. The stranger was followed by Alex, who was saying, "Now if you get any problems setting it up just give me a ring and I'll talk you through it. I'll be back down in a couple of weeks to set up your network and webcam. Oh, hi dad."

The next two hours were spent packing Alex's belongings into the hired van. "Why have you got so much stuff?" Gary kept asking, as the boxes kept on coming.

"I'm starting my own empire, dad, This time next year I'll be right up there with Bill Gates and Elon Musk on the billionaire's list."

I tried to avoid Gary as best I could, but he was very persistent and very determined. He grabbed me every chance he got and whispered things in my ear.

"We can make it work," he breathed on the stairway.

I prised his arms away and ran up to Alex's bedroom, where he grabbed me again. "I'll make it up to you, Suzanne, I'll do anything you ask, anything you want, *anything*."

"I want you to stop, Gary."

He grabbed me in the kitchen, where I was throwing random food into a carrier bag for Alex to take with him. "I love you," he said. "Don't I deserve a second chance, to prove myself to you? Aren't I allowed to make one mistake? I've learned from it, I really have."

"You've learned that you're not very good on your own, and you're not very good with an iron by the look of it." I deftly avoided an oncoming embrace. "You buggered off and left me, Gary, how do you think that felt? For me, I mean, I know how it must have felt for you, bloody marvellous I'd imagine."

He dropped his head. "Is there someone else?" he asked. "Have you met someone?"

"No."

"Are you sure?"

"I think I'd know, Gaz."

"Then why won't you let me come back?"

"Because I don't *need* you. I don't *want* you. I don't … I don't love you, not any more."

He looked at me then, properly looked deep into my eyes. There were tears in his. "I'm sorry," he said. "I really am sorry. I'm sorry I messed up, I'm sorry I hurt you, and I'm sorry I didn't realise what I had until I lost it."

"I'm sorry too, Gaz." I touched his arm. He gave a weak smile.

"You're sure?" he asked. "You can have as much time as you want to think about it. I won't hassle you. Just think about it. Please."

"I'm positive," I said, not wanting to give him any semblance of false hope. "And I've had plenty of time to think about it."

He turned away slowly and walked out of the kitchen all slumped and miserable. And then he was gone. And Alex was gone. And the house seemed very empty and quiet.

But I was okay with that.

* * *

I worked as a receptionist the following week. I hadn't wanted the assignment, but it paid well so I allowed myself to be talked into it. It was at a small family law company, small as in one solicitor, one secretary (who spent all day filing her nails and talking to her boyfriend on her mobile), and me. It wasn't too bad because the only time the phone rang was when Sarah called on my mobile, insisting I meet her for lunch.

"It's happened," she beamed in the wine bar, positively bouncing up and down on her stool. "James asked me out on a date last Friday."

"A *proper* date?" I grinned, "With a posh restaurant and walking home hand-in-hand and making mad passionate love on the living room floor?"

"They haven't invented a word to describe what we did on the living room floor," she grinned.

"Good, then?"

"*Way* beyond good."

I was pleased for her, I really was. If anyone deserved true love and happiness it was Sarah, the nicest person I'd ever met. The fact that I, personally, hadn't had sex in months, if not a full year, didn't make me the least bit envious. Well, not much.

"He's amazing!" she cried, clapping her hands together and grinning like a maniac. "He's so loving, so kind, so perfect, so – "

"Calm down or they'll throw us out," I laughed, buoyed by her happiness. Several customers were already staring at us, and I'm sure one of the bar staff had rushed off to get an emergency bucket of cold water. "How come you're only *just* telling me this, anyway? Aren't I your best friend? Aren't you supposed to tell me the instant it happens?"

"I am!" she cried.

"But you went on the date on Friday."

"We've only just emerged," she giggled.

"But today is Wednesday."

Sarah nodded vigorously.

"You've been at it for *five days*!"

Sarah's head was almost like a piston at this point.

"Bloody hell, the poor man must be exhausted!"

"No, he isn't. Isn't that *amazing*? I think this is it, Suze, I think this is the real thing. I've never felt like this before, and James says the same. We were meant to be."

"Just ... just don't marry him," I said, "Not yet, anyway. Give it at least ten, maybe twelve years and see how you feel then."

"Marry him?" she laughed. And then she stopped laughing and pondered the wall behind me for a moment.

"Don't do it, Sarah. Don't get carried away and make mistakes you might regret for the rest of your life." Did I sound bitter? Surely not.

"Trust me, Suze. James McCreath is *no* mistake, he's a bloody miracle!"

"Take it slowly, Sarah. Don't rush into anything."

"Rush?" she cried, "I've waited almost a year for this."

This was true, and if anyone deserved to be as happy as Sarah was right now, it was Sarah herself. I reached out and took her hand. "You go for it, girl," I said.

"I will." She glanced at her watch. "In three more hours. God, *three more hours*! Employers should give new lovers special time off work to indulge in fabulous fornication, don't you think?"

"It's not something I need to worry about," I drawled.

"What about you? How are you doing? Any men on the horizon?"

"Not on the horizon, over the horizon, or even in the same solar system," I said, and sighed heavily, just as Sarah's mobile phone rang.

"James!" she cried, winking at me. "Yes, I miss you too, darling. What? You're going home? You don't feel well? Oh," she giggled, glancing mischievously at me, "It must be contagious, I don't feel well either. Meet you there in five minutes." And she jumped up, grabbed her coat, promised to call, and was gone.

To her fabulous fornication.

Leaving me to my enforced and rather uncomfortable celibacy.

* * *

I spoke to Katie almost every day, lunched with Sarah every week. Some of the girls I worked with on temping assignments kept in touch and we exchanged text messages, including Annabel at the tiny solicitors' office I'd worked at. "How much would it cost for a divorce?" I texted her once. She called me straight away, said words like 'nisi' and 'uncontested?', which I didn't really understand, but I certainly understood that Legal Aid didn't exist any more and that I'd have to pay for it all myself.

"I'll see if I can get you a free half hour with Mr Smyth, who handles this sort of thing," she said, "He'll quickly run you through the process."

I got invited to birthday drinks after work one night with the girls from Stepps & Partners, and even met up with Olive, who collected teapots, a couple of times in a cafe. I felt very buoyed up and happy, I was enjoying myself.

But I was always brought back down to earth by endless text messages and phonecalls from Gary, either begging to come home or raging about not being able to come home. The last one was at 2 o'clock in the morning. He sounded drunk.

"I want to come home," he cried. "I'm so lonely, Suze, I hate living on my own. I miss my family, I miss my house, I miss you. Please, let me come home."

I almost fell for it, almost felt sorry for him, but caught myself just in time. I was doing fine without him. I didn't want to go back to the way things were before, I liked the way things were now. In the end I had to hang up when his wheedling voice started to turn angry again.

A couple of days later Elliot came home from work, went straight to the fridge, and casually said, "They're moving."

"Who?"

"Dad and Popeye."

I stopped stirring the gravy and turned to stare at him. He stared back with widening eyes. "Oh," he said, "You didn't know."

I couldn't speak.

"Did you think they'd broken up? Did dad tell you they'd broken up?"

I nodded my head.

"They haven't, they never have. He's been staying with her, but she lives in a shared house and I guess the other girls didn't like having him around all the time and he kept moaning that he had no privacy, so they're moving to a flat in town." He came over and gave me a quick hug. "Sorry, mom," he said, and raced up to his room.

Leaving me standing there, feeling stupid because I'd believed all the lies he told me and felt bad about his loneliness and his misery because I thought I'd caused it.

I burst into tears. I cried for a long time, sat at the kitchen table. And then I wiped my face dry and said, "Enough now, I'm not shedding one more tear over this ever again."

It was cathartic.

* * *

On Friday TemPers finally produced an assignment to get excited about. A secretarial stroke PA position in a major commercial property company, if not *the* biggest property company in the country. And it was in the Building Consultancy department, my perfect niche. Three months of temping work leading to possible permanent.

"Want it?" they asked.

"More than you'll ever know," I said.

I was going back to working with surveyors and dilapidations and reports again. I was delighted. And nervous. What if I didn't like the job and was stuck there for three months? Or worse, what if I really liked it but they didn't offer me a permanent position at the end of it?

Just turn up, I told myself, and take it from there.

On Monday morning I was wearing a suit I'd taken a shaver to to get rid of the bobbles and was sitting in a reception area waiting for a supervisor to take me to my desk. The signs so far were good – a gleaming building on Colmore Row, right in the heart of the city centre, with people who smiled as soon as they saw me, and the atmosphere seemed light and casual. I'd been on so many temping assignments I'd developed a sixth sense and could tell which ones were going to be good and which ones were going to be bad as soon as I walked through the door. This one was definitely a good one, I could feel it in my bones.

"She won't be too long," the receptionist kept saying. "Mondays are always pretty busy round here."

"It's when the surveyors discover all the work they should have completed on Friday," I said.

The receptionist laughed. "You've worked for property companies before then?"

"Yes, I was at Richard Sovereign."

"Oh!" she gasped wide-eyed, "Isn't that where James McCreath works?"

"You know him?"

"I know *of* him. Is it true he's possibly the best-looking building surveyor in the country?"

Before I could answer the doors from the lift to the reception area opened and a man stepped out. A man I recognised. "No," I breathed at the receptionist, "Not any more."

The man looked at me and our eyes locked for what seemed like the longest time. There was recognition in his he remembered me. "Hello," he said. I felt the blood rush up through my body to congregate in a reddened mask on my face. "Haven't I seen you somewhere before?"

"Does that line still work?" the receptionist laughed.

"At S-Stepps & Partners," I spluttered. "I worked there as a receptionist for a while."

"Not a very long while," he smiled, "I was there the following week and you'd gone."

"I was just temping."

"Ah." He stood looking at me for a moment. His eyes were truly amazing, the palest of blue, and his voice was deep and smooth, like a warm cotton wool in the ears. "Are you temping here?" he asked.

"In the Building Consultancy department."

"Really?" He gave a broad smile. "That's my department."

No! Could I be that bloody lucky?

"I'm Alan Talbot," he said, extending a hand, "Partner and Head of Building Consultancy."

I shook his hand, smiling like an idiot. I was touching his skin, making *physical contact*! I couldn't speak. I felt very hot. I seriously needed to pull myself together.

"You're Pauline, aren't you?"

Pauline? *Pauline*? Oh great, he thought I was someone else, it wasn't me he remembered at all.

"Suzanne," I told him. "Suzanne Philips."

"Oh? Adam Palmer told me your name was Pauline."

I suddenly remembered the predator at Stepps & Partners, who had so shocked me with his lechery I'd told him my name was Pauline just to get rid of him. "He was mistaken," I said, coolly, professionally, while my heart pounded like a bass drum.

"Well, Suzanne, I look forward to having you around the department. Hope you can type, we're pretty busy."

Type? Could I type?

Hell, yes. For him, *anything*.

'Get a grip, woman!" I told myself, as I followed him through the doors and down the corridor.

* * *

"Something's happened," I said.

"What? Oh you haven't take gormless Gary back, have you?"

"No, I've ... I've met someone."

"Met someone?"

"At work."

"At work?"

"Is there an echo on the line? Yes, I've met someone, at work."

"Oh Suzanne!" Katie suddenly cried, "That's *brilliant!* What's his name? What's he look like? Is he rich? Tell me *everything.*"

"I've only just met him."

"And?"

"And nothing really. Well, something, obviously, but I'm not quite sure what. I've seen him before and he made me go all funny inside, and I met him again today and he made me go funny again."

"You're not making much sense, Suze."

"That's because I don't understand it. I've met this man – "

"Which man?"

"He's ... my boss – "

"Oh no, not the old boss syndrome."

"He's not old, he's ... bloody gorgeous, actually."

"How gorgeous?"

"As gorgeous as they come." I sighed, remembering his ice blue eyes and warm, soothing voice.

"Good for you," she declared, "You deserve to have something nice in your life for a change."

"It's just a three month temping job at the moment but they might keep me – "

"Boring," Katie cut in, "Tell me more about the man, like his name."

"Alan Talbot." The name rolled off my lips like a magic incantation, *Alan Talbot.* "I think I'm a bit old to be feeling like this about anyone."

"Nonsense, you're breathing, aren't you?"

"Not much when he's around, I have to admit. All the secretaries in the department, if not the whole company, are madly in love with him. They say he's an absolute gem to work for, the best boss in the world, so not only is he gorgeous but he's nice too."

"He's not married, is he?"

"I don't know."

"Bloody well find out before you start throwing your heart or any other part of your anatomy at him. And check he's not gay while you're at it."

"You want me to provide a detailed profile?" I laughed.

"Fax it to me. I've got to go," she suddenly cried, "If I leave my customer under the dryer much longer she'll come out bald. Keep me posted, have fun, don't get hurt. Love ya, babes."

For the next few days I leapt out of bed in the morning almost fizzing with enthusiasm. I took great care with my makeup, hair and, as best I could, my clothes, and as I walked into the office I felt I was floating on a cushion of happiness. I threw myself into work with gusto, breezing through schedules and reports, letters and faxes, like a dervish. I was in my element and I wanted this job, wanted it so bad.

"Wow," Alan said, after I'd worked up the courage to walk into his office with an urgent schedule of dilapidations, "You got that done quick. I didn't expect you to finish it today."

I just smiled. I found it difficult to talk around him without spluttering and turning puce, so I kept conversations to quick nods, huge smiles and the occasional noise from the back of my throat. Terrible way for a grown woman with teenage sons to behave, but I couldn't help myself, I really couldn't. I'm sure he thought I was a bit 'slow' – an *idiot savant* who could produce reports fast but wasn't up to much in the old talking department. I was letting myself down, not giving a good impression, but then, what chance did *I* have with a man like Alan Talbot? None whatsoever. He was so handsome, probably knew he was handsome, and most likely had a posse of gorgeous women chasing after him. I was just the secretary, and a temp one at that.

Still, he was nice to look at, nice to work for, and nice to dream about. Which I did, almost every night.

No way for a woman of my age to behave at all.

On Friday, when I arrived at work, Alan wasn't in his office.

"He's gone to check on the building works in Digbeth," Christine, the Senior Secretary, told me. "Should be back by lunch, which might give us enough time to clear away the week's debris." She sighed as she surveyed the piles of paperwork on her desk. Mine looked the same, and so did Jennifer's, the junior secretary who popped bubblegum all day and slumped motionless in her chair when she had no work to do.

I began to make neat piles out of the papers. Jennifer suddenly leapt up from her chair and cried, "Last one to finish has to buy a round at lunchtime."

A moment of silence, and then Christine cried, "You're on!"

Suddenly papers were flying everywhere, mostly in the bin. Jennifer was a blur at the filing cabinets, whipping out files, punching papers and tossing the files back into the cabinet in one fluid movement. It was almost artistic to watch, and all of it punctuated by the popping of her bubblegum.

Christine went mad with a stapler, and I collated random papers into piles – a perfectly neat pile of James' work, which I reverently placed on his desk (noticing no photographs of wife or kids as I did so), a fan of papers for the surveyors, and a loose bundle for Russ, the graduate who didn't appear to do anything except make paper planes all day.

In the midst of all this hyperactivity, Christine threw up her hands and shouted, "Photo!"

"Who of?" Jennifer snapped.

"Alan at the Bromsgrove site."

"Is it needed for the Bromsgrove report?"

"Apparently not," Christine grinned.

"Is it a close up?"

Christine inspected the photograph in her hand. "Well, you can tell its him."

"Give it to Diane," Jennifer said, "She offered a box of *Krispy Kreme* doughnuts for a good one."

"But didn't Susan offer a whole tray of Philpotts sandwiches? And she hasn't got one of Alan yet."

"You sell surveying photographs?" I asked Jennifer later, when her filing had brought her closer to my desk.

"Only when the surveyors get caught on a picture and only to the girls, although there's been some rumour about a partner who collects pics of secretaries, which is why we all pull faces when Danny Bloom comes round with his phone out." Files were opened and closed like a flurry of giant butterflies in front of her. "Photos of Alan always do well, of course," she continued. "Louise Mansfield gave actual cash for one of him once, but it was a really good one and the money went straight in the charity tin. Carl is our next top selling surveyor, he's built like Superman, followed by Pete, who's the image of Keanu Reeves, Paul, who could easily be a male model, and John, who has exceptionally good hair."

"Don't they mind?" I asked, amazed.

"Who? They surveyors? Oh, they don't know," she laughed.

Christine shuffled over to us. "I've finished," she declared.

Jennifer slammed the last file into the cabinet. "Me too. Time for nail care, me thinks."

"Nail care?" I asked.

They both looked at me strangely. "Don't they do nail care where you come from, Suze?"

"No, never heard of it."

"How do you take care of your nails then?"

I held them out in front of me. Both Christine and Jennifer lowered their faces to inspect the ends of my fingers. "Oh," they both said. "Nasty," Jennifer added, and dragged me over to her desk.

I was having my nails painted bright red when Alan walked into the office at midday. I expected him to say something about it, but he didn't. He just smiled and sailed into his office saying, "Tidied up pretty well, girls."

"We do our best," Christine shouted after him.

"Yeah, I know you do. Thanks for all your efforts this week, much appreciated. And you're a positive whizz on the old computer there, Suze."

I made a noise at the back of my throat to indicate acknowledgement.

"Right, it's Friday." He clapped his hands together. "It's pretty close to lunchtime, so, let's go."

Christine, I noticed, went all girly and started applying lipstick. Jennifer popped a particularly large bubble in celebration and, after picking the gum off half her face, said, "You paying, Alan?"

"Don't I pay every time, Jen?"

"Not every time, no. You didn't in February."

"February." He made a great show of trying to remember the incident, rubbing his hand across his square chin and staring up at the ceiling. "That wouldn't be the time when I was off for a whole week with flu, would it, Jen?"

"Yeah." She popped another bubble. "That's right."

"The 'flu episode' that you remind me about every single Friday?"

"Yep, that's the one."

"Once again I offer my most sincere apologies and can only promise that it will never happen again."

"Oh, isn't he a card," Christine giggled. "Come on, we're wasting valuable drinking time."

"Where are we going?" I asked, as she bustled us out of the office.

"Where?" she gasped. "Where every self-respecting surveyor is on a Friday lunchtime. The Old Joint Stock, of course."

CHAPTER 15

It was Friday lunchtime and I was in The Old Joint Stock with some of the department secretaries and … Alan Talbot. I didn't know how to act, how to behave, and certainly not how to speak. I was still making sounds at back of my throat whenever he was within earshot and glowing like a bloody firefly whenever he spoke to me directly. I had reverted to teenage inadequacy. Was he looking at me? Was I making a complete fool of myself by basically not talking? Did he think I was a complete moron?

My three month assignment at Grimbles MZ Property Consultants working for Alan Talbot was going to be very long and arduous if this kept up.

And then someone handed me a pint of Stella. Which I drank. On an empty stomach. To the consternation of Russ, the graduate, who had to make do with my glass of wine instead.

And suddenly I was talking again. Couldn't shut up, in fact. And I had a rapt audience who thought a minor miracle had occurred and the temp could speak after all. I regaled them with tales of my teenagers, and then, when I mentioned some of my work experience, somebody asked, "What was Callum Redfern like to work for?"

"Oh, don't even get me started on that one!" I screamed.

"Go on," they persisted.

"We've heard rumours," Christine said.

"Whatever you've heard is probably true," I told them.

"No! Really?"

"How long did you work for Callum?" Alan asked.

At the back of my head, submerged beneath a half-pint of Stella, my brain was prodding me, saying, 'Isn't that the bloke you've got a crush on? And hasn't he got the most amazing eyes? You can't speak, of course, not to *him*.'

"Four years," I said, surprising myself.

"You must be one tough cookie."

"A cookie forged out of grim determination with a backbone of steel."

He laughed. And I laughed. And then everyone was laughing, until someone mentioned that, as it was now 2.30 in the afternoon, we should perhaps be thinking about returning to the office. Where we found Carl, our Chief Surveyor, having a major fit at his computer terminal.

"I forgot the dilaps for the Stoke job," he cried, pounding at his keyboard. "They wanted it today and I just *completely forgot!*"

"I can't stay late," Jenny immediately said.

Christine pulled a face.

"Just like old times," I said. "The Friday lunchtime drink followed by the Friday afternoon panic. I'll stay and help," I offered, "I don't mind." It's not as if I had anything to rush home for, and it didn't hurt to suck up to an employer who might offer you a proper job later. "I'll need food to soak up the alcohol though."

A McDonald's was sent for and brought in. Carl took up position on the edge of my desk and dictated directly. I typed. Christine and Jennifer did what they could, gathering together all the necessary photographs and photocopying them, and left at 5.30 on the dot.

I printed. Carl edited. I amended. Alan came over and read the dilaps, then made more amendments, which made me and Carl groan out loud. I amended. Printed. Alan read the report again while Carl and I fervently crossed our fingers at my desk. The report came back untouched and we let out a cheer of jubilation. I rushed to the binding machine as Carl stood by and waited, open envelope at the ready.

"I'll drop it in personally on the way home," he said.

"Covering letter!" I cried.

"Done it," Alan said, coming out of his office with a sheet of paper. He glanced at his watch. "7.30. Not bad. You're fast, Suzanne."

"Thanks." I was looking straight at him and not blushing, not stuttering, maintaining steady eye contact. I was a grown up again – and thank God for that.

"Let me give you a lift home," Alan said. "It's the least I can do after all the effort you've put in."

Panic coursed through me. Okay, I'd mastered the art of talking in front of him, but being trapped in a car with him for any length of time was pushing my adult capabilities a bit too far. "I'm meeting someone," I lied.

And so it was that, at 7.45 on a Friday night, whilst the city centre all around me vibrated with raucous revellers, I stood at the bus stop on Colmore Row in the pouring rain. And, of course, I had no umbrella.

I eventually got home an hour later, drenched and absolutely knackered, to find Elliot and Kelly making out on the sofa.

"Don't mind me," I shouted, rushing into the kitchen, "I just want a bath and my bed."

"Mom!" Elliot yelled.

"It's okay, you're a grown up, I respect your need for privacy. Though why you couldn't do it in the safety of your own room I don't know. Would have been better, but I'm not one to criticise your grown-up choices."

"Mom." Elliot was at the kitchen door now. "I couldn't go to my room."

"Why not?" I was busy pouring hot water into a very strong cup of coffee, thinking I might be able to stay awake long enough to have a bath. "Too messy, eh?"

"No. Well, yes, but that's not the reason we're not in it. Katie's there."

"Katie?" The coffee spoon clattered across the kitchen counter. "My Katie? My sister, Katie? Katie from Canada?"

"Yeah, all of them."

"She's *here*?"

"Surprise visit, she said."

"Surprise? I'm bloody gobsmacked!"

"You don't look very happy, mom."

"Oh, I am, I am. I'm just ... surprised." I hadn't seen my sister in over a year. "Oh my God, I look a mess."

"I don't think she's bothered what you look like, mom," Elliot laughed. "She's your sister, she's probably seen you look a lot worse."

"Yes, yes, you're right, you're probably right." I raced towards the kitchen door, hardly daring to believe that my sister, who married a rich Canadian accountant and had been whisked away from the Midlands, was here in my house, in the flesh. I stopped dead in my tracks, turning slowly to face Elliot. "You let her sleep in your bed? Why, exactly?"

"I didn't *let* her. She turned up, hugged the life out of me, talked a lot, went to the bathroom, then didn't come back. When I went to check to see if she was still alive, I found her slumped across my bed, fast asleep."

"You sure she was asleep and not in some kind of coma induced by the stench emanating from your room?"

"Mom!"

"Sheets," I gasped. "Have you changed your sheets recently? Vacuumed recently? Has your room ever seen a duster?"

"What's a duster?"

"Elliot!"

"Okay, okay. What do you mean by recent? How recent are we talking here?"

"This month?"

Elliot laughed, I groaned. Then it began to sink in to my befuddled, rain-soaked brain that my *sister* was *here* in *my house*.

My sister!

I raced up the stairs taking two steps at a time, God only knows where I found the energy, and arrived at the top with shredded tendons. I hobbled along the landing, pushed open Elliot's bedroom door, and there she was, lying face down, legs akimbo, arms outstretched, snoring.

"KATIE!" I screamed.

She leapt at least three inches off the bed, perfectly horizontal. I threw myself down on the bed next to her and wrapped my arms tight around her. "Katie! Katie! You're here! What are you doing here? Oh god, it's so great to see you!"

"Wait," she dribbled, hauling herself into an upright position and holding up a hand. "Jet lag victim coming round."

I bounced up and down with barely contained excitement, making Katie bounce up and down with me.

"If you could just stop that, I'd be grateful," she groaned.

"Oh Katie! You look ... well, you look pretty shit, actually."

As if! My sister was perfect in every way, with her tall, slender body, huge blue eyes, blonde hair, and a husky voice that felled grown men like bowling pins. Usually immaculate, her makeup had shifted like a mudslide down her face and her long hair was splayed out like Medusa. And still, to me, she looked like a film star.

Her bright blue eyes stared at me. And then life came into them, as if someone had turned on a switch in her brain, and she looked at me properly and screamed again, this time in delight. We hugged, both of us shrieking hysterically. From downstairs, Elliot shouted, "If you kids could just keep the noise down a little?"

"Why are you here?" I cried.

"Business trip for Aiden."

"In Birmingham?"

"London, for the weekend, but I couldn't resist coming to see my little sister and catch up with all the gossip. It's okay, isn't it?"

"Okay? Of course it's okay!" I hugged her again. "It's so bloody great to see you."

She patted down her hair and leaned her back against the headboard. "It's been a nightmare," she said. "First the flight was delayed from Toronto, then we hit bad weather, then we couldn't land in London for an hour, then I had to jump on a train to Birmingham and catch a taxi from New Street, so basically, I'm knackered."

"You and me both!"

"You just got home?" Katie asked, struggling to focus on the dusty alarm clock on Elliot's dusty bedside table.

"Yeah. There was an emergency at work."

"Ah, so you're a doctor now."

"No," I laughed, "A surveyor's secretary."

"Wasn't aware there were any life-or-death situations in surveying."

"You'd be surprised. Come on." I grabbed her hand and hauled her off the bed. Katie pulled away for a moment to brush down her expensive, wrinkled clothes, grimacing and saying, "What's he do, collect dust as a hobby?"

"He's a teenager."

"Say no more."

I took her into my bedroom and threw back the duvet. We glanced at each other and grinned at the memory of our teenage years spent lolling in bed, gossiping and watching TV. We quickly changed into pyjamas and leapt into bed. Katie turned on the TV and began flicking through, muttering, "All these channels and still nothing to watch." I picked up my phone and called Elliot.

"Mom?" he answered, "Where are you?"

"Upstairs."

"Now *that's* what I call *idle!*"

"We need that bottle of whisky out of the kitchen cupboard, and a bottle of lemonade out of the fridge. And glasses."

"And ice," Katie yelled.

"And a takeaway."

"A takeaway!" Elliot laughed, "And what exotic delights would the madams prefer from the local delicacies?"

"Katie, what do you want to eat? Indian? Chinese? Fish and chips?"

"We're in the Balti Triangle, aren't we? It *has* to be curry. Chicken. With rice. And naan bread." Katie's eyes were now so wide I thought they might pop out. "I haven't had a proper curry in *years!*"

"Heard it," Elliot said, "Both in my ear and from up the stairs. You two are *loud!*"

"There's bugger all on," Katie suddenly cried, leaping out of bed. "Where's your DVD collection?"

"Under the dressing table."

Katie bent to have a look. "Five DVDs, that's all you've got?"

"236 episodes of Friends, what more do you need?"

"You're absolutely right," she said, slipping one into the machine and diving back into bed again.

Elliot came in with a tray laden with our drinks. "Where did you get the ice from?" I whispered to him.

"Chipped it off the inside of the freezer," he whispered back.

"Is that safe?"

"Dunno." He nodded at Katie, who was shovelling ice into her glass. "If she turns blue or starts screaming in agony, let me know. I'll bring your curry up when it arrives." He stood up straight, draping a tea towel over his arm. "Do you ladies require anything further?"

"Thank you, Jeeves," Katie said, dismissively waving her hand in the air. "That will be all for now."

Elliot tutted and left the room with his eyeballs rolling like loose marbles.

We didn't get to see our curry.

* * *

"How far did you get?" I asked at breakfast the next morning.

Katie, wrapped in a dressing gown and with her hair up in a towel, munched hungrily on toast. "I got as far as them dancing in the fountain with umbrellas. After that ... nothing."

"We just can't hack the late nights any more. It's fine to

lounge in bed, eating and watching TV until the early hours when you're teenagers, but no good when you've just flown in from Canada or done a 12 hour stint at work."

"Plus, of course, we're old."

"I wasn't going to mention that."

"Well, it's true. But we're still unutterably gorgeous, no doubt about it. Genes are a wonderful thing, thank you, mother." She ran a sweeping hand across her face, then burst out laughing. "Spending a fortune on creams and gym member-ship helps too."

"How old are you then, Katie?" Elliot asked, coming into the kitchen and immediately making for the fridge.

"How rude!" she cried. "Does the boy have no manners? What kind of philistine are you raising that *dares* to ask how old a woman is? If you must know, I'm thirty-eight."

Elliot laughed out loud. "But you're mom's older sister and mom's thirty-nine."

"I am not!" I retorted. "I'm thirty ... five."

"Weren't you thirty-five last birthday, mom?"

"No, thirty-four, *obviously.*"

Elliot grinned and nodded. "Glad to see you two got your beauty sleep, anyway, you certainly needed it."

"The cheek of the child! Have him thrashed immediately!"

"Stop drinking milk out the carton, Elliot."

"Just checking you were fully awake, mom."

"I am, and you're still doing it."

"Your curries are in here, by the way, should you fancy them later. I brought them up but you were both out cold." He slammed the fridge door and, with a high wave, said, "Right, I'm off, taking Kelly shopping. You two have fun. Try not to fall asleep anywhere public."

And then he was gone, slamming the front door behind him.

"So," I said, sipping coffee and still finding it hard to believe that my sister was here, in the flesh, "What do you want to do today? Go into Birmingham? Shop till we drop at Merry Hell?"

A strange look came over Katie's face, a look I recognised all too well. "What?" I gasped, "What dastardly deed have you got planned?"

Katie sauntered over to the kitchen counter and picked up a mobile phone. "I was up early," she said, "and ... I've been very naughty. Your phone pinged and I glanced at it and saw a text message."

"Okay."

"It was from Gary."

"Ah."

"Why are you letting him text you like this?"

"I don't let him, he does it all on his own without any provocation. He's quite good at it, actually."

Katie was tapping the screen furiously with a manicured finger. "The language," she gasped. "How dare some Neanderthal with the IQ of a dung beetle call my sister these horrible things."

"I didn't read them. Well, not all of them."

"They're disgusting, Suzanne. He's disgusting."

"He's just angry."

"There you go, making excuses for him again. There is no excuse for this, its abuse."

"Like I said, I didn't read most of them, I just replied with a LOL or an OK."

"He needs sorting out, Suzanne, and I'm not joking."

"No, I can see you're not, but short of flashing the Batman logo into the sky there's not a lot I can do about it."

"We don't need Batman," she said. "We're sisters, and we're going to teach that little scumbag a lesson. But first, we need to have a little talk."

"Sounds ominously ominous."

"Take a look around you, Suze."

I did, shrugging, confused.

"This place is a dump."

"It's not a dump," I cried.

"It is." She stared at me as she reached out an arm and pulled open a top cupboard. The cupboard creaked, then fell heavily at a slant.

"It just needs a new hinge."

She stepped back, still looking at me, and pushed the mixer tap above the sink. It rocked from side to side, sending up little spurts of water.

"Just needs a washer."

She stepped back again until she was level with the cooker. "I haven't seen a cooker like this since mom had one when we were little."

"I think," I said, slowly starting to get her point, "that *is* mom's old cooker."

"Did he invest *anything* in this house, Suzanne? His time, his effort? Certainly not his money. The carpets are threadbare, the wallpaper's old and so damp in places it's created its own pattern, and the bathroom is a bodge-job of pipe fittings."

"I know what you're saying, Katie, but we can't all have lovely houses in the Canadian countryside."

"I'm not talking about the house, I'm talking about the love and care that's gone into making a house a home."

"I try my best," I said, frowning.

"I know you do, Suze, I'm not having a go, none of this is your fault. I'm just pointing out that Gary's a narcissist who clearly had no intention of ever looking after his family properly. He gave you nothing and took everything, and that *is* your fault."

"How is that my fault?" I was starting to feel angry now. Why was everything always my fault? And wasn't my sister supposed to be on *my* side?

"You're a 10, Suze. Gary's a 3 at a push, but he thought he deserved you because you let him believe he deserved you, which boosted his ego, which turned him into the arrogant arsehole he is today."

Silence while I digested this. Katie waited. Then she said "Get dressed, we have unfinished business with your erstwhile husband. It's time we paid him a little visit. Where's he living now?"

"No, you can't! We can't!"

"I can and we will. Nobody treats my sister like this," she said, picking my phone up off the counter and shaking it at me, "*Nobody*. So, where's the slimeball living?"

I didn't know and, even if I did, I wouldn't have dared tell her. So Katie rang Elliot.

"Devious plan? Moi?" I heard her say, "I don't know how you can think such awful things about your delightful aunty! I just want to pay him a little visit, that's all, haven't seen him in *ages*. No, of course I won't cause him physical harm, I'm a beauty technician, not a heavyweight boxer. Look, just tell me where he lives or I'll tell your mom about the stash you keep hidden underneath your mattress." She ended the call. "Got it," she grinned.

* * *

"I don't think this is a good idea, Katie."

"I do."

"He won't do it."

"He will."

"He'll never agree."

"He'd better."

"You're scaring me, Katie."

"I haven't even started yet. It's going to be biblical, and I'm going to enjoy every second of it."

"That's what I'm afraid of."

We were sitting in the back of a taxi, on our way to Gary's new flat near the city centre. "Do you remember me asking your permission for Aiden to look at your joint account last week, so he could draw up a budget to make life easier for you?"

"Yes."

"Well, he had a look and he's worked out roughly what Gary owes you," she said.

"Owes me?"

"Yes. The joint account is paying all his direct debits for the gym, a golf club, a few dodgy websites, payments and insurance for a car *you* never got to use, plus personal expenses, like flowers and jewellery and – "

"Yes, I know all that."

"But did you know he's still doing it?"

"What? No!" The shock was like a bolt of electricity running through my body. He couldn't. He wouldn't.

"Aiden checked to make sure the figures were right before we left home and saw that a BACS payment has been made to a letting agency in Birmingham. It's the deposit for his new flat. He's completely cleaned you out, Suze, there's nothing left. He owes you for everything he ever spent on himself and her, and everything he's taken since he left."

My mouth moved but nothing came out. I could hardly believe it. Katie squeezed my hand. "Don't worry," she said, "We're going to fix this once and for all. I've got your back, and so has Aiden."

"What are you going to do?" I finally asked, as the taxi made its way down the Bristol Road. "There won't be any blood involved, will there?"

Katie looked thoughtful for a moment.

"Katie!"

"No, of course there won't be any blood! A bit of begging, maybe, a lot of grovelling perhaps, and hopefully an apology for being such a little shit, but definitely no blood. There's no blood in testicles, is there?"

"Oh," I groaned, "I don't want to do this."

"Yes you do. You *need* to do it. I've seen the inside of your wardrobe, Suze, and, quite frankly, it's a disgrace. You need money and he's going to give it back to you."

"And he's just going to hand it over without any argument, is he?"

Katie tapped the side of her nose. "Fear not, little sister, I have a cunning plan."

"Oh god."

* * *

The taxi pulled up at the kerb and I looked up at the tower block above me. I passed it almost every day on the way to work on the bus, and now Gary was living there. The Cube. It had a uniformed doorman sitting in the lobby.

"How can he afford this?" I gasped, as Katie sidled up to the doorman and said, "We're here to see Gary Philips."

"Who shall I say is visiting?" he asked, reaching for the phone on his desk.

Katie leaned provocatively across his desk; how her boobs didn't fall out of her low cut top I've no idea. "Oh," she breathed, "Don't announce us, we want to surprise him?"

We walked to the lifts, my legs like jelly, Katie with a frozen look of grim determination on her face. We rode up to the 16th floor. Outside his flat door Katie looked at me as if for confirmation. I nodded slowly. She rang the bell

When Gary first opened the door he was smiling and appeared quite casual and relaxed in a fluffy dressing gown. Once he clapped his eyes on us his smile vanished and his demeanour turned stiffly defensive.

"Gary, darling," Katie cried, faking a kiss on the cheek and sidling past him into his flat, "How absolutely wonderful to … " She didn't finish the sentence.

"Suze?" said Gary.

"Gary," I said, hurrying after Katie, who had, by now, reached the living room area.

"What a lovely place you have," she said, wandering around and picking up expensive looking knick-knacks. It had a floor to ceiling window along the far wall, showing exactly how high up we were. I pressed myself against the near wall with my heart pounding in my throat

"Does this place come furnished?" Katie asked, spotting a huge TV screen on the wall.

"Yes," he snapped, thrusting his chin out.

"Nice. Expensive, is it? The rent I mean."

Gary shrugged, his jaw clenching and unclenching.

"Gary?" A girl wearing a flimsy kimono appeared in what I imagined was the bedroom doorway, a girl I recognised.

"Poppi just ... just came round to see if I was settling in okay," he spluttered.

Katie pushed open the door Poppi had come through. Inside was an very unmade bed.

"Gary," I growled.

"Gary?" Poppi whimpered.

"Gary," Katie drawled, "We need to talk."

* * *

Katie and I were sat on a plush sofa, Gary in a plush arm-chair, Poppi perched like a little bird on the plush arm next to him.

"So, you see," Katie said, pointing at the piece of paper on the coffee table in front of him, "all your direct debits from the joint account have been cancelled. Aiden's very kindly drawn up a list so you can transfer the payments to your own personal account, isn't that nice of him? He's also worked out everything you've taken from the joint account for your girlfriend, and everything you've taken since you left the house, including," she said, tapping a nail on the paper, "the deposit for this flat, I've added that at the bottom."

"Gary?" the bird wittered.

He threw up his arms. "That was a genuine mistake," he implored, "I got the account numbers mixed up, that's all."

"Sure you did," Katie said. "Now, looking at this column of figures, it does appear that you owe my sister quite a substantial amount of money. She'd like it back now, to tide her over until the courts step in and issue a financial order."

"Ridiculous!" Gary spat. "I won't agree to it, not in a million years."

The fragile bird decided to speak. "You can't expect him to

pay any more than he already does!"

"Poppi, please – "

"Excuse me?" I said, "Pay me more than he *already does*? He doesn't pay me anything, he only ever takes."

"He gives you more than enough," the bird continued, as Gary surreptitiously tried to stop her, "It's not fair to ask him for more, you're bleeding him dry as it is, he's almost broke."

"Broke?" I gasped, raising my arms to take in the opulent surroundings. "Duh."

"Oh dear," Katie said, shaking her head. "It seems telling the truth isn't your strongest point, is it, Gary."

He jumped up out of the armchair, bursting with indignation. "Listen," he snapped, "I won't have you two barging in here demanding money with menaces – "

"Menaces?" Katie laughed. "We're not menacing you, you little weasel, not yet anyway. We're here to get the money my sister is owed, and we're not leaving until we get it."

"Really? We'll soon see about that."

Katie casually crossed her legs, not looking the least bit perturbed, as Gary started pacing backwards and forwards in front of the panoramic window. "What are you going to do, Gary, call the police and say your visitors have overstayed their welcome? I don't think so. We want the money back, and an apology for the way you've treated her."

The bird looked at us with both fear and contempt, while Gary spluttered a bit, clearly trying to figure out what he could do. "It was Suzanne who threw me out of the house, I need money to build a new life for myself."

"Pretty lavish lifestyle you're building, Gary, while your wife struggles, has always struggled. You're a selfish, pathetic excuse for a man, aren't you, but I can be reasonable, I can give you choices."

"Choices?" I'd never seen Gary's eyes so wide, his face so annoyed.

Katie let the heavy silence linger in the air for a while before she began talking again. "There are a few things I can do here.

I can take what's-her-name to one side and tell her what's *really* been going on." A pause. Gary looked at the bird. The bird cocked her head. "Gary?" she squeaked.

"She's bluffing ... lying." he said. He turned to Katie. "Poppi knows everything, she knows Suzanne will do *anything* to get money out of me."

I laughed out loud at that.

"No worries", Katie said, "What's-her-face will find out what you're like soon enough." She stopped at that point and diligently began inspecting her nails. It was while we all waited for Katie to speak again that I realised I hadn't taken a breath in quite a long time. I was so tense I thought I might implode. I had no idea what Katie was going to do next but, like Gary, I was on tenterhooks.

"Aiden sends his love," she drawled. "He sent me a text to read out to you, do you want to hear it?" Gary said nothing. Katie took out her phone and cleared her throat. "It reads, and I quote verbatim, 'If the moron doesn't cough up the dollars and fall to his knees in abject apology for his appalling behaviour, I might have to pop up and see him, just like old times', end quote. You remember Aiden popping in to see you once before, don't you, Gary?"

Gary's mouth tightened. He glared furiously at Katie. Katie glared right back. "Transfer the money, Gary."

The bird started to say something, but Katie snapped, "Stay out of this," so abruptly that we all jumped. The bird pulled the kimono tighter around her skinny body.

Gary threw himself back in the armchair and said, "I won't. It's *my* money. I'm not going to *give* it away."

"You're not giving it away, you're reimbursing, refunding, replacing, compensating, whatever you want to call it. Make the transfer, Gary. You wouldn't want to upset Aiden now, would you?"

Gary looked flustered, confused, angry. He ran a hand through his hair several times. He turned his head as if to say something to the tiny bird, but the tiny bird was no longer in the room, she'd fled back to the bedroom, slamming the door behind her.

He turned to me instead, his eyes beseeching, his face a mass of misery. "Suze," he whined, "We can work this out, I know we can. Okay, so I've done some stupid things and I should never have cheated on you, but I'm only human, no man can resist when it's handed to him on a plate. I swear I'll never do it again. Give me another chance, *please*, Suzanne."

He reached out towards me, to take my hand, but I snatched it away. I felt nothing.

His face contorted. He glared at me, then turned to Katie. "You're bluffing," he snarled.

"Am I?" She began tapping on her phone. "Why don't we ring Aiden and ask him to pop in for a visit? How long does it take by train from London, two hours, is it?"

The bird, now fully dressed, suddenly burst out of the bedroom and clacked her way across the room to the front door. She opened it, stepped through, and slammed it shut behind her without a backwards glance. Gary seemed to deflate like a balloon in the plush armchair.

"Do it, Gary."

With a heavy sigh and a sagging of shoulders, Gary picked his phone up off the coffee table and slowly started tapping the screen. "It's done," he eventually said.

"Check it," Katie said to me. I took my phone out of my bag and logged into the account. "Has it been transferred?"

"Not yet."

"It says on my screen it can take up to four hours to transfer funds," Gary said.

"Not from the same bank it doesn't. Now?" she asked me.

I refreshed the screen. "No."

I waited, looking idly around Gary's flat, looking at him, looking at Katie, before pressing the refresh button again. "Still not."

"You'd better not be trying it on, Gary."

More idle stares, more awkward glances at each other, Gary

rubbing harshly at his face in fury and frustration. Another refresh.

"It's there," I said, relieved, "It's been transferred."

"Good. Now, there's a couple more things to wrap up before we go, Gary."

He sighed loudly and flopped back into the chair, defeated. Katie put another piece of paper on the coffee table in front of him. "Sign this," she said, "It's to take your name off the joint account so you can't plunder it like your own personal piggy bank again."

"I told you, that was – "

"Don't care," she cried, "Just sign the damn thing."

He leaned forward and signed it with an angry flourish, throwing the pen down when he'd done.

"And the debit card."

More huffing as he jumped up, went to a cupboard, snatched out a jacket and searched the pockets. He pulled out his wallet, opened it, and took out a card.

"Give it to Suze."

He came towards me. I snatched the card out of his hands and hissed, "Don't use the joint account, Gary."

He flopped back into the armchair like a man truly defeated.

"Finally," she said, and Gary threw his head back and groaned out loud, "Suzanne, could you give me your phone?"

I handed it over. Katie tapped on it and then turned it round to show Gary the screen. A list of his text messages were displayed. "This," Katie growled, her face twitching with barely restrained fury, "This stops now, do I make myself clear?"

Gary nodded again.

"If I hear that you've sent her any more abusive texts or left one more abusive message I swear to god I will hire a private plane to get here and I will personally remove your testicles using a blunt implement. Do you understand?"

Gary nodded frantically.

She stood up, smiling. "Right," she said, "I think we've got everything we came for, we'd better be off now." She marched to the door and I fell into step behind her. "See ya, Gaz," she cried with a wave in the air, "Have a nice life."

CHAPTER 16

"Oh my god, you were *brilliant!*" I screamed, when we fell out of the building and onto the street.

"I know."

"Absolutely bloody amazing!"

"I know."

"You're totally wasted as a beauty therapist, you should be an A-list actress being wooed by the media and winning multiple Oscars."

Katie flicked her hair back dramatically and said, "I know."

I kept hugging her and kissing her cheek in gratitude. "You've just solved all my problems in one fell swoop, and it was *magnificent* to behold."

"Any regrets?" Katie asked. "Do you still have feelings for him?"

I laughed. "Are you kidding? Man's a moron, don't know how I stood him for so long."

"Good. Now you're free and I'm happy. Let's celebrate. We are mere inches from The Mailbox and a short taxi ride to the Bullring. Let's go shopping, my treat."

"Your treat?"

"I'm going to buy you a whole new wardrobe and I won't take no for an answer."

"I'll buy lunch," I squealed excitedly, "And I'll pay for the taxi home. Oh," I added, scrambling in my bag for my purse, "You couldn't lend me some money, could you?"

* * *

We arrived home late that afternoon laden with bags, some of them bearing designer logos and a few containing garments that were wrapped in *tissue paper*. I felt like Melania Trump.

"I'm just on my way out," Elliot said, laughing as we struggled into the living room with our purchases. "Looks like you two had a good time."

"The best!"

"Dad rang."

"Oh?"

"He didn't sound happy."

"No, well he wouldn't," Katie grinned.

"We haven't done anything bad," I assured him. "He owed me some money, that's all, and your brilliant aunt got it for me."

"There wasn't blood involved, was there?"

"Sadly not," Katie said, then, noticing both mine and Elliot's shocked expressions, quickly added, "Oh I'm sorry, Elliot. I keep forgetting he's your father. Where are you off to, anyway?"

"Clubbing with Kelly and a few mates."

"Oh? Which club?"

"No!" Elliot gasped, "You're not coming!"

"I was only asking, but now that you mention it – "

"No!" Elliot gasped again.

Katie glanced at me. "Me thinks the boy doesn't want us around, Suze?"

"Probably for the best," I told her.

"No worries, we'll find you." While Elliot protested, Katie repeatedly poked him in his side with one finger. "Be afraid, little boy," she cackled, as Elliot crumbled backwards onto the sofa laughing his head off, "Be very afraid."

A wrestling match ensued with Katie crying, "You can't touch me, I'm a woman," every few seconds as she continued to poke Elliot to the brink of convulsion. Then she suddenly stopped and, brushing back the hair from her flushed face, said, "Here, take this."

"£50?" Elliot gasped. "What for?"

"Pocket money."

"I'm too old for pocket money."

"You're right, buy me a drink with it later."

Elliot's eyes narrowed into suspicious slits. "What do you mean, buy you a drink later?"

"Oh, nothing," she smiled innocently.

"Mom!"

"We won't," I said.

"We might," Katie said.

Elliot left shortly after, rather nervously I thought. Katie and I immediately began pulling clothes out of our bags and trying them on, parading in front of the full length mirror in the hallway. I had a new pin striped suit, very smart, very well cut and *very* expensive.

"You see what I mean about the tiny shoulder pads and slightly wider trouser bottoms," Katie said, "Perfect for balancing out your hips."

"Thanks!" I cried. "Easy for a skinny bint like you to say."

"Suze, we're the same shape, the same size, and probably the same weight as well."

"Yeah, right!"

"It's true! I just look better because I wear the right clothes. And now you do, too."

I had to admit, she *was* right, I did look surprisingly good.

"You want to impress that gorgeous new boss of yours, don't you?"

I sighed heavily. "He thinks I'm a good secretary, that's it, end of story. I don't stand a chance with a man like him, I'm just glad I came to my senses before I made a fool of myself."

"You're kidding, right?" Katie was glaring at my reflection in the mirror. "Look at me, Suze." I moved my eyeballs from my reflection to hers. "Am I not gorgeous?" She put her hands on her hips and posed like a supermodel.

"Yes, of course you're gorgeous, Katie. You've always been the good looking one."

She stared at my reflection. "And aren't we exactly the same except for the hair colour? Look, Suzanne, look *properly*. Same bone structure, same facial features, same mannerisms, we even talk the same, though you want to work on that Brummy accent a bit."

"I like my accent!"

"Okay, keep it, it's cute in a kind of Peaky Blinders way. But *look*, Suzanne, we could almost be mistaken for twins. So, if I'm gorgeous, what does that make you?"

"Gorgeous?" I laughed.

"Again, with conviction."

"I'm *gorgeous*."

"One more time!"

"I'm *gorgeous!*"

"Yes, Suzanne, you are. And if you wear those new tops with that suit – "

"Those low cut tops?" I gasped, holding them up, "For work?"

"Absolutely! With your boobs you shouldn't be wearing anything else. Why, what do you normally wear with a suit?"

"Roll neck jumpers or high collar shirts."

Katie had to steady herself against the banister rail. "If you ever wear a roll neck jumper or high collar shirt again I'll disown you, I swear."

"How do you know all this stuff, anyway?" I asked, trying on a pair of heeled shoes that made my legs look amazingly long. I'd have to learn to walk in heels or else look like Bambi on ice for the rest of my life.

"Well, it *is* part of my job, and also, I live in a country that's obsessed with shopping malls."

"Malls?" I laughed, "*Malls?*"

"Don't mock your big sister."

I preened in front of the mirror for a few moments, then said, "Katie."

"Yes?"

"What did you mean when you told Gary about Aiden paying him a visit again. The blood seemed to drain from his face when you said it."

Katie looked at me with wary eyes. "Come and sit down." She moved into the living room. I followed with a sense of foreboding. We sat together on the sofa and she took hold of my hand. "Do you remember that garden party you had about four years ago?"

"Yes."

"Do you remember when Gary came out of the house with a red mark on his face."

"Yes."

"And do you remember he said he'd been play fighting with Elliot?"

I did. Elliot had looked quite surprised. I was surprised too, since Elliot had been doing his man-act at the barbecue all afternoon, wouldn't let anyone else touch his tongs.

"He made a pass at me, Suzanne." I gasped. "He said he'd married the wrong sister and tried to kiss me. I belted him, I mean, really smacked him one. It was my hand mark on his face."

"Oh my god!"

"Wasn't the first time he'd tried it either, but it was the last. I told Aiden this time. He was bloody furious, went round to Gary's work the next day and, by all accounts, Gary screamed like a hyena as soon as he saw him, must have been the manic look in his eyes. Aiden only managed to land one punch, that's where his black eye came from."

"He told me he'd walked into a door."

"He told you a lot of things that weren't true, Suze."

"Yes, I'm beginning to realise that."

"I couldn't tell you then, I didn't want to cause any trouble, but I think it's time you knew the truth. He tried it on with your friends too, that's why they stopped coming round."

I couldn't speak for a long while. Katie kept hold of my

hands. Eventually I raised my eyes to hers and said, "I've been a bloody idiot, haven't I."

"Let's just call it a learning experience."

"Oh, trust me, I've learned my lesson and learned it well."

I rested my hands on hers. "Thanks, sis, for everything."

"Any time." She exhaled loudly. "Glad that's off my boobies. Anyway, let's not think of the old lech any more, we've got other things to think about, like what are you wearing tonight?"

I laughed, as relieved as Katie looked. "Tonight?"

She glanced at the huge pile of clothes spread out across the back of the sofa. "Yeah, tonight. It's Saturday, it's Birmingham city centre and it's *party time!* But first ..." She picked up a carrier bag and winked at me. "There's something I've been *dying* to do."

* * *

"Does it look alright?"

"Yes, stop fussing."

"Are you sure?"

"It's perfect!"

"It feels strange."

"Well, it will do for a bit, until you get used to it."

"It's not too short?"

"Suze, I've only taken a couple of inches off and put some highlights in."

"Yes, but is it *me*?" I persisted, gently running my fingers through my new hairstyle, courtesy of my sister, the beauty therapist.

"Is it you as an ex-wife-to-be and mother of teenagers? No. Is it you as a sophisticated city slicker who knows what she wants and grabs it with both hands? Absolutely!"

"You're sure?"

"You're asking for a fight. Have you no faith in my abilities?"

"Yes, but – "

"Don't 'but' me, it's annoying. It's taken ten years off you, Suze, and another 10 for the well-fitted clothes. You're practically a teenager again. Now stop faffing and start enjoying."

The taxi pulled up outside a bar on Broad Street. Katie got out first and I clambered out after her. "You look like you're struggling to get out of a tight hole," she laughed. As I walked across the path towards her she slapped the palm of her hand against her forehead and cried, "You walk like a John Wayne after a long ride across the prairie."

"Stop picking on me or I'll punch you," I hissed.

"Look." She pushed me in front of the bar's glass windows, where we were both reflected in all our finery. "You're gorgeous, you have every right to strut your stuff, girl, so *strut*."

I straightened myself up. The delicately flowing dress I was wearing took on an elegant shape and my startlingly exposed cleavage – which I still couldn't believe was mine and not on loan from some porn star – held forth like a Goddess on the bow of a ship.

Katie laughed, "I hope the men have strong constitutions around here, they're going to need them once they clap eyes on us."

She wasn't wrong, as soon as we entered the bar a multitude of male gazes fell upon us. I wasn't used to so much attention and hunched against it, until Katie elbowed me in the ribs and hissed, "Straighten up and wear those boobs with pride!" A couple of men rushed over and offered us seats and drinks. Katie haughtily waved them away, but they kept returning with more men in tow until we were surrounded by a crowd of them

"Persistent little buggers, the Brummies, aren't they," Katie said.

"I don't like it."

"You don't?"

"No, I'm not really interested in meeting men, having so recently disposed of one."

"Okay, we'll just soak up the adoration from a distance and enjoy ourselves then."

"But what about them?" I asked, nodding towards the throng all around us.

"Men-types," she said aloud, throwing a possessive arm across my shoulders, "If you could just give me and *my wife* a bit of space please?" They sauntered away pretty quick after that.

Even so, an hour later I found myself talking to a man from Dagenham who sold plastic parts to a motor company and was straining to keep an interested smile on my face. Beside me, Katie was laughing outrageously at a man from Great Barr who, from what I could gather, didn't actually do much at all. I was feeling more than a little tipsy, but even that didn't help curb the boredom of my companion.

"Toilet trip," I hissed in Katie's ear.

We trooped off with our handbags.

"So, how's it going?" she asked. "Yours is extremely good looking."

"He is, but he's boring the pants off me."

"That's probably his strategy."

"Katie!"

"Okay, we'll move on."

"What do we tell them?"

"Tell them?" she said, wide-eyed in mock shock. "We don't have to tell them anything, we just move on."

And, laughing, she grabbed my hand and dragged me out of the toilet, through the bar, right passed the table with the two expectant but now confused men, and out onto the pavement, where she cried, "Brindleyplace!" and off I was dragged, across the road and into another bar.

"Harrison Ford," I heard her telling one of the men that continued to approach us. "That's who you look like, a young Harrison Ford. Who do I look like then?"

We were both a bit squiffy by now, but Katie told me not to worry, she had pepper spray and a fold-up cattle prod in her handbag.

"Charlize Theron," he told her, and Katie screamed with delight.

"Jennifer Lawrence," said the bloke from Dagenham, who had followed us like a lost dog desperate for a home.

"Pardon?" I said.

"That's who you look like, Jennifer Lawrence."

I was so chuffed I let him buy me another drink.

"You wouldn't, would you?" I asked, when Katie and I paid another visit to the ladies' loo later that night.

"Wouldn't what?"

"Wouldn't ... you know."

"Shag him?"

"Yes. I mean, I thought you and Aiden were happy – "

"Let me tell you something," she said, turning away from the mirror and poking her lipstick at me. "Aiden is possibly one of the best human beings on the planet and I love him completely. I would rather chew off my own leg than hurt him in any way, so no, I wouldn't shag him out there or anyone else for that matter. What I'm doing here is teaching my little sister how to enjoy herself, since she obviously hasn't enjoyed herself for quite a long time. We're here to have fun, Suze. *Harmless* fun. You follow?"

"I follow."

"And are you enjoying yourself?"

"Well, actually the man from Dagenham is getting less boring with every drink."

"Then let's get another round in."

It was while Katie was at the bar, waving her credit card around and demanding immediate attention, which she got, that I saw him across a crowded room. At first I couldn't believe it was him, just someone who looked like him, but then he turned and saw me looking at him, and smiled. My heart started banging out a cinematic beat when he started walking towards our table.

"Oh God!" I gasped, grabbing Katie's arm and making her spill half the drinks on the tray she was carrying to the table. "It's him. It's *him*."

"Him who?"

"*Him!* My boss!"

Katie spun round like a spinning top, peered into the

thronging masses, and then smiled. "It's Leonardo DiCaprio!" she cried, "Its bloody Leonardo DiCaprio!"

"Help!" I begged. "Hide me. Throw something over me, quick!"

"Panic not, little sister, you look like a million dollars, Canadian dollars, that is. Now straighten up, let the dress do its work, and pump up those boobs."

I did, and the man from Dagenham stared at my cleavage with wide eyes. I instantly slumped. Katie slapped my arm, quite harshly I thought, and hissed, "Teeth and tits, Suze, teeth and tits."

"But he's my boss," I whimpered. "I can't let my boss see my *naked chest*."

"It's not naked, but it bloody well will be if you don't straighten up right this minute."

"You wouldn't dare!"

She raised a hand to my shoulder. I flinched when I felt her fingers curling under the straps of my dress. "I bloody would," she said, as Alan Talbot came to stand in front of us.

"Fancy seeing you here," he grinned.

Despite the fact I was ever so slightly intoxicated, the teenage angst was back and I couldn't bring myself to speak. My boobs could probably carry off a better conversation than I could, and who needed conversation when stiff C-cups were staring right at you? Katie let her hand drop from my shoulder and turned to Alan.

"Hi there," she cooed, "I'm Suzanne's sister."

"I guessed as much. You look very alike."

"See," Katie said to me. Then, turning back to Alan, she said, "So, you're Suzanne's boss?"

"Lucky sod," the man from Dagenham said.

"Yes, she's a great asset to the department."

"I'll bet," Dagenham man muttered. I moved my foot back and pressed a high heel hard into his foot until I heard him squeak.

"I'm just out celebrating a mate's birthday," Alan said. "Suspect we need to soak up some of the alcohol, so we're going for a meal, if you'd care to join us?"

Inside my head I began to scream "No! No! No!" desperately hoping that my almost twin sister would be able to pick this up telepathically.

"We'd love to," she replied, and inside I began to cry. "Wouldn't we, Suzanne."

I was smiling and nodding my head, but inside I was already a quivering blancmange of shredded nerves. Even worse, Dagenham man and Katie's companion assumed they were invited too. Alan would think boring Brian who sold plastic parts to car companies was my date or, God forbid, my boyfriend, or, worse, my *husband*!

"We're off to a pretty good restaurant just over the road," Alan said, pointing through the window, "Come and join us when you've finished your drinks."

"Oh we will," Katie said, "See you there."

Just as Alan was turning to leave, he briefly glanced down at my chest. Was it me he was inviting to dinner or *them*, I wondered. Did he glance at them in awe or stare at them in horror – his secretary's boobs, exposed.

Alan wandered back to his group, weaving his way through the crowds like a lithe athlete.

"*Very* nice," Katie drawled, watching after him.

"We can't go."

"Yes we can." She looked surprised. "Why wouldn't we?"

"Because … because he's my *boss* and … " I leaned into her ear and breathed, "Because I'm totally incapable of speech in front of him because I fancy him so much."

"Oh, we'll soon sort that out," she said.

"No, you can't! I can't! We can't!"

"Drink up, Suze, we have places to go, people to see."

I sipped delicately at my glass of wine, figuring I could make it last at least another three hours, by which time Alan and his party would hopefully have eaten and left.

"Neck it!" Katie hissed.

"I am!"

She pushed up the stem of the glass, forcing me to drink or drown.

* * *

We were walking across Broad Street again towards the restaurant, Alan's party in front, laughing and joking, Alan turning constantly to include us in the conversation, which meant I was grinning inanely most of the time and my face ached.

"How do we explain *them*?" I asked Katie, indicating the man from Dagenham and her lost soul, Derek. Brian and Derek, could it have been any worse? "I don't want Alan to think they're our boyfriends or anything like that."

"I think you're passing up a brilliant opportunity to make him jealous," she said. "They're pretty good looking, a real credit to our pulling power."

"They may be good looking, but they're not exactly the sharpest tools in the toolbox, are they."

"Then we'll just tell him the truth."

"What? That we've only just met them, that we *picked them up in a bar*! How's he going to introduce me to his friends? 'This is Suzanne Philips, my slut of a secretary who picks up strangers in bars, and by the way, isn't she displaying an enormous amount of cleavage?'"

"I'll think of something," Katie soothed. "And your cleavage is fine. You're thirty-seven … thirty-six? … thirty-something years old, you've had two children, and those two beauties still stand up on their own. You should be proud."

"Proud? I'm struggling to keep them contained and terrified they might burst forth at any moment. It's no good, Katie, I'm going to have to fake my own death. I'll drop to the floor and you start screaming about me having a heart attack. I feel like I'm having one anyway."

"You're panicking, Suze."

"Of course I'm panicking! I'm going to dinner with a boss

who renders me speechless. Right barrel of laughs I'm going to be, *not.*"

"These are your instructions," Katie said, "Breathe in. Breathe out. Continue until you start enjoying yourself. You remember how to enjoy yourself, don't you?"

"Oh God."

* * *

I couldn't eat, of course, not in his presence, I was bound to drop something down my cleavage or catch something in my throat and have to be Heimliched in the middle of the busy restaurant. So I didn't eat, I just drank. White wine. Copious amounts of it.

I got really, really drunk.

There were several advantages to being really drunk, I discovered. First, I forgot my tits were pretty much on full display for the whole world to view at their leisure. Whenever I caught someone looking at them – Brian, Derek, a few of Alan's friends, the waiters, half the customers in the restaurant – I assumed they must be admiring the necklace I wasn't wearing.

The alcohol also loosened my inhibitions, chilled out my self-consciousness, and positively fired up the motor on my tongue; fired it up but didn't link my mouth to my brain, bypassed it completely, in fact, and once I got talking I found I couldn't stop, fully aware, despite the alcohol and because of the alcohol, that I was slurring and spouting utter rubbish but too wasted to care.

Suddenly, I was having a good time. Katie was laughing almost constantly and only taking pauses to draw breathe or pick delicately at her food. I held loud conversations up and down the table and had everyone laughing, at what I couldn't remember, I just kept thinking, 'Eat your heart out, Gary, and *hello Alan.*"

I was hammered.

I staggered to the toilet at one point, accidentally pushing Brian off his chair and falling into Derek's lap; he rather creepily tried to hold me there, until I screwed the heel of my shoe into his foot, which I was getting quite good at. As I weaved my way from one chair to the next and using the walls for support, I passed Alan coming back from the bar, credit card still in hand.

"Oh, you must let me pay my share," I insisted.

"No, it's my pleasure, really."

"Well, that's very kind of you, Mr Talbot."

"You're most welcome, Mrs Phillips."

"Miss," I said, grinning and leaning against the wall to keep myself upright. "Or Ms, although I'm told from unreliable sources that only lesbians call themselves Ms, which I'm not." Another huge grin.

"You're not married, then?"

"No. Well, yes, I was until very recently. I have two grown up-sons, so obviously I was married at some point because I'm just not the type to have children without having a husband to complete the whole happy family scene. 'Cept it turns out the husband wasn't happy after all and buggered off to shag his secretary instead."

"The man's clearly an idiot."

"I totally agree. How about you, are you married?" I asked, struggling to keep my eyes focused – there seemed to be two of him but I wasn't complaining.

He shook his head. "No, never married, never had the time, to be honest. Too busy building my career."

"I see." The wine was churning in my stomach and I was struggling to concentrate on his words so that I could remember them for all time.

"So, who are your two male friends?" Alan asked, nodding back towards our raucous table. "You don't have to tell me if you – "

"No, no, I don't mind. They're just people we met tonight. They were having a good time, we were having a good time, so we decided to have a good time together for a bit. They're nice enough blokes, just a bit boring, you know?" Alan laughed and nodded. "I like sharing your good time better."

"And I yours." He looked at me then, so intently that I literally felt myself go weak at the knees – I was 80% sure it wasn't the alcohol. I slipped sideways a bit. Alan quickly reached out to steady me.

"You think I'm drunk, don't you," I giggled. Rather ambitiously, I stretched out an arm to try and lean casually against the wall, but failed, missed the wall completely and almost fell flat on my face. Alan gripped my shoulders firmly, which saved me from a possible broken nose/ribs/arm. He was so strong. "You're right, of course," I admitted. "I'm absolutely bladdered, but I haven't been out for a while, years in fact, so I guess I can't hold my booze like I used to."

"I think you're holding it just fine," he said. "Even drunk, you're still an attractive and very funny woman."

"Ah, you're a man who likes his women drunk and unsteady."

He laughed. "I guess I must be."

"I think it's the tits," I said, looking blearily down at them. "Bosses don't tend to imagine their secretaries with tits, do they, and probably for very good reason. I mean, how can you concentrate on work when you know your secretary's sitting right outside your office with tits like these." I lifted them up with both hands and wobbled them a bit. "Even I didn't know I had them until tonight, when my very bossy sister shoehorned me into this dress. Did you say I was attractive?"

"Yes, I did."

"Can you do me a favour?"

"Of course."

"Can you remind me you said that on Monday morning, when I'm still recovering from possibly the worst hangover in history?"

"Yes," he laughed, "I will. Now, do you need assistance finding the ladies, or would you prefer to get lost on your own?"

I lifted up an elbow, he took it and escorted me to the ladies.

And then, too soon, it was time to leave. The restaurant emptied and the waiters hung around our table, glancing pointedly at their watches.

"I've had a really nice time," I said to Alan, as he helped both me and Katie into a black cab. Brian and Derek lurked miserably in the background, obviously realising they weren't going to get so much as a goodnight kiss.

"So have I," Alan said. "See you on Monday, Suzanne."

"Yes, bye, Alan."

I managed to restrain myself until the taxi had pulled at least six feet away from the kerb, and then I turned in my seat and grabbed Katie by both arms, shaking her feverishly and screaming, "Alan Talbot! I just spend the night with Alan Talbot! Oh my God, how fantastic was that? Katie? Katie?"

Katie's eyes were shut and she was quietly snoring with her head on one shoulder. "I'll get that cattle prod out your bag and use it on you," I said.

"Don't you dare," she croaked, and went back to snoring.

CHAPTER 17

Hell hath no fury like white wine consumed. And that's what it felt like when I stirred from my drunken stupor the following morning, like I was in hell, my body and brain in purgatory. Katie was lying with her back to me in bed.

"Hey," I gasped out of the cess pit that was my mouth.

"Leave me to *die*," she breathed.

"You okay?"

"No," she croaked. "If I'm not dead then I bloody well ought to be."

"We didn't even get undressed."

"Have you moved yet?"

"No."

"Try it and tell me how bad it is."

I tried to sit up. Far too difficult, so I gave up and slumped back onto the mattress. I tried to turn my head on the pillow. Impossible. I raised an arm. All the blood in it rushed down into my body and straight up into the screaming cavity of pain in my head.

"Not good," I reported.

"Then I won't bother. I'm thirsty."

"Me too." Trying very hard not to lift my arm too much or too fast, and without moving my head or my eyes a single millimetre, I felt for the mobile on the bedside table. I struggled to focus on the numbers on screen. When I started pressing them

Katie hissed, "Stop the beeping! Make it stop!"

It took me ten minutes and three agonising attempts to finally get through to Elliot's mobile phone. "We're dying," I gasped, "Bring water."

"You had a good time last night then?" he laughed.

"We need help."

"I've been telling you that for years."

"Elliot, please don't joke, your mother and aunt are dying. We need fluids, and fast. Can you bring us – ?"

"I can't," Elliot said, "I stayed at a friend's house last night."

"Is it far? Can you come home and look after us?"

"I'm in Wolverhampton, mom."

"Oh." I ended the call and turned my head very slightly towards Katie, who still hadn't moved. She was hunched up beneath the blankets, only her hair, splayed out in a blonde explosion, visible on the pillows. "He's not coming," I croaked.

"Who?" she gasped.

"Elliot, he can't come. We're on our own."

She groaned miserably. I reached out and pulled her onto her back. Her mouth opened in a silent scream. Then her mouth closed and she muttered, "Give me the phone."

It took long minutes of deep concentration for her to remember Aiden's mobile number. I could feel my body shrivelling with dehydration with every passing second.

"Aid," she gasped, "Have you left London yet? Well, how long will it take you to get here? Two hours?"

"Oh god," I sobbed.

"Can you come as soon as you can? No, we're fine, we're just a bit hungover, that's all."

"Two hours," I breathed at the ceiling.

"Why?" she cried, "Why did we drink so much?"

"It seemed like a good idea at the time and … *Shit!*"

Suddenly, despite the incredible pain shooting through my head and making my stomach turn like a rotary spit at full speed, I sat up straight in bed. The whole room spun around me and the urge to heave was great.

"What?" Katie whimpered. "What's the matter?"

I couldn't speak. I was wailing and rocking backwards and forwards on the mattress. Katie eventually dragged herself up beside me, her face – and no doubt mine – looking like something a truck had crashed into. "What's the matter?" she asked again.

"Last night," I gasped, "I remember. I remember some of the things I said last night. Oh god, kill me now."

And I went back to wailing.

Worse was to come. Memories continued to surge up through the detritus of alcohol until I felt my only option was become a recluse or leave the country at the earliest opportunity. I had flirted outrageously with my boss. I had flaunted my body at him, *had jiggled my boobs in front of him*. Every flashback brought on a fresh bout of wailing.

"I'm supposed to work with him tomorrow," I howled. "How can I work with him after what I did?"

"That's tomorrow," Katie said, slowly peeling back the duvet to reveal her fully clothed body underneath. "We have to concentrate on the here and now and do our best to survive on our own." She gave a little whimper as she began to move. "I'm supposed to be flying back to Canada later. Frankly, I don't rate my chances of living that long."

Following Katie's example, I rolled myself out of bed and onto the floor, where we both crawled on all fours out of the bedroom and down the landing to the bathroom. I helped Katie onto the toilet, where she sat with the sink tap running beside her, furiously cupping water into her mouth. Then it was my turn.

Still on hands and knees, we slid down the stairs to the kitchen. Katie made it to the fridge first and, slumped against it, reached up, opened the door, and pulled down a carton of orange juice. We took it in turns to drink the contents and, when it was empty, she reached up and brought down a carton of milk. After a while I felt confident enough to pull myself up a kitchen cabinet and reach the Paracetamol. After gagging two down, we sat on the floor, not moving, not speaking, until they took the edge off our self-induced agony. An hour later, we made it to our feet and managed to make mugs of strong coffee before staggering into the living room to collapse on the sofa.

By the time Aiden arrived from London we had risen to the ranks of sitting upright. Katie went to answer the door very, very slowly. They came back into the living room with Aiden holding Katie very tightly in his arms, gasping, "What's wrong? Are you ill? Are you injured?"

"Only on the inside, Aid. Inside, everything hurts."

"Oh, my poor baby."

Mercifully, the very wonderful Aiden took care of us. He covered us with blankets on the sofa and made dry toast, kept our water glasses topped up, and raced to the nearest chemist for hangover cures. When Elliot finally came home in the middle of the afternoon, he discovered his mother and aunt almost fully conscious in the living room.

"You did have a good time, didn't you," he laughed, giving Aiden a delighted hug, "Just look at the state of you both."

"Thank you, Elliot, that really helps."

"And can you not shout."

"Darling," said Aiden, "Do you think you could make it up the stairs to pack your things? I really wouldn't rush you, only we have to leave for the airport in less than an hour."

"I'll try," Katie said wearily.

Aiden helped her up the stairs, Elliot pretty much carried me up after them.

"I can't believe you're going so soon," I cried, as I sat on the edge of the bed watching Katie on the floor, slowly throwing things into her suitcase. "You've only been here five minutes and it's been great. That's my blue top, by the way."

"It has been great, hasn't it, Suze. I've really enjoyed it. I'm not going to let the salons tie me down any more. I'll come over as often as I can. Are you sure this blue top is yours?"

"Come over anytime, you're more than welcome, you know that. Thanks for everything, Katie, you've been a real help, and you, Aiden." I looked up at my sister's handsome husband and gave a smile of gratitude. "And I bought that blue top to go with the blue skirt, but take it, what's mine is yours."

And then we were both struggling to our feet, crying and hugging each other. It was horrible to see her go, I liked having my big sister around.

"Call me as soon as you get home," I sobbed, when they were heading out the front door.

"I'll call you every day," she sobbed back. "And good luck at work tomorrow."

That was something I certainly didn't want to think about. I gave each of them a final hug and watched them walk out to the waiting taxi. "Bye, Aiden, and thank you. Bye, Katie. Love you both."

"See ya, Suze. Love you, too."

I went to bed immediately after their car drove out of sight. Elliot came up to me a short while later with a large jug of water, a glass and a packet of Paracetamol. "Just keep drinking and taking the tablets," he said.

"Thanks, mom."

* * *

Week two at Grimbles MZ Property Consultants. First day after making a complete and utter fool of myself in front of my boss, Alan Talbot.

Oh, this was going to be such fun.

I was wearing my new pin stripe suit and shoes, and a roll neck jumper (no point rubbing it in, I told myself – one peek at my cleavage and the whole sorry episode might immediately come back to haunt him). I strode to my desk as confidently as I could manage, greeting everyone as if I hadn't a care in the world.

"Nice suit," someone said.

"Like your hair," said someone else.

I was doing well, until I got to my desk outside Alan's office. He was already there, head bent low over papers. I tip-toed the rest of the way to my desk, hoping against hope that he might not notice me or say anything for the remainder of my time here – two months and three weeks.

I should be so lucky.

I'd barely turned on my computer when Alan came out of his office. I couldn't interpret the expression on his face as he approached me, but I instantly froze. One week and three minutes spent at Grimbles, and then I was thrown out for gross misconduct in a public place, or something. My agency were going to love me. I'd gain a reputation for heavy drinking and even heavier flirting with management. I'd never work in this town again.

"Suzanne," he said.

"Alan," I said, as calmly as I could manage, while I felt puce heat creeping over my entire face.

"Had a good time on Saturday," he beamed.

"Yes, so did I. Bit drunk, though." I tried a laugh, but it came out as a grunt. "Might have said a few things I maybe shouldn't have."

"No, you were fine, a good laugh. Mates loved you."

I'll bet they did. Probably hadn't seen a woman display her assets so blatantly before. "Good." I said instead.

"So anyway." He stood next to me, looking down at me, still beaming. He really was the most incredible looking man I'd ever seen, and also the nicest, and I'd behaved like a total idiot in front of him. "Got lots on today, so I hope your you're up for it."

The words 'up for it' hung in the air between us.

"Yes," I lied, feeling like death.

"Good, good. So, anyway, to work." He turned to go back into his office, then looked at me with an almost shy smile on his face. "By the way," he said, and I braced myself for the worst, "You asked me to remind you of something today."

"Oh, please," I groaned, "Whatever I did, whatever I said, *please* don't remind me, I'm embarrassed enough as it is."

"Embarrassed? You shouldn't be, you did nothing to be embarrassed about."

"You're very kind to say that but – "

"No," he insisted, "You were very ... what's the word?" I could think of a few words myself; moron, drunken bum, loser. "Sweet," he finally said. "Very articulate and amusing."

"Really?" The heat was creeping across my face with a vengeance. He didn't sound at all like he was lying through his back teeth, but maybe he was a good liar, like Gary. Or perhaps, maybe, he meant it.

"Anyway, I'm to remind you that I said you were a very attractive woman." My heated face now boiled like molten magma. How I didn't spontaneously combust I don't know. "You were attractive on Saturday, and you're even more attractive today." I was going to die a very happy woman at that moment. "But we'll just keep that to ourselves for now, shall we? Wouldn't want to make any of the other secretaries jealous, we'd never get any work done."

I nodded mutely and, with a final smile, Alan went back into his office.

Hangover? What hangover? My life had just opened up like a flower. My gorgeous boss had just told me that he thought I – a 39 year old who used to be married and had grown-up sons – was attractive! Me! Suzanne Phillips!

I wanted to wave my arms in the air and batter my feet on the floor like an over-excited child.

Instead, I logged into my computer with a very large smile on my face. When I dared to look up, I caught Alan looking at me with a very large smile on his face too.

I wasn't too shy to speak to him after that. I mean, once you've wobbled your tits in front of your boss you just can't go back to being the quiet little temp again, can you.

* * *

Work over the next few weeks was absolutely manic. First Christine was off sick with some intestinal bug, and then Jenny went down with it too, so there was just me in the department, valiantly struggling to keep up with the surveyors, who were working as if they were on commission. I came in early in the morning (not that I minded because Alan did, too), usually worked through lunch, and stayed late most nights. Within a week I was more exhausted than I'd ever known and terrified I might also come down with the bug – I couldn't cope with not seeing Alan for any length of time. Fortunately, pure adrenaline and, I suspect, happiness kept me going and kept all viruses at bay.

I'd never enjoyed a job more.

Alan and I didn't have much time to talk except about work, which suited me fine. As long as I could admire him from afar, I was happy. Even though he'd told me I was attractive, I was still under no illusions. I knew that someone like Alan Talbot, Partner and Head of Department, would never harbour any serious feelings for someone like me, a mere secretary, and a temp secretary at that. That's just the way things were. And I'd never dream of flirting with him at work, it wasn't professional and it just wasn't me. So I was perfectly happy to keep it a strictly professional relationship.

One Friday lunchtime when we were particularly busy, I was in the photocopying room binding up reports. Alan came in and stood next to me. "These are nearly done," I said, thinking he was checking on progress. "Another ten minutes and I can make a start on the Kingsbury dilaps. Hopefully we can get them all out tonight."

"You're a star," he said, "But something's been bothering me."

When I turned to look at him he did seem a bit worried. He wasn't smiling, which was unusual. "Is it the work?" I asked. "I know it's been a bit frantic without Christine and Jenny, but we've managed and I'm sure they'll be back soon."

"No, it isn't that."

"Is it … is it my work?" I dared to ask. "Is there something I'm not doing right, because – "

"No, no, your work is fine, bloody brilliant in fact. Don't know how we could have managed without you these last few weeks."

"You'd have got temps in," I said.

"That wouldn't necessarily have solved the problem, Suzanne." I loved it when he said my name, it sent a little shiver up my spine. "We've had some pretty bad temps working here, you're the best we've had. Best secretary we've ever had, in fact, but never mention that to the others."

"My lips are sealed," I told him with a laugh. "So, if it's not my work, what is it, what's wrong?"

"You," he said, staring straight at me with his ice blue eyes.

My heart actually stopped beating. I suddenly couldn't remember how to breathe. "Me?" I gasped. "Why? What have I done?"

"You're here every day," he said.

"But that's good, isn't it?"

"Yes ... and no."

"No?"

"I'm sorry, I'm not putting this across very well. What I wanted to say was – "

"Excuse me." Emma Smith from Marketing burst into the photocopying room with a pile of papers in her arms at that moment and, without even glancing at us, sighed heavily and began to feed the papers into the photocopying machine. "Rush job!" she cried, "They're all bloody rush jobs. Just kill me now and have done with!"

Alan stared at me. He certainly looked like a man who desperately wanted to say something, but couldn't.

"I'll ... I'll bring these to your office when they're done," I said.

"Please do," he said, and left.

I've never bound documents so fast in my life, and all the time I was frantically wondering what Alan wanted to say to me. Were my new clothes not appropriate? Was Katie's Canadian fashion sense a bit over the top? Did I not get on with people (I thought I did)? Did someone not like me? Was I causing problems in the department? *What?*

By the time I raced into Alan's office I was a nervous wreck. I wanted to scream, 'What? What have I done?' Instead, I put the reports on his desk and said, very professionally, "Will there be anything else?"

He looked at me with troubled eyes. "Yes," he said, "Could you shut the door please, Suzanne?"

Alan Talbot *never* shut his office door. When I shut it now several faces in the office looked up in surprise, every expression cried, "What's going on? What's happening?"

I was definitely getting the sack.

"Sit down," Alan said.

"This is all very formal." I was so nervous my hands were shaking in my lap.

"I'm sorry, I didn't intend for it to be formal. I wanted to keep it casual, but ... "

"What have I done?" I urged. "Is it serious?"

"Yes." He leaned back in his chair while my heart pumped feverishly and my breath came in shallow gasps. "I'm sorry, Suze, I'm going about this all wrong, and I practised it so well beforehand." He gave a little laugh. "I'll start again. I've just heard from Lorraine, my previous secretary, who you're covering for. She went to America with her husband but said she wouldn't be any longer than three months."

"Yes, Christine told me. Is she coming back early, is that what you're trying to tell me?" Tears were stinging the back of my eyes.

"No. She rang to say her husband's plans have worked out better than anticipated and they're staying out there permanently. She's not coming back." He leaned forward in his chair, staring down at his hands on the desk, not looking at me. "Under normal circumstances I'd offer you the position like a shot. Like I said, you're the best secretary we've ever had."

"But?" I dared to ask.

"But I'm not going to, and I'll tell you why ... if I can just find the right words."

When he paused my brain went into turmoil. This was the

best job I'd ever had, working for the best people, not least of all Alan himself. I enjoyed the work, I was *good* at it and Alan had said I was good at it. I wanted this job, I wanted it *so* bad, but he wasn't going to give it to me. Why not? What had I done wrong? Was it that episode on Saturday night when I'd flaunted myself at him? Was he afraid I might try something like that again in the office?

"Suzanne," he began, and I braced myself. "Suzanne, working with you has been amazing. You're hard working, know what you're doing and just get on with it without any fuss. And you get on with everyone here, which is no mean feat in itself."

"Then why can't I have the job?"

"Because ... because, whilst working with you and getting to know you – " Yes? What? Was I smelly? Did I have a personal hygiene problem that nobody wanted to tell me about? Did I make strange snorting noises I wasn't aware of whilst typing? "I've really come to like you," he eventually said, saying it as if it caused actual physical exertion. "I like you a lot. So much so that I'd like to see more of you. But not as my secretary. I can't mix business and pleasure, I'd find it too awkward and it's not very professional. Do you understand, Suzanne?"

I stared at him for the longest time. "No," I said.

"Okay, let me put it another way." He shuffled in his seat, stared at his hands for a moment, then looked up at me with the full force of his blue eyes. "Suzanne, will you go out with me? Do they still say that, 'go out with me'? I'm not sure, it's been a while."

"Pardon?"

"I'd like to see you outside the office. I'd like to see you a *lot* outside the office. I'd like to take you out somewhere, just me and you, and get to know each other better. And I'd quite like to do that on a regular basis."

"You would?"

He laughed. "Yes, I would, very much so."

"Oh." I couldn't think what else to say. I was in shock. Stunned. Amazed. Was this really happening or was I still hungover from Saturday and imagining all this, having some sort of a psychotic episode?

"You're not saying much, Suzanne. Are you disappointed about the job? It's entirely up to you, of course, I just thought that maybe the feeling was mutual, but perhaps I was wrong. I'm not very good at these things." He took a deep breath and added, "I can certainly make a recommendation to HR about your abilities to – "

"Say it again," I managed to gasp.

"What?"

"Say it again, what you just said."

"I can recommend you to HR – "

"No, not that, the other bit."

"The personal bit?"

"Yes." I wanted to laugh and cry at the same time. I was *obviously* dreaming, no doubt about it, and if I didn't get my unconscious carcass out of bed soon I was going to be late for work. But just one more time. "I liked it," I said. "I liked what you said."

Smiling his wonderful smile, he said, "I think you're a wonderful, incredible, extremely attractive woman, Suzanne Philips, and I'd be very honoured if you'd agree to go out with me?"

* * *

"And what did you say?" Katie screamed down the phone.

"I didn't say anything. My heart was pounding and I was hyperventilating. I honestly thought I was going to pass out. Then the fire alarm sounded and everyone was herded out of the building."

"You are joking!"

"I'm not. Timing, eh?"

"You didn't get the chance to say yes, 'Yes, please, take me, I'm yours'?"

"No. Carl, our fire officer, burst into the office and told us to get out, he was really quite adamant about it. Then we were all herded down the stairs and, once we were outside, we were surrounded by people and could only stare at each other across a crowded car park." Never have a set of staring eyes thrilled me so much. "When I tried to edge over to him so nobody would notice this *incredible electricity* sparking between us, his mobile went off and he and Carl had to rush to some emergency at the Kingsbury site. They never came back."

"You are bloody joking!"

"I'm not!"

"Couldn't you have just shouted, 'Yes!'?"

"I was confused," I said, "I still am."

"Confused? Get a bloody grip, woman. You've fancied this bloke for the longest time and, having met him myself, I don't blame you, the man is sex on legs. Now you're telling me you're *confused*?"

"There's other things to consider," I said lamely.

"Name one!"

"Money. I know we got that money off Gary, and that will tide me over for a bit, but long term I really need a well-paid job. And I like *this* job."

"You'd pass up the delectable Alan Talbot for a *job*? Are you really my sister or some imposter? How would you feel working with him every day, knowing you'd passed up the chance to *sleep* with him and make all your dreams come true?"

"I have my future to consider," I said firmly. "I have to let my head rule my heart or I'll be back where I started. Love doesn't conquer all, you know, and it certainly doesn't pay the bills. I have to take care of my family and the house. I *need* a decent job. I can't afford to stay with the agency much longer, they don't pay enough and – "

"I don't believe this. Phone him," she snapped furiously, "Phone him right now and say yes."

"I can't."

"Why not?"

"I don't have his number."

"You're his bloody secretary, aren't you? You should know his number!"

"Well, I do *at work*," I snapped back, "It's on my desk, but I don't know it off by heart."

"It might be too late by Monday," she said. "He might think you don't really fancy the bloody pants off him and go all cold on you."

"I know," I whimpered.

"Not likely, I'll admit, but possible. Are you sure, *absolutely positive*, you don't know his number, or anyone who knows his number?"

"No, I'm just making it up to make you feel bad, Katie!"

"Well, you're certainly doing a good job of that! Do you even know where he lives?"

"Somewhere in Kidderminster, I think. But even if I did know I couldn't just turn up on his doorstep and say, 'Hi, I was just passing and thought I'd drop in to accept your kind offer'."

"Yes, you bloody could."

"Well, maybe, if I knew where he lived I would, but I don't, so I can't."

"Well," Katie drawled, "I'm too depressed to talk to you now, I'll call you later."

"Yeah, thanks, Katie, that makes me feel so much better."

"You brought in on yourself, Suze. I mean, for God's sake, how long does it take to say the word 'yes'?"

"I know! I bloody *know!*"

CHAPTER 18

The weekend that followed was a complete nightmare. Alex was home from uni but I hardly saw him, he was either cooped up in his bedroom building computers, handing over computers to customers who turned up at the door, or out celebrating his lucrative new business venture with his friends. And Elliot was out all the time, too.

Which left me. All alone. Chewing on my nails and wondering what I'd done, what opportunity I'd missed, if I'd ever have the opportunity again, and if I'd accept it if I did. It was true, I needed a well-paid job, but was this the right one to take when I felt so strongly about the boss?

And then, to top it all, like the cherry on the top of my cake of misery, Gary came.

"The boys are both out," I told him on the doorstep.

"Good," he said, "Because it's you I've come to see."

He wasn't aggressive, he didn't look angry. If anything, he just seemed tired. I let him in and we sat in the living room.

"Has she left you again?" I asked, noticing his wrinkled shirt. "Because you can't come back here, Gary. It's over between us."

"I know," he said, looking agitated. "I know it is, Suze."

"Would you like a cup of coffee?"

"No. I'll just say my piece and then I'll go."

"In that case I'm having a stiff whisky. Want one?"

"Yes, that would be nice." He watched me pour two glasses out on the coffee table and said, "You used to say I drove you to drink."

I laughed. "You clearly still do."

We sat there with our whisky, me staring at Gary, Gary staring at the swirling glass. "Right," he said, "This isn't easy to say, so I'll just come right out and say it. But before I do, I'd ... I'd just like to tell you that you're a wonderful woman, Suzanne, and you've been a really good wife to put up with me for so long. I've been a bloody idiot, and I mean that from the bottom of my heart, and I'm not trying to wheedle my way back or anything, I know there's no chance of that, and I really don't blame you. None of this is your fault, it's all mine."

I took a huge gulp of whisky, not sure I could deal with more emotion in my delicate state.

"Poppi didn't leave me," he said. "I left her. She was too young for me, we had nothing in common." He laughed harshly. "She's with someone else now. Well, she's young, who can blame her? And I've downsized. Bloody stupid idea living in a flat in The Cube, I had some wild fantasy about being a James Bond sex symbol or something equally ridiculous, so I've sublet it and found a smaller place, more modest. Anyway, what I've come to say is, I think we need to tie up loose ends, settle unfinished business."

"Such as?"

"The divorce," he said. "Do you still want a divorce?"

The question seemed to hang heavy in the air between us. He was staring at me so intently. "Yes," I said, "I do."

Gary exhaled slowly. "Right, I'll start that then, it's cheaper for you if I instigate it. I'll admit it was all my fault, that I committed adultery. Is it still called adultery these days or is it emotional abandonment? Anyway, you'll need to get your own solicitor, although I won't fight you for anything, I'll let the courts make a fair judgement on the house and finances and stuff."

I couldn't speak for a moment or two. This was unexpected, and uncharacteristic. "Thank you," I finally managed to say.

I half expected him to jump up, point at me and scream, "Ha! Got you there! Thought I was serious, eh? Well I'm taking you for every penny you haven't got." Only he didn't.

"It's true what they say about not knowing what you've got until you've lost it," he said, staring into his glass. "I certainly didn't. Didn't know when I was well off, thought the grass was greener and all that. Well, it wasn't, it isn't, and now, of course, it's too late. I've ruined everything, lost everything, and I've only myself to blame. What an idiot." He took a deep breath, as if composing himself. I just sat still and let him talk. "I've dated a couple of women since Poppi but they're all just ... well, odd, really. I haven't met anyone who's a patch on you, Suze, and that's the truth. I'm sorry for all the hurt and pain I've caused you, I won't be causing you any more, I promise."

I was speechless. Gary emptied his glass in one gulp and finally looked up at me. "Well, that's all I came to say," he said, "I'll leave you in peace now."

"Thank you," I said again, standing up with him, "I appreciate it."

"Just trying to make amends, Suze, and get on with my life the best I can."

"Well." We stood facing each other in the living room, Gary with his hands in his jacket pockets, looking uncomfortable. I still didn't know quite what to say, so I said, "I hope you find what you're looking for."

He huffed. "I did. Then I threw it all away. Be happy, Suze, you deserve to be happy."

He kissed me gently on the cheek.

And then he went.

* * *

Afterwards, I started cleaning the house from top to bottom, unable to stop. I was still in shock from Gary's visit, still in shock about Alan, and I didn't have anything better to do anyway. If I'd said yes straight away I might now be at some country pub getting to know the man I'd adored from afar for so long, the man who had made me go weak at the knees the first time I saw him, and who'd been utterly brilliant to work with all these weeks. As it was, I hadn't answered him at all, which was, I suspected, equivalent to saying no. Instead of a cosy drink in some country pub I was maniacally cleaning the toilet. Going to work was going to be *very* awkward after this. Like Katie said, he could have gone off the boil over the weekend and decided I wasn't worth it after all.

Why hadn't I just said yes?

Because it was a good job and, having worked as a temp all these months, I knew better than anybody that there was a scarcity of good jobs out there, and I needed a good job. I *had* a good job, and I wanted to keep it.

But I would lose Alan. Was any job worth that?

But I had my family to consider, a house to keep. Was any man worth that?

"Bugger!" I snarled, cleaning the toilet with furious energy.

That night, as I sat alone in my pristine living room, idly watching TV and wondering where my life was going, the phone rang. I picked it up immediately. Alex might be having a financial emergency, or Elliot might need my help in some way. Somebody, somewhere, might want me.

It wasn't Alex. Or Elliot. It wasn't Gary, or Katie, or my mother making one of her bi-monthly calls. It wasn't even Alan, who'd somehow managed to track down my number through sheer hard graft because he simply couldn't bear not to speak to me for a whole weekend.

The voice on the other end of the phone was the last person on earth I expected to hear from.

"Mrs Philips?" the familiar voice said.

"Yes."

"Mrs Suzanne Philips?"

"Yes."

"I'm sorry to bother you at home, but are you the Suzanne Philips who used to work at Richard Sovereign & Co?"

"Is that … ?" I could barely bring myself to say the name. It couldn't be, could it? "Is that *Callum*?"

"Yes, it is."

"What are you doing ringing me at home on a Sunday night?"

"I realise it's an awful imposition, and I really wouldn't trouble you at home if I didn't have to."

"What do you want, Callum? Have you lost a file? Are you looking for someone to take the blame for something?"

"It's taken me a week to get your phone number," he said. "I've had to bribe and cajole and eventually managed to elicit it from someone in the HR department at Richard Sovereign. I really hope you don't mind."

"Well, it depends what you're calling for, Callum. If it's to inform me I've won the office lottery, then of course I don't mind."

"No," he said quickly, "It's not that."

"Pity."

"It's taken me over a week to work up the courage to call you, Suzanne."

Suzanne? He hardly never called me Suzanne, not in all the time we worked together. He was up to something, I could tell. He *wanted* something from me. Well, whatever it was, he couldn't have it.

"This isn't easy for me," he said.

"Just spit it out, Callum, I'm missing Antiques Roadshow."

"I want you to come and work for me."

Silence. A heartbeat. A kind of glitch in the time structure of the solar system. I was obviously going mad to believe that my old boss – the odious man who made my working life a misery – was calling me to offer me my old job back.

"*What*?" I gasped.

"I've had three secretaries since I've been at Flogg & Float and they've all been useless."

"Have they?" I grinned. "Are you sure it wasn't you being useless, Callum."

"Yes, yes, I expected that," he said. "I need a secretary who knows what she's doing, who can work with me – "

"As I recall, I did all the work and you got all the glory. You conspired to have me *fired*, Callum! What on earth makes you think I'd ever want to work for you again? You were a nightmare!"

"I'm aware of that, Suzanne, and I'm prepared to make compromises. I'll agree to any terms you might have."

"Yeah, right."

"No, I'm serious. Lay down any rules you like and I'll stick to them, I swear. I'm desperate, Suzanne."

"Yes, you sound it."

"I'm … I'm in danger of losing my job."

"I said you would, didn't I, Callum?"

"Yes," he said, and I could tell it took a lot of effort for him to say that one word. "You were right, I was wrong, and for that I apologise. I apologise for everything I've ever done."

Two men apologising to me in one day! Was this a conspiracy or had I finally lost my tenuous grip on reality and was now having insane delusions?

"I'm prepared to make you a very generous offer if you'll just come and work for me," he said.

"What kind of offer?"

He told me. I had to press a hand to my mouth to stop myself gasping out loud, my brain screaming 'How much? *How* much?' Then I took stock and managed to control myself. It was, indeed, a very generous offer. The price was high, but not high enough to make me even consider working for Callum Redfern again as long as I lived.

"No," I said, thinking, even as I said it, how easy it would have been to say yes – to Callum *and* to Alan.

"Is that a definite no?" he asked.

"Sounded pretty definite to me, did it not sound definite to you?"

"I urge you to at least consider it."

"Okay." I paused for a heartbeat. "I've considered it and the answer is still no."

"I know I haven't been the best boss to work for, but – "

"You were a bully, Callum! You put me down at every pos-sible opportunity and treated me like the lowest of the low, or does your selective memory not recall that."

"No, I recall it, and I admit I may have been a little unfair."

"A little unfair?" I repeated, laughing.

"If I could up the offer would you reconsider your answer?"

I hesitated for just the briefest moment. It was so, so tempt-ing. "Not in a million years," I made myself say.

"I'm desperate," he said again.

"I'm not, Callum. I've changed, I've moved on, I'm not the same person any more."

"Me neither," he said quickly, "You're an excellent secretary, kept my files in order, made sure I never missed an appointment, kept everything running smoothly."

"Corrected your spelling and grammar."

"Yes, that too, and nobody can pull a report together on time like you can."

"The answer's still no."

"Name your price," he suddenly cried. "Whatever salary you want, I'll give it to you."

"You want me to come up with a figure?"

"Yes. Anything. *Please*, Suzanne."

"Okay." So I named a figure off the top of my head. A ludi-crous, impossible number I knew he'd never agree to. Anything to get rid of him.

"What?" he cried, and I had to hold the receiver away from my ear.

"You said anything."

"Yes, but I meant within reason."

"That's my price, take it or leave it."

"I ... I ... "

"I have to go now, Callum, I'm a very busy woman." I flicked idly through the TV channels.

"No! No, wait! I'll ... I'll find out. I'll contact Flogg & Float's HR department first thing in the morning and – "

"Don't bother," I told him, knowing full well that no company would pay what I was asking.

"I'll get back to you," Callum said quickly.

"Okay, whatever."

And I put the phone down.

* * *

"Are you completely out of your mind?"

"I don't know. It's possible, I suppose."

"Maybe you have a problem with that particular word. Let's practice it together, shall we? Y-e-e-s."

"Katie, I – "

"No, come on, say it for me, Suze. I want to hear you *say* it."

"Yes," I said.

"There! See? It wasn't that difficult, was it?"

"Look, I had choices – "

"And screwed them both up by the sound of it! First you can't say yes to Alan because you need more money and would rather keep the job than him, then someone offers you – "

"Not someone," I corrected, "My old boss, a terrible boss. Think Scrooge in a suit."

"I could put up with him for *that* money, Suze! Hell, for *that* money I'd offer him regular blow jobs!"

"Oh, that's more disgusting than you'll ever know."

"You ditch Alan for a well-paid job, then an alternative and much more lucrative job offer turns up just when you need it and you ditch that, too. What *is* the matter with you?"

"I ... I ... I stick by my decisions," I said fiercely, not really sure that I did. "This is *my* life and I'm going to live it the way *I* see fit."

"Alone and poor. Is that really what you really want, Suze?"

I wasn't sure any more, about anything.

"Suze, go into work tomorrow and say yes to Alan, go straight to his office and blurt it out, sing it if you have to. Then ring your old boss and accept the job. Are you listening?"

"I don't know," I said. "Working for Callum was such a nightmare."

"But Alan's such a dreamboat!"

"Dreamboat?" I laughed. "*Dreamboat?*"

"You know what I mean," she snapped. "You're just dithering because you know I'm right."

"You might not be right."

"When am I ever *not* right, Suze?"

"Well ... "

"This could be a very long and very expensive phonecall if we have to wait for you to remember something I've not been right about!"

"Paul Raxter," I declared. "You went out with him in secondary school and he *certainly* wasn't right, he was a complete lunatic who rode a motorbike."

"Er, excuse me, but I did *not* make a mistake about Paul Raxter. He may have been a rebel, but believe me, Suze, I learned a *lot* from him."

"How so? He barely came to class. How could you possibly learn anything from *him*?"

"Oh I didn't learn anything *academic*. Far from it. Best teacher of *that* I could have had, he was bloody marvellous and had the most amazing – "

"Oversharing, Katie."

"Just proving a point, Suzanne. I'm *never* wrong, about anything. Now what, exactly, are you going to do about the mess you've got yourself into?"

"I don't know, I really don't. Alan's probably dismissed me from his emotions by now, and Callum will never come up with the salary I asked for in a million years."

"So, basically, you screwed up."

"It would seem so. Thank you for pointing that out."

"What are big sisters for if not to point out little sister's mistakes?"

"Again, I thank you."

"See Alan tomorrow, beg him to take you back, grovel if you

have to. And call this Callum, accept anything he offers you."

"I'm not sure – "

"Just do it, Suze!"

* * *

I had decided. I had lain awake half the night thinking it all over, considering what Katie had said, what Callum had said and, most of all, remembering what Alan had said.

At 3 o'clock in the morning it came to me like a revelation, like someone had given my brain a good kicking and the light had come on, the cogs had started turning again.

I knew exactly what I had to do. I didn't know if it was already too late, but I had to try.

I had to try.

* * *

I was a complete bundle of nerves when I walked into the office the next morning. My heart was pounding so hard it made my whole body pulsate, and my stomach! I'd never felt so sick in all my life.

I'd deliberately arrived before anyone else so I could, hopefully, give Alan my answer. I prayed that he would be in and not out on some job in some far off county.

I had practised my speech in front of the bathroom mirror until the early hours of the morning, choosing my words carefully and adding an inflection here, a subtle nuance there. As long as I could remember it and put my point across, I would be fine. I wasn't going to flake it, I wasn't.

When I saw Alan already in his office, pouring over papers on his desk, my heart skipped a beat. Just to see him made me feel happy inside. I stiffened my resolve. I had to do this.

I put my bag on my desk, not wanting to take my eyes off him. And then I approached his office, slowly, full of terror. How would he take the news? Would he be pleased or not? Would my nerves cause me to throw up all over the place?

"Come on, Suze," I chanted under my breath, "You can do this, you can do – "

"Suzanne!" He was rising from his seat and, yes, he was smiling, he was pleased to see me. That was good, it was a good sign. "Didn't expect you in so early," he said.

"I ... I ... " Speech, where was the speech I'd so diligently practised for three solid hours in front of the bathroom mirror? I fumbled around inside my head but it wasn't there, I couldn't remember any of it. "I ... I ... "

"Are you alright? Here, sit down." And he came towards me, touched my bare arm, led me to a chair. He perched on the edge of his desk, looking down at me, still smiling but with concern in his beautiful blue eyes. God, he was gorgeous. I could feel the warm imprint of his hand on my arm.

"T-this isn't easy for me to say," I managed to splutter. "I ... "

"Would you like a drink? A coffee, perhaps?"

"No, I just want to say my piece. If I can remember any of it, which I doubt. In fact, I know I can't." I racked my memory cells but they were empty. I looked up at him, at his fabulous smile and startling blue eyes. "I've really enjoyed working here. I mean, I like the job, I like it a lot."

"Oh," he said, and his smile diminished.

"No, I mean I've really ... well, the job is ... The thing is, I have commitments at home, and my almost-ex-husband is suddenly being uncharacteristically reasonable and that's thrown me a bit, and I have boys to support, although they've been doing a better job of supporting me lately, and I'm aware that I'm rambling but I can't seem to stop." I stopped, took a deep breath, couldn't bring myself to look at him but I could feel his eyes on me. "I had it all planned, you see, I knew exactly what to say at 5 o'clock this morning, but now I ... I ... "

"Take a deep breath," Alan said softly. "Take your time."

"It's just that I need a good job and this is a good job, but then Callum, my old boss, rang me last night and offered me a job and I turned it down and, in retrospect, and everything is so much easier in retrospect, isn't it, I wondered if maybe I'd done the right thing."

"Breathe, Suzanne."

I inhaled deeply and almost passed out at the sudden rush of oxygen to my brain. Alan leaned forward. "This job," he said quietly, "You want to keep this job, is that what you're trying to say, Suzanne? I understand and I respect your – "

"That thing you said," I said, struggling to get the sudden onslaught of words out of my mouth before I lost my nerve or passed out, "That thing you said on Friday about going out on a date together and getting to know each other better. It was nice. I liked it. And I was wondering, perhaps, if you wanted to, if you hadn't changed your mind or anything, if … if you'd say it again."

EPILOGUE

CHRISTMAS EVE THE FOLLOWING YEAR

"Did you get the after-dinner mints?"

"Yes."

"Are you sure?"

"Positive!"

"Show me."

"There, are you happy now?"

"Pretty much," I grinned. "Oh! You didn't forget to buy the punch bowl from M&S, did you?"

"No, I didn't forget to buy the punch bowl from M&S."

"Only your wife sounded pretty stressed about it when she rang earlier."

"My wife is pretty stressed out about everything at the moment."

"Living with you, Callum, I can well understand why. Right, now the Shawditch tender is finally in the post and they should receive it sometime next week, so there's no worries about that. I've left a note for you to start work on the Nottingham report as soon as you're back in the New Year."

"You mean, *that* note?" he sneered.

We both looked at the massive sheet of planning paper taped across most of one office wall with 'START NOTTINGHAM REPORT!!' written across it in thick black marker pen.

"Yes, that one," I said. "Don't say I didn't remind you. I've also left a note on your desk in full view about the meeting Bill Peterson wants with you about the Farqhuar building."

"The Farqhuar building? What Farqhuar building?"

"I *told* you," I said, rolling my eyes. "They want a Schedule of Condition on the Farqhuar building."

"I don't remember you telling me about that."

I pushed him over to his desk and pointed at a pile of papers perched on the edge, the top page of which read FARQHUAR BUILDING SCHEDULE OF CONDITION. Attached to it was a sticky note giving the date I'd told him about it, along with Callum's initials to prove that I'd told him about it. Most of his work was covered in these sticky notes.

"Okay, okay," he groaned. "Is my tie straight?"

"No."

"Could you just – ?"

"No, I couldn't, it's not in my job description. Go to the loo and do it in the mirror like normal people, Callum. I'm not your dresser."

"No, bloody expensive secretary is what you are," he muttered.

"Personal Assistant! I thought we agreed that my job title was Personal Assistant."

"Bloody expensive Personal Assistant then."

"I'm worth it though, aren't I?" I grinned.

"Yes, yes, don't keep going on about it. Here," he suddenly said, taking a wrapped parcel out of his desk drawer, "I got you this. Merry Christmas."

"You … you got me a present?"

"It's nothing much, just a little something to say thank you for all the hard work you've put in around here this last year. If you don't like it you can exchange it for something else."

"Can I open it now?"

"If you want." A tiny grin tugged at the corner of his mouth.

I tore off the wrapping paper. Inside was an ornate silver photoframe.

"It's gorgeous!" I gasped.

"I thought you could put a nice photo of your boys in it."

"Thank you, Callum."

"And?" he shrugged.

"And what?"

"Where's my present?"

"You're looking at her," I laughed. "No, seriously, you can have it when you and Mildred come round on New Year's Eve. You are still coming, aren't you?"

"Of course."

"Good."

"What is it?"

"What's what?"

"My present," he grinned, "Tell me what my present is."

"No."

"Oh, go on."

"It's a framed print," I relented. "For your office."

"What kind of print? Dali? Picasso? Vettriano?"

"It's motivational." Callum shrugged and shook his head. "An inspiring picture with inspiring words underneath."

"What do the words say?"

"It says, 'Behind every boss is a brilliant and thoroughly knackered secretary stroke PA,'" I laughed.

"Really?"

"No, not really. You'll have to wait until New Year's Eve, Callum."

"Oh. *Oh!*"

"What?"

"Oh," he said again, staring at me with wide eyes.

"What have you done, Callum?"

He tapped on his computer screen. I moved around his desk to take a look. It was the dictation software. There was an audio file still in it. "I'm sorry," he said, "I forgot all about it. It's the contract letter to Proxy & Sons."

"You're kidding!"

"It needs to be there when their office opens up again after the holidays."

"But its 4.30 on Christmas Eve! Everyone else went home hours ago!"

"I know. I'm sorry. Please?"

"No."

"I'll bring good champagne on New Year's Eve."

I narrowed my eyes. "How many bottles of good champagne?"

"Two?"

"Four."

"You drive a hard bargain."

I rushed back to my desk, brought up the audio file, brought up the contract template, and typed faster than I've ever typed in my life. When I'd printed it out, Callum glanced through it – under my watchful, reproachful, slightly squinted eye. "Sign it," I growled.

He signed it. I turned off my computer, grabbed my coat, picked up several bags of last-minute shopping and presents from colleagues, shouted, "Happy Christmas, Callum," and raced from the building.

A car was waiting for me outside. I tossed my bags onto the back seat and leapt into the front.

"He kept you late."

"What can I say?" I sighed, "The man's a tyrant. Usual last-minute panic, but he's bringing champagne on New Year's Eve to make up for it."

"Talking of which, I rang Gary to check he's still coming for dinner tomorrow. He is, but he asked if he could bring someone called Felicity with him."

"Did he say mention old this Felicity was?"

"No, but he did say the boys wouldn't be interested in this one."

"That's good. And Katie's arriving around 8 o'clock tonight."

"Excellent."

"Yes, it's all very excellent." I sat in the silent car outside my office building and took a deep, very happy breath. Then I said,

"Sarah's threatened to bring her wedding magazines with her on Boxing Day."

"Oh god, poor James."

"I know. How's everything going at home?"

"Well, Elliot and Kelly are busy preparing dinner for tonight. She can't seem to get enough of your new kitchen, Elliot keeps moaning that he never sees her, she's always cooking something."

"I know, I've never eaten so well."

"And Alex has gone to collect his girlfriend from the train station." He blew out air. "I think it's all under control."

I let the happiness waft over me in warm, endless waves. "So," I said at last, "Aren't you driving us home then?"

"Haven't you forgotten something?" He was staring straight ahead with mock indignation on his face. "This car isn't going anywhere until I get it."

I smiled and leaned towards him. He turned his head and we kissed – a sweet, loving, tender kiss that never failed to turn my insides to jelly. "Happy Christmas, Suzanne," he breathed, running a gentle hand down the side of my face.

"Happy Christmas, Alan."

BOOKS BY THIS AUTHOR

Pitching Up!

A thoroughly entertaining read with a wonderful cast of charismatic characters in caravans who romp from one dramatic catastrophe to another. Touching captivating, and very, very funny.

My Mom's A Witch

FOR YOUNG TEENAGERS written as Debbie Aubrey
Funny magical fantasy fiction that's ever so slightly bonkers

GET IN TOUCH!

If you enjoyed TIPPING POINT please do leave a rating or a review (for extra brownie points) on: Amazon or Goodreads.

I thank you.

I'd also be thrilled to hear from you about anything.
Email: deborahaubrey01@gmail.com
Facebook: AuthorDebbieAubrey
Amazon Author Page: Deborah Aubrey

Please do 'like' or 'follow' my Facebook page, AuthorDebbieAubrey, for some free, upcoming stories that tie in with this book, and also up-to-date news on the next book.

Until then, ta ta. D x

Printed in Great Britain
by Amazon